Conflict in the Home

Conflict in the Home

Tan Kheng Yeang

ISBN: 978-1-4269-4941-8 (sc)
ISBN: 978-1-4269-4942-5 (hc)
ISBN: 978-1-4269-4943-2 (e)

Library of Congress Control Number: 2010918029

Trafford rev. 12/08/2010

 www.trafford.com

North America & International
toll-free: 1 888 232 4444 (USA & Canada)
phone: 250 383 6864 ♦ fax: 812 355 4082

CONTENTS

Chapter 1

The Teahouse

Groups of laughing, chattering people sauntered with leisurely indolence and grace in and out of the spacious halls devoted to pleasure and conversation. In vain might the inquisitive observer trace any shadow of care on their warm faces, which shone with as brilliant a flame as the brownish walls, proving, beyond any possibility of dispute, that here at least there was perfect harmony between man and his surroundings. The well-proportioned rooms were adorned with a picturesque array of red and green lanterns, which in themselves were sufficient to inspire any reasonable man not hopelessly engulfed in the morass of worry and discontent with feelings of freedom and gaiety.

Moving from table to table, urbane waiters pushed tiered trolleys furnished with all manner of delicious viands. Pretty waitresses from time to time stepped forward and filled the teapots with hot water or brought warm towels to departing customers so that they might leave with their hands as clean as when they sat down. These damsels formed an essential part of the establishment, their duties encompassing as much of the ornamental variety as the useful. For a great part of the time, they stood in an attitude of impassive elegance, silently scanning the proceedings from various vantage points. What thoughts, if any, coursed through their minds could not be divined. Blue blouses with high collars and sleeves stretching a bare three inches below the shoulders and trousers of the same celestial hue covered their slim, lithe figures. White rubber shoes tipped their feet, and their aprons were so stainless and pure that their use was a confounded problem to exercise the wits of the curious.

All the tables possessed their full quota of patrons, and the moment a seat was vacated it was promptly reoccupied so that the quantity of heat, scientifically described as molecular motion, it absorbed considerably exceeded what it emitted, with the net result that its colossal hordes of unfortunate molecules were in a chronic state of extraordinary commotion. It was a matter for conjecture whether the new occupant found the warmth left by his predecessor a pleasurable sensation. Besides the large central halls, there were smaller closets containing only a single table each; these secluded spots bore an extra charge and, as a rule, were made use of by mixed parties of men and women. Confucian restraint and placidity were characteristics very little in evidence: noise and jollity shot through the atmosphere.

Round a square table, which was placed near a window on the right side of the front room on the second story and from which could be obtained a comprehensive view of the humming street below, sat four men, who were certainly not yielding an inch to the others in the matter of enjoyment.

"Have another dumpling," politely remarked a young man dressed in brown, addressing a stout, middle-aged individual.

"Thanks, Siu Kam," replied that person, whose name was Mak Gaw Lok. He kept a general store that had maintained a consistently flourishing trade for such a long time that any decline in business would have seemed to his friends the act of a particularly malignant demon. "I wonder how many have rolled into my stomach."

"No need to count them," interposed a lawyer, whose face, though it still bore its usual air of portentous gravity, now betrayed a distinctly perceptible flush. "I'll have one too."

He stretched his hand toward a porcelain plate, got hold of a dumpling about the size of an orange, and began to peel off its glistening skin, on which was stamped a tiny, red circle, signifying to a connoisseur the fact that this particular specimen contained fried pork. Other varieties were distinguished by different marks or sizes or shapes. When the outer creamy layer of flour was removed, the lawyer gingerly placed it on a small plate beside him. Then, breaking what he had in his hand into two more or less identical portions, he ate them ceremoniously, moving his mouth as little as possible in his excessive gravity.

Yuen Siu Kam, he who was dressed in brown, was twenty-seven years of age and was just a bit short of five feet six inches tall. His face tended toward the square and his mouth toward the large; his chin bore little trace of a beard, and a razor was well-nigh a superfluity as far as he was concerned. His meticulously groomed jet-black hair was parted on the left. His neck sat well on his shoulders, and his arms drooped from them with undeniable grace; though they did not reveal any bulging biceps sticking out like huge eggs and insistently shrieking for the admiration that is supposed to be the legitimate due of such phenomena, they were by no means flabby. His figure was slightly on the thin side, and his movements were of a leisurely character, conveying the impression that his will was not particularly strong. His expression was usually gentle and would often light up with an ingenuous smile so that he could not be charged with exhibiting an impassive exterior beneath which lurked mystery and subtlety. From his appearance one could easily discern that he was neither of a forward nature, reeking with the desire to be extremely modern, nor anxious to cling desperately to his ancestral ideas and customs. Doubtless he had reached the conclusion that, for the sake of being in harmony with society, he should follow its fashions to a considerable extent and avoid coming into violent collision with it.

He cherished truth and an easy existence.

"This lichee tea," he said, apparently intending the remark for the edification of his companions, though his eyes were on the beverage in question, "is remarkably good."

"I dare say so," replied the lawyer, "but I prefer Ceylon tea with milk and sugar."

"The tiger roars; the duck quacks," smiled Choi Ching Kee, an unobtrusive, pallid schoolmaster with round shoulders and bulging eyes. "Every man has his own taste. For me the ordinary, bitterish, unflavored tea suffices. The infusion from the green leaf, dried in the sun, is all I want."

"The four of us seem to have four different tastes," put in Gaw Lok, emitting three short coughs, which he intended for a laugh. "Give me the fine chrysanthemum, the golden blossom. I drink a huge bowl every night before retiring. How it soothes the throat!"

The lawyer, whose name was Wong Tak Cheong, assumed an awful expression and seemed disposed to thrash out the point with formal eloquence, probably using arguments of a learned character. He opened his mouth to deliver his harangue, but due to one of those inexplicable impulses that insidiously determine man's conduct, though often not present in the field of his consciousness, he closed it again and bent his head over his cup. His argumentative nature was proverbial, and Gaw Lok heaved a mild sigh of relief when he surprisingly left the field after showing unmistakable signs of wishing to do battle.

"What a superb blessing is tea!" declared Ching Kee with emphatic conviction. His sallow face was all aglow with poetic enthusiasm, and his long, thin fingers lovingly caressed a tiny cup full to the brim with the liquid. "I can think of nothing more beneficial to man. I often wonder how our ancestors managed to pass the day agreeably before the discovery of the leaf. They were compelled to drink more wine, which is harmful and not so stimulating. Tea has made us a nation of peaceful, contented people. It is inexpensive and is ever at hand. Its influence on our life and conduct is enormous."

"Very true," murmured the merchant, Gaw Lok. "The one who first singled it out from among the plants as a thirst-quencher and taught its use must have been an immortal."

"Tea is one of the greatest gifts heaven has given us, and its discovery, after that of agriculture by Shen Nung, the Divine Farmer, is the greatest. Rice makes for existence; tea makes for happiness. Existence without happiness is not exactly desirable," said Ching Kee with a touchingly benign smile.

"No man in his senses would contradict you," asserted Gaw Lok with evident satisfaction. "The peasant has been said to have seven causes of anxiety every day: firewood, rice, oil, salt, soy, vinegar, and tea. Without a doubt the last is his greatest solace."

"I must confess," said Tak Cheong, a look of disdain flitting across his solemn countenance, "that the praises you two shower on it are too excessive. Modern science tells us that it contains a substance called caffeine that is nothing more nor less than a poison and acts badly on the nervous system. Every time you drink a cup, you are swallowing a certain amount of poison. If you take too much, you are deliberately killing yourself. I shall not be surprised if, at the rate you are going, you soon pass out of the world altogether. As for me, I drink only a little, and that must be very dilute." He drew himself up in his chair to show that he was in no danger of quitting the world for a long time to come.

"With all due respect to your esteemed learning," replied the unconvinced Ching Kee mildly, "I cannot believe in your statement. I have never heard of anyone who was killed in that way yet, and although I am not particularly strong, I trust I shall live to a venerable age."

"Many substances are not as innocent as they appear," interposed Siu Kam. "Coffee also contains caffeine, and the delicious cocoa produces similarly injurious effects with what is called theobromine."

"What are we supposed to drink then?" asked Gaw Lok in a faltering tone. "I never imagined before that what so many people regularly take could have the slightest harm. Shall we confine ourselves to water only?"

"Water contains germs that can kill a person in a day," replied Siu Kam, not very encouragingly. "It's a wonder to me how, when almost everything we eat and drink is dangerous, there are people who live up to three score years and ten."

"In such a case," said Gaw Lok vastly relieved, "I shall continue to stick to the pleasant drink." He looked round the room with a broad smile and was very much delighted to find the people at the other tables gulping away with all their might, quite unconscious of the momentous discussion that he had just heard and that had so shaken his peace for a moment. A smart waitress caught his eye and immediately stepped forward to pour hot water into his pot. After a couple of minutes he filled his cup with the infusion and drained it off slowly, placidly passing his hand over his abdomen to express his satisfaction, which was a treat to behold.

"Ah!" he exclaimed, "what shall we take next? I feel quite hungry. I suggest stuffed duck." Prosperity was stamped on his figure, and he had no desire to look thinner.

"Excellent," said Siu Kam. "Add steamed carp and abalone soup and we'll have a splendid repast."

The order was given, and while waiting for the appearance of the delicacies, Siu Kam scrutinized the other patrons with a languid expression. From a large group of people there erupted, at regular short intervals, hilarious bursts of laughter; as a florid individual was doing almost all the talking, he was clearly relating some tickling story. "A rare raconteur he must be," thought our hero, "to be able to excite such mirth." In one corner of the room was a withered man with hollow cheeks and a furtive, unsteady look on his dark face; he consisted only of skin and bone. "Doubtless an opium-smoker," said our commentator to himself. "I wonder what pleasure he finds in wasting his money that way. He has lost his health into the bargain." At a neighboring table a party of staid individuals in long gowns was engaged in an amiable wrangle, each extremely desirous to pay the bill and urging the waitress to accept his money, pushing aside the hands of his companions. "True old-world hospitality and politeness," pondered our philosopher, "fast disappearing in our day. We are now all anxious that our friends should do the paying. In many respects our modern behavior is that of the trivial man, not that of the distinguished man." His eyes alighted on a group of dandies who were gazing at the waitresses libidinously and laughing among themselves. "I bet their main preoccupation in life is sex," he uttered, almost aloud.

He looked down into Queen's Road below. Along the principal thoroughfare of Hong Kong motor cars rolled past in a continual stream and pedestrians jostled one another in pleasant confusion. The asphalted street, though neither as wide nor as level as some others, was the busiest in the city and was lined with cinemas, cafés, and shops of various descriptions.

Red neon signs flashed, and innumerable customers swept in and out of the brilliantly lighted buildings. He was still gazing with interest at a curious puppet show used as an advertisement that was taking place in front of a large department store opposite him when his attention was suddenly recalled to his companions.

"Society," the teacher, Ching Kee, was saying, "is nowadays getting worse and worse, more and more corrupt. I feel that much of all that can be classified as good will never come back again. We are living in a most unfortunate age, which I would gladly change for the golden periods of the Han and Tang Dynasties. Ah! Those were real times of greatness and happiness. What peace, simplicity, and culture reigned then! How well were the precepts of our great sage, Kung Fu-tze, applied! All the social relationships were properly maintained with benefit to all under the sky. But present times are different. 'Those conversant with virtue are rare,' said the sage. How right he was!" he concluded mournfully.

"As right as you are," said the lawyer, Wong Tak Cheong, sarcastically. He had been fidgeting with impatience the whole time that the enthusiastic Ching Kee was chanting eulogies to the past. "Your unfortunate quotation was applied by the sage to his own age about twenty-five hundred years ago. Just as you have your mind fixed on his example, so he had his fixed on the legendary emperors, Yao and Shun, who are supposed to be, except for a few centuries less, as far away from him in time as he is from us. I shouldn't be surprised if the two virtuous sons of heaven also found their prototypes in some uncouth barbarians before their time."

Ching Kee was profoundly shocked. "Ai-ya!" he exclaimed in remonstrance: "You shouldn't refer to our sages so inconsiderately.

What do you mean by saying that Yao and Shun are legendary rulers? Their existence is as certain as that of the sky. I am more willing to believe that I don't exist than that they didn't."

"I dare lay a bet that they were purely fictitious beings," was the emphatic reply. "In any case their existence is of no concern to the modern world. Whether they actually lived or not is of no interest to me, nor, I presume, to any practical man who has enough to occupy his days." Here he fixed a severe eye on the embarrassed Ching Kee. "We are always harking back to the past. That is why we have not made any progress for centuries on end. Even now, for the first time in our history, when we have the opportunity to cast away the shackles of the past, we still have people like you talking with regret of antiquity."

Ching Kee blushed in confusion; nevertheless, he remarked firmly, "The so-called shackles of the past are not shackles at all, except to those who don't like them. You may regard them as such; to me they are glories, great treasures. To my limited understanding it doesn't seem just that one mode of life should be regarded as a chain and another as mighty free. I don't prize a thing merely because it is old, but whatever is good seems to me more valuable still if sanctified by the experience of the ages. I don't object to antiquity, as you do, on its own account. And I must deny your gratuitous statement that we have remained completely still for centuries. On the contrary, we have made the real kind of progress; gradual, solid progress. Every dynasty has shown progress in some direction. Great philosophers arose in the Chou period; Buddhism was introduced and paper was first made in the Han; the Tang was the Golden Age of Poetry and printing was invented; Sung scholarship is famous; porcelain first made many centuries earlier reached its perfection under the Mings. In fact, we have discovered and invented a vast number of things step by step. What we haven't done is to do away with an entire civilization as we have been busily trying to achieve during the last few decades."

"Unfortunately we haven't completely accomplished it yet; I wish we could cut out the old culture with one stroke of a knife," said Tak Cheong. "What kind of progress is that which you call gradual—inventing odds and ends in a haphazard way through so many centuries? The West has made such a lot more discoveries and inventions in a hundred years than we have done in a thousand. Look at that wonderful instrument—science. It has given us true knowledge of the world, not imaginary stuff out of the so-called sages' fertile brains. In contrast to the mystical nonsense that Taoism preaches, science has given us airplanes, motor cars, machines that do the work of men, the radio that supplies you with music without your having to see the musicians, and a host of other amenities too numerous to name. Our happiness has increased proportionately," he concluded with a magisterial air.

Siu Kam and Gaw Lok had hitherto maintained a respectful silence, listening to the arguments so freely bandied between the two learned gentlemen.

"Ah! I beg to—to state a different view. My—my opinion is a bit different," Gaw Lok now interposed timidly with a self-depreciatory smile. "Happiness! That is the real object of our life. I personally feel though that the ease and dignity of our former mode of existence gave greater happiness. Our present life is too hurried. Everything is keyed up to a feverish pitch. We seem to be trying to rival the speed of the airplane in all we do. The ancient gentleman is said to have obtained his happiness from the pursuit of the seven arts—writing, painting, playing chess, performing on the lute, composing poetry, drinking wine, and growing flowers. All these are leisurely occupations. I am unable to do most of them. Indeed, wine drinking is the only one at which I really excel." He smiled a still more apologetic smile. "But I am convinced that he who follows these pleasures is far more contented than he who dashes round madly on a motorcycle, and his life will be quite safe, with no danger of losing his limbs. And this is a great point to consider."

"A man can find happiness in anything," said Tak Cheong contemptuously. "The mere pleasure one can get from a pursuit does not prove that it is desirable. Boys like to play marbles and leapfrog. I know of an idiot whose sole happiness consists in drawing zigzag lines on the pavement. The flying birds and walking beasts seem to be supremely happy without doing anything. Are their examples to be imitated? The important point is whether, besides giving amusement, a pursuit is worthy of a man." Here he drew himself up to indicate that all his activities were of stupendous merit. "Besides, all the joys you mentioned could be pursued only by the cultured, who could afford to waste their time. The illiterate masses, consisting of the peasants, were completely deprived of any form of luxury and even the necessities of life. They had literally to toil from dawn to dusk with their hands instead of merely looking after machines for a few hours. Utilitarianism, the greatest happiness of the greatest number of people, is what should be promoted."

"Really," smiled the accommodating Siu Kam. "There is a good deal to be said on behalf of the old civilization. Of course, some changes are needful to suit present-day life. Our ancestors were more virtuous and gentle. Competition for success in life with all its attendant jealousies and rating a man according to his wealth was not so keen. Contentment was more easily achieved. True, they enjoyed few amenities, and their knowledge of the natural world was very limited. Still, as happiness is chiefly subjective in its character, what they lacked is not very important. The seven arts were undoubtedly instruments of pleasure superior to those recently cultivated."

He bowed his head and the upper half of his body with affable grace to Gaw Lok, whose face beamed with delight. "Like Mr. Choi, I regret the passing away of the Han and Tang periods." Here he made an identical bow to the teacher, whose face, compared to the merchant's, registered a fainter smile, though fully as much satisfaction.

Just at this juncture, the blue curtain of a room but a short distance from the broad staircase was drawn back and out stepped two men and two girls. The men were arrayed in Western clothes; one, tall and thin, had on a gaudy crimson tie with tiny blue squares and the other flashed a grass-green jade ring. Both the girls wore long, tightly fitting cheongsams and carried themselves erect. One of the girls had evidently forgotten to take out with her some particular article, for the man with the ring, after a hurried explanation, re-entered the room. She whose property was being retrieved turned around and glanced at the tables on the front part of the floor. She noticed the lawyer, acknowledging his bow with a frank smile, and whispered to the man by her side, who wheeled around and, after raising a hand in greeting, bent down to tie a shoelace.

Siu Kam stared at her in surprise, and his mouth promptly fell open to such an extent as is seldom achieved by any man; if his tongue had also lolled out, he would have looked very much like a dog. The object of his admiration, aged twenty, possessed a fair measure of beauty, of which she was fully conscious, judging from her expression, which was by no means remarkable for excessive modesty. Her height was five feet three inches, her figure was thin and graceful, and her face was a perfect oval. Her dark hair was bobbed and curled and lay close to her head, not a single tress being out of place. Her dress was of bright silk and revealed all the curves of her body. Her eyes caught those of Siu Kam, and though she felt secretly amused at his ludicrous expression, she pretended to frown ominously and turned away with a dignified gesture of disapproval such as no mere male could ever hope to emulate. The egregious Siu Kam did not seem to construe her action as having any reference to himself and continued to stare just as hard as ever, rather more so in fact. All this took place in the space of a few minutes only, for the man who had entered the room soon emerged, holding tightly a fine handbag made of silvery beads. The girl received it with a smile, and the party descended in a lift that had stopped near them at that moment. The fantastic Siu Kam immediately thrust his head out of the window to wait for their emergence, and only after they were no longer visible did he turn back and look with a dazed expression at his chopsticks.

In the meantime Gaw Lok and Ching Kee were applying themselves assiduously to finishing the stuffed duck, steamed fish, and clear abalone soup that had appeared awhile ago and for the time being were oblivious to everything else. As for the lawyer, Wong Tak Cheong, after performing his cursory gesture of greeting to the girl and the man, he was brooding with resentment over the fact that all his three companions seemed to be arrayed against him in his view of the superiority of modern life. He was marshalling his wits to deal a crushing blow to them and make them feel convinced of the rightness of his irrefragable logic. Consequently, with his eyes glued to his cup, he failed to observe his friend's unusual behavior.

He frowned, creating three perpendicular wrinkles between his bushy eyebrows, and said heavily, addressing Siu Kam, who was, however, not looking at him, "I am surprised, Siu Kam, that you value the ancient civilization more than the modern."

Siu Kam here awoke from his state, which was dangerously balancing on tiptoe near the brink of the comatose. "Contentment and virtue are all very excellent, but we can be just as contented and virtuous nowadays. Surely the more conveniences we possess and the fewer hardships we have to put up with the more we approach perfect contentment. And as for morals, I think that we are essentially far better than our grandfathers. We exercise a more developed social sense and care more for the welfare of men in general. Formerly people were exceedingly cruel. Nowadays, we can never produce such monsters as the infamous emperors, Chieh and Chou."

"I agree with you," replied Siu Kam. "I did not say though that our former life was superior; I only said it had some good points. No doubt our society is vastly more preferable."

His three companions were astonished, for at first he had given them the impression that he preferred olden days. As a matter of fact, he was contradicting his previous statements, and his opinion had shifted its emphasis to the other side, the reason being his vision of the girl. He argued to himself that a society that could produce such an enchanting maiden must be very excellent, and he could not associate her with antiquity. Ladies of previous generations had bound feet—golden lilies, as the perverted taste of those times termed such monstrosities—and she, whom he loved, could not possibly possess such a figure and gait if she had lived not so many decades ago. Besides, there were a great many other changes to differentiate her from her former counterparts, all to her advantage. True, the improvements were not peculiar to her, but somehow or other he singled her out from all others and condensed all the excellences into her person. From thinking about her glory he came to feel many other advantages denied to previous eras.

"I am glad you have come over to my point of view," said Tak Cheong triumphantly, drawing out a pipe with a curved stem and starting to smoke. "My proofs, I trust, are sound." He looked solemnly at Gaw Lok and Ching Kee.

The polite Siu Kam refrained from pointing out that the argument that had wrought his conversion was not a verbal one but corporeal in its nature; to wit, an extraordinary specimen of the Yin, or female, principle. He dropped his eyes and blushed in embarrassment.

They had sat there for such a long time, nearly three hours, that the waitress who had charge of their table was seething with impatience and every now and then cast an eye at their pots to see whether the tea had by this time, owing to frequent infusions, lost its color. Thinking it was now high time to get rid of them, she brought forward moist towels and politely inquired whether there was anything more they wanted. The four friends looked at one another with an uneasy glance, took the hint, rose, and departed.

Chapter 2

The Mah-jongg Party

On a slight eminence in Kowloon, in a more secluded part of the town, reposed a brown, three-storied mansion, square and compact, with a flat roof and verandas running round the various floors, flanked by arches of brickwork. Only a feeble crescent moon darted pale rays from behind a cloud, looking as if she was feeling very weary indeed of climbing the self-same sky again and again for untold eons. But the stars winked brightly, holding animated conversations in close contact, whispering among themselves how happy they were that their common foe lay, for the time being at least, prostrate, enabling them to enjoy the heavens. These urchins seemed to be particularly interested in the house mentioned above, for a whole crowd of them lay huddled together right above its terrestrial position. Like the inquisitive and mischievous Puck, they were anxious to play some light-hearted pranks, though, being able neither to leave their heavenly perches nor to penetrate the concrete, chinkless roof with their light, they contented themselves with shedding mellifluous smiles round its environs.

The girl who had excited such cruel commotion in the heart of the unfortunate Siu Kam and the tall man with the gaudy, crimson tie were standing at the door, waiting for admittance. They had returned home after crossing the ferry that separates the island, dubbed "Fragrant Port," from the town of "Nine Dragons." The door was opened, and the girl and her brother entered the house. After going to her room and divesting herself of the more superfluous portions of her outdoor attire, she entered a bright hall from which issued the hum of ceaseless conversation, occasional bursts of laughter, and the unmistakable sounds produced by the striking of mah-jongg tiles.

Round a blackwood table set right under a large electric bulb that expended its hundred-watt power in solitary grandeur, though it formed part of a chandelier whose other bulbs had to endure the ignominy of taking no part in the pleasant scene, was gathered a group of members of the fair sex, old, middle-aged, and young. Four of them had a more personal interest in what was taking place; the rest were spectators. On the table was spread a smooth, white sheet of paper, and on the paper was a collection of about 150 rectangular blocks made of ivory backed by teak. They were arranged face downward, in four straight rows, having the appearance of an unsymmetrical square. One of the players was about to throw two dice, rolling them between her fingers with obvious enjoyment. They had already played one game but still remained as enthusiastic as ever; they had now reached the beginning of the "South Wind" of the second, the rounds of each game being classified under four groups bearing the cardinal points of the compass, in the order east, south, west, and north. A study of their expressions would form quite a worthy branch of psychology, for each face registered its own peculiar reaction, mental and emotional; chiefly the latter. They knew full well that the complicated game with its multifarious rules and picturesque names—many people are devotees without knowing all its traps or even how to calculate their winnings, for when a round is over each player has to count how many "sticks" he is entitled to gain or lose, and some have never learned to do this, allowing the other players to do the job for them—demands not merely luck for success nor even skill added, but much more the ability to gauge what their opponents, every other player being one's opponent, are trying to achieve and what tiles they hold.

"Ah, Wai Hing!" exclaimed a well-preserved, buxom lady on seeing the girl. "Where have you been? It is quite late."

Wai Hing dutifully informed her mother, Mrs. Chu Weng, of the cause of her absence, greeting the assembled company gracefully.

"You are always out," grumbled Mrs. Chu Weng, bending her head over her tiles, thirteen in number, and stretching out one hand to take a new piece to replace a "flower" that was laid open before her line of upright pieces. "I don't think you have remained at home for even a single day. Always one thing or another, now shopping, now the cinema, now a party; in fact, everything that produces injury and no benefit."

"Ahem!" coughed old Mrs. Sheung, who was such a familiar friend of the family and had, as she often proclaimed in season and out of season, assisted at the birth of Wai Hing that she treated the latter with more severity than Mrs. Chu Weng herself ever did. "Young girls nowadays are hopeless, absolutely hopeless."

She shook her head in confirmation of her lamentation and was proceeding to utter something more drastic when she suddenly gave a sound resembling that produced by a tile and down came her hand on a piece bearing the character "middle," engraved in red, which the player opposite her had just thrown down. She immediately took out of her pile two other pieces of a like nature, and the three "red middle" pieces gleamed in triumph before her.

"Hee! hee!" laughed Mrs. Sheung, revealing only one tooth in her mouth. Then, seeing Wai Hing standing near her, she recalled her other mission in life, namely, the condemnation of young women, and said, half to herself, for she could not afford to take her eyes off the tiles for more than a fraction of a second, "Formerly we were shut up in the house and dared not allow a man to see us. Nowadays the hussies think themselves mighty important if men turn around to look at their bewitching faces! I don't blame the men for our corrupt morals. Their natural relationship to women is like that of ants to sugar! A man who would refuse a woman who purposely sets out to entice him is yet to be found."

She threw down a tile inscribed with six circles. The player on her right, a frail lady on whose face an unfading smile was minted, picked it up and turned down all her pieces, indicating that she had secured a complete "hand." After "sticks" were exchanged between the different protagonists in the drama, each gamester being initially provided with an equal assortment of slips of wood bearing diverse arrangements of dots that served as an easy method for keeping the score, four pairs of hands were stretched out and a grating sound was produced as the tiles were shuffled.

"When is Wai Hing going to get married?" asked the frail lady of nobody in particular as she arranged her tiles.

"High time she does!" exclaimed Mrs. Sheung. "What says the proverb 'An adult daughter resembles an illicit bag of salt'? The moment girls reach puberty they should be safely provided with husbands. Why, I was wedded when I was fourteen!"

"Indeed!" exclaimed Wai Hing. "And how did you relish the experience?"

"My feelings had nothing to do with the matter" was the severe rejoinder. "If I had dared to put in a word to my parents about the affair, I would have been disgraced for life as a monstrous specimen of immodesty. I don't find that any harm has come of it."

"Could you possibly understand what you were in for at such an age? You must have received the shock of your life on your wedding night," remarked Wai Hing serenely.

"What—what did you say?" almost screamed Mrs. Sheung, unwittingly laying one of her tiles open in her thunder-stricken surprise. "Could such devil's language be spoken in my hearing? What kind of a girl is this, over whose birth I presided?" She directed her face toward every person in turn with a helpless look, as if beseeching someone to tell her whether she was in the presence of a malignant fox that had assumed the form of a human being.

"How dare you utter such nonsense!" cried Mrs. Chu Weng.

She cast on her daughter a wrathful glance, partly because she herself had been profoundly startled and partly because she was constrained to make some remark to relieve Mrs. Sheung of her paralyzed state. The frail lady and one or two others smiled secretly to themselves, while the majority were bereft of speech altogether. They gazed at Wai Hing with mingled awe and excitement, scarcely daring to breathe or stir. The tense atmosphere was happily dispelled by the frail lady, who was unhappily seized with a racking fit of coughing, causing everyone to stare at her with anxiety.

"Drink this warm water," said Mrs. Chu Weng with the solicitude of the perfect hostess.

"Are you better?" asked Mrs. Sheung, thumping her patient's back with an energy that she deemed gentle and beneficial, but that, though it produced the desired effect, was rather too rough for the frail lady, as she began to feel her back with her hand to soothe the pain produced.

"Quite well now; many thanks" was the hurried response.

Taking a fresh tile, she dragged it toward her between the thumb and fingers. Without looking at its face and only just by its feel she knew what its value was; not being the tile she needed, she rejected it.

After an interval of silence lasting ten minutes, a most unusual occurrence among the assembled company, one of the spectators, who wore her hair in a massive, compact chignon on the nape of her neck, said, "Oh dear! I have clean forgotten. I don't know what is the matter with me; my memory must be getting bad. I must hurry home now to do what is needful for worshipping the Weaving Damsel tomorrow night."

The hour was already quite late; so it is doubtful what she could possibly contribute, if she got home at that time, toward making the necessary preparations for the festival dedicated to the two constellations, Aquila and Vega, known as the Cowherd and the Weaving Damsel, respectively.

"Plenty of time for that," asserted Mrs. Sheung decisively. "The morning will suffice."

"What is the festival meant to celebrate?" questioned Wai Hing innocently, turning for no reason whatsoever to the frail lady for an explanation.

"The ignorance of the younger generation!" exclaimed Mrs. Sheung in an incredulous tone before the frail lady could utter a word. "A girl not knowing the object of this festival, when it is specially intended for girls. Really, this is monstrous! Have you never taken part in the celebration before?"

"Festivals hold no special interest so far as I am concerned," replied Wai Hing unblushingly. "Formerly I used to participate in them as a matter of course; now I avoid them as much as possible. They are so boring, what with candles, incense sticks, crackers, etc."

"Goodness!" groaned Mrs. Sheung, viciously flicking down a tile with a resounding bang. "I really don't know what the people of the present age are coming to. Their behavior is getting more and more astonishing."

Thereupon she launched forth into a vituperative harangue, which, though it lasted a worthy length of time, could easily be recorded in the words: *quae fuerunt vitia, mores sunt*—what were once vices are now in fashion.

The frail lady mildly tried to turn the flow of her torrential eloquence into a more pleasing channel by saying, "The story of the Cowherd and the Weaving Damsel is very enchanting. I am never tired of listening to it. Won't you please kindly recount it to us, Mrs. Sheung? It will serve to banish the ignorance of the youngsters concerning the origin of tomorrow's worship."

Mrs. Sheung composed her countenance into a dignified state of solemnity at this appeal and said, "Long, long ago …"

"Her words are strangely like those that begin every legend," whispered Wai Hing to a girl by her side.

Luckily for the smooth continuation of the story, Mrs. Sheung did not catch her comment and so was able to carry on with the same grave composure: "There lived in heaven a very beautiful and modest damsel, the daughter of the God of the Sun. This girl was very good, and was, like all good girls, of a domestic turn of mind. She was never tired of working at her loom and wove with tremendous skill: hence her name, Chih Nu (the Weaving Damsel). She worked so hard that she seldom smiled. Her father thought that this tended to make her unhappy and was worried over her industriousness."

"Naturally," whispered Wai Hing to her companion; "I would die of ennui in three days if I had to pass such a life. I wonder how she could stand it."

"Hush, pray," admonished her companion in the same subdued tone, for Mrs. Sheung was gazing at them and she thought the story charming and did not want it to be interrupted.

"After turning the affair over in his mind," went on the narrator, "the God of the Sun came to the conclusion that the problem could only be solved by marrying her away. She would then be more cheerful, and having to look after a man, her thoughts would be diverted to some extent from her loom."

"The story is decidedly getting more interesting, or at least more romantic," murmured Wai Hing to herself.

At that moment the round came to an end, Mrs. Chu Meng having managed to carry it off. After the count was over, Mrs. Sheung continued, in a voice that trembled just a little from emotion, "So the God looked round for a suitable bridegroom. Soon afterward he found just the right person. You know that a bright river runs across the sky. This Tien Ho (Celestial River) is always full of water. You can see it quite clearly, if you care to do so, at night."

She instinctively looked toward the window as if the Celestial River, or the Milky Way, was anxiously inviting her gracious attention; from her position not even the fringe of the sky was visible. Withdrawing her eyes from the darkness outside, she continued, "An excellent man, known to us as Niu Lang (the Cowherd), had his dwelling on its bank, where he tended his cattle. The God was very pleased with him and chose him for his son-in-law. The marriage accordingly took place, and you can imagine that it must have been quite grand. The Cowherd and his bride were pleased with each other, and a change of character came over the girl."

"This is truly become very exciting," said Wai Hing to her companion. "Why should marriage have made her different?" Her companion shook her head to indicate her ignorance.

"She more than fulfilled her father's expectations," went on Mrs. Sheung after another pause produced by the play, which was itself getting more and more engrossing owing to its increasing tempo. The mah-jongg often interfered with the recital; the recital never interfered with the mah-jongg. "Instead of being gloomy, she was now exceedingly gay and lively. She sported the whole time. She ceased to work hard and lost her interest in her former occupation. The transformation of her nature is really surprising."

"Very much so indeed," said Wai Hing aloud, for the first time in the course of the story venturing to utter a comment audible to the entire company.

Mrs. Sheung wrapped her with an uncertain glance, not knowing what the implication was behind the remark, delivered in a flat, expressionless tone. She could not refrain, however, from giving vent to her usual theme in a few words, as a laudable preliminary to the further unfolding of her narrative. "Lively though she became, she was certainly less so than the modern girls who have never known a moment's gravity," she said, pretending to look at the wall above her opposite player's head. "Her conduct now became annoying to her father. He did not relish such an excessive show of good spirits, to say nothing of her extreme laxity with regard to her work. He naturally attributed her change to her preoccupation with her husband, who had likewise ceased to be a diligent man, serious and appropriate in his manners. He was angry with both of them and devised a means of putting an end to their undesirable conduct." The good old lady became rather tedious, for she spoke very slowly. "He decided to part them …"

"He sounds very tyrannical," averred Wai Hing with some heat.

"How can you speak like that of a god?" put in her mother quickly. "Be more reverent."

Mrs. Sheung, thus checked from giving rise to any further reprimand, gulped down her anger and said, "He made the husband set up a new house for himself on the other side of the Celestial River. Sadly, the two parted. There was no bridge across the river, and so they could not meet each other. But, owing to the entreaties of his daughter, he agreed to allow them to come together once a year."

"This is frightful," involuntarily murmured Wai Hing with a pretended shudder. "How hard-hearted some parents could be!" No one heard her or noticed her tremor.

"On the seventh day of the seventh moon each year the husband and wife were given an opportunity for a meeting. How was the man to cross the river?" She made a dramatic pause to heighten the effect of the climax.

"The simplest solution would have been for him to swim over," said Wai Hing, whereupon most of the audience laughed.

Mrs. Sheung tried hard to conceal her annoyance at this unseemly levity, like the grandiloquent orator whose sense of the sublime is damaged by the irresponsible sallies from the crowd. She looked at that moment as if her greatest happiness would be to grab hold of Wai Hing, strip off her skin, and put her to stew in a tank of salt. She closed her mouth with a peremptory snap, maintaining such a prolonged silence that she was obviously not going to carry on with her tale at all. Everybody began to look uncomfortable, and the more timid glanced at the clock to see whether it would be decent to make the time an excuse for taking an abrupt departure.

"Please, Wai Hing," expostulated the frail lady, after an uneasy glance in the direction of the irate Mrs. Sheung, "don't make jesting remarks. They do not suit the lofty nature of the story, which should inspire in us only a reverent interest."

"Why!" interjected Wai Hing in mild surprise. "I didn't mean any harm. I was just making a reasonable suggestion."

"What may seem reasonable to you is senseless to your elders," was the frail lady's response. Turning to Mrs. Sheung after this admonition, she said, "Pray, Mrs. Sheung, tell us how the two spiritual beings were able to triumph over the obstacle of the river."

"The man couldn't swim," categorically affirmed that worthy dame, stabbing a vindictive look at Wai Hing. "The Celestial River is not Repulse Bay or Shek O, where, I am told, men and women strip themselves seminaked for all to see and flounder about in the water. Still less was the unlucky girl a swimmer. If she were born today and living in the world, doubtless she would be able to show her prowess as a fish and might even take the initiative and swim over to her man."

After this pointed observation, which, being received in abashed silence, restored her complacency to a slight extent, she went on, "The magpies were required to serve as a bridge. They collected by tens of thousands and, remaining stationary wing to wing, formed a narrow path along which the Cowherd could tread. He still continues to perform the journey to this day. After they have finished their conversation, the magpies fly away to their nests to gather again the following year. This annual gathering of the birds is called 'Po Niao Ta Chiao' ("the myriad birds form a bridge"). Naturally, the special day is sacred to the couple; and if he couldn't travel whenever it is due, then he would have to wait another year for his chance. They are therefore anxious that nothing should arise to mar their meeting. Sometimes indeed they are deprived of their pleasure. If rain should chance to fall on that day, then it would be impossible for him to cross the river. Never containing less than its full capacity, any additional water would produce an overflow, and the birds would be unable to maintain their steady road under such circumstances."

"What then is the aim of our prayers?" asked the girl who stood by the side of Wai Hing in a faltering voice.

"Surely it needs no explanation," said Mrs. Sheung emphatically. "We will pray tomorrow that the weather be fair and the sky clear." She looked benevolent and ecstatic.

"But what special benefit do we get?" persisted the same interrogator, who thus showed herself to be of a pragmatic temperament, wishing to get good value in return for her devotional exercises.

"The Weaving Damsel inspires us with skill in needlework and embroidery. That's why we worship her," pronounced Mrs. Sheung in a conclusive intonation. "In addition, she will arrange suitable marriages for girls; hence it's their special duty to offer her their prayers."

The young lady who was so interested in the narrative looked happy and satisfied.

"How do we celebrate the festival?" continued Mrs. Sheung, casting a venomous glance at the unlucky Wai Hing. "We worship these celestial beings with fruits and cakes."

"What a beautiful love story!" said Wai Hing dreamily. "I never knew before that our ancestors could make love or thought so highly of it as to commemorate a pair of lovers with a festival. Plainly love is not a modern product."

"Outrageous!" exclaimed Mrs. Sheung, starting from her chair and dropping down again abruptly. "I never heard such profanity. How dare you link a festival with such an indecent idea?"

"What is wrong with my remarks?" asked Wai Hing, genuinely startled out of her reverie.

In her excitable state, the good lady carelessly tossed away a tile, which was immediately picked up by the player to whom no special reference has hitherto been made, for she was of an inconspicuous appearance, being one of those persons whose presence in a room is as little felt as the atmosphere. Besides, she could hold her tongue with phenomenal facility, focusing her entire attention on the play. The moment Mrs. Sheung saw her grab the tile with evident greed she regretted its rejection and quickly remarked, "I want the piece back. I threw it down by mistake …"

"Sorry" was the reply. "People say, 'What has fallen on the earth has grown roots.'"

With this appropriate and decisive utterance, the lucky player turned down her tiles with a gurgle of delight and revealed to the astonished gaze of all present her triumph, having won the maximum score possible in one round. According to their particular play, this was worth eight hundred "sticks" from each of the two other minor players and double the amount from the chief player. In every round, according to regular rotation, one of the four players was the leader; the score between her and any of the other three was twice what would be the case between two minor players. Mrs. Sheung happened to be the leader at that moment, and so she had to bear the brunt of the loss to the lucky player, who till then had been poorer by about two thousand "sticks" but with this successful feat found herself richer by more than a thousand.

Angry indeed was Mrs. Sheung with Wai Hing for this calamity. She did not, however, charge her with the loss in so many words; instead, in reply to her question asked about five minutes earlier, she said, "What is wrong with your remarks! Do you think I have nothing better to do than to tell an idle love story? I was not conscious that the tale had to do with—ahem!—love. And the very mention of the word in your sense is obnoxious and indelicate and extremely unbecoming, and it's high time you learn some manners. Your behavior and your conversation are most abominable!"

After this scathing indictment silence reigned, and soon afterward the game of mah-jongg came to an end; thereupon the company dispersed. Wai Hing retired to her room and, before falling asleep, ruminated over the dolorous plight of the Weaving Damsel, allowing a gentle sigh to escape from her as she wondered why love, in legend as well as in real life, should be synonymous with sorrow. But her worry did not last for even so long as an hour because she was soon enfolded in blissful slumber.

Chapter 3

The Factory

Siu Kam bore an air of anxiety and restlessness as he sat in his office with his feet on the littered table in front of him and his head tilted sideways on his chair in a position that could not possibly be deemed comfortable unless his anatomical structure deviated from the normal. His mental depression did not owe its origin to the repercussions of a business depression, for he was in blessed enjoyment of a soothing bath in the lapping waves of prosperity, which had endured a goodly span of time. His income was regular, he was able to lay aside considerable savings, and his bank manager always greeted him with garrulous affability. He was a prominent member of the chamber of commerce and the subject of enthusiastic eulogies from philanthropic workers carrying subscription rolls, the envy of many a lesser folk; in a word, he was a fine specimen of commercial success.

He deserved his prosperity. When it came to his particular variety of work, he approached the proverbial bee in diligence, though his character in other respects tended toward indolence. He was ready to bear all troubles in connection with business but was extremely averse to meeting any other kind of misery, however trivial. The presence of a quality in one direction does not mark its necessary existence in another. The mathematician may be wonderful for his accuracy and orderliness in regard to the infinitesimal calculus and at the same time strike one dumb with surprise for his slipshod incompetence in arranging ordinary affairs. "Virtue is the foundation and wealth is the product" runs a precept in the Great Learning. Consequently, with his instinctive recognition of the value of this truth, he was virtuous according to the conventional code. We do not mean to depreciate the worth of his morality or to say that his conduct was actuated only by one motive. Doubtless, many influences molded his character, such as natural inclination, custom, and desire for public approbation, for it is also stated: "Wealth glorifies the house; virtue glorifies the person." The brigand also works for riches by a different method; we certainly deny that Siu Kam would ever have been a brigand at all. Concerning the merit of virtue motivated by an ulterior intent, when one comes to think of it, nobody ever practices the good life purely for its own sake; the saint may not wish for success in the present world, but he earnestly desires it in the next. Siu Kam was neither a saint nor a villain; he only wanted to lead a pleasant existence, which is most easily secured by conforming to the rules of society and ministering to its needs.

When he reached manhood, his father, who had made a fortune in the jewelry trade, in order to launch him in the world set up for him at his request a textile factory for the production of cotton goods; in the course of a few years, he had made it hum. The prices of his commodities were excellent and the profits gratifying. The factory, situated on a dingy street in an uninteresting suburb of the city of Victoria, employed scores of workers and was personally run by him with the assistance of a manager.

Almost every day he would be working hard in his office in one corner of the factory on the upper floor with his sleeves tucked up if it was summer and closely buttoned if it was winter. On this day he should have been working as usual, but he wasn't. Instead, he was apparently lost in an idle daydream to the consternation of his manager, who found it hard to explain to him any special requirement as occasion arose. What was he thinking about? Inglorious to tell—what would his elders have said of it? He was contemplating the form of the girl he has seen last night. Just a fleeting glimpse, nothing more, and there he was in a stupor—what degenerate posterity his spotless ancestors had produced! They might well cause their spirit tablets to tremble in their anger. Hitherto, he had not been susceptible to the charms of the opposite sex. Marriage had been repeatedly suggested to him by his parents; indeed, on one occasion when they insisted on making an engagement for him, he threatened to leave home altogether. It is doubtful whether he would have actually carried out his intention if the deal were concluded and they were to compel him to stick to what they had transacted on his behalf; but they ultimately gave up the attempt for fear that he might turn out more resolute than they expected with the result that the engagement would have to be called off, with immeasurable loss of face to them. He did not refuse marriage on any set principle; he just felt that, somehow or other, the problem held no special interest, and he kept repeating to himself that he would think about it later on.

"What a beautiful face!" he murmured, getting up from his chair and walking toward the window. "How noble was her mien! I have never seen such a wonderful person before; absolutely crushing!"

The prospect from the window was rather dismal—a gray sky bulging with layers of dyspeptic clouds and tenement houses that looked exceedingly dark and dirty indeed. Nevertheless, his lyrical rhapsody was not dampened by such uninspiring surroundings. Under the influence of passion, his imagination must have become touchingly poetical, and probably in his mind's eye, he was gazing at a scene lifted straight out of the pages of the Arabian Nights entertainments.

"Really," said he, scratching his head, "she resembles a fairy. I wonder who she is and where she lives. What a pity that I was not even aware of her existence formerly! How blissful my life would have been if I had known her intimately these last few years. It's all very sad, but fate is omnipotent." He smiled a faint smile, as one often does in derision of one's own misery.

Suddenly a new thought raised its powerful pistol and fired right into the middle of his cranium, making him start with horror: "Suppose she is already married ... This would be fine! Excellent! Two men were with her. One of them was possibly her ..." He clenched his fist and brought it down—feebly, on empty air. He gritted his teeth, but finding that the sensation was not very pleasant, he relaxed his mouth again. "Truly life is a misery. The only happy man is the Buddhist monk, who escapes from life and wishes to attain nirvana. If, as seems most likely, I couldn't marry her, what should I do? Become a monk?"

The idea delighted him in his mood of desperation. For a while he enthused over the simple, peaceful life of the monastery, with its freedom from all desire. His eyes gradually possessed a vacant look; nirvana was apparently fast closing in upon him. Then the figure of an ordinary monk sidled through his mind: bald head, yellow robe, wooden bowl, and all complete.

"How I would look with not one hair! How my friends would laugh at me! To eat only vegetables and murmur the whole day long: 'Na-mo O-mi-to-fu' ('I rely on your grace, Amitabha')! What an uncomfortable life!"

He regretfully but firmly dismissed the monastery as a solution to his difficulties.

"Oh!" he exclaimed impatiently. "Why was I ever born? I am so fed up with everything." He walked back to his seat and sat down with a flop. For some time he shook his mind and his body. "But what am I being so miserable about?" he finally asked himself. "I used to be very happy. Why all this pother? A girl. Ha, ha! Now think properly, Siu Kam. How can you be so foolish as all this? How can you allow your life to be ruined for such a trifling reason? Girls are inferior to men. Your honorable ancestors were right. Do you mean to say that a man of any dignity like you could find nothing better to do than to worry his head and waste his time over a mere woman? You are getting very absurd. As if she is the only girl on earth. Now consider this fact. The population of the Middle Nation alone, not to speak of the rest of the world, runs into several hundred millions. Half of it is sure to consist of women. What is there so unique about that particular specimen then? If you are anxious to have a wife, why, you can easily get one. You have seen many girls far more beautiful. She has many faults." He tried to enumerate her deficiencies; to his chagrin he could find none. "Besides, your behavior is immoral. If you go on at this rate, you will disgrace your family and your reputation."

Having arrived at this highly satisfactory conclusion, he bent over some papers and forced himself to work. But his mind continually wandered off from the room against his will and frolicked about with extraordinary agility, visions rising before his eyes as gracefully as Venus from the billows, visions of the rosy future that might conceivably come to pass. At one moment he soared into the pure empyrean of bliss; the next, he plunged as precipitately into the murky abyss of woe. Now a smile glided over his face; then a frown contracted his brow; then a groan of anguish, which would have reduced a heart of stone to as liquid a state as tin in the furnace, shot from his throat. Try as he might, and there is no denying that such a heroic struggle is admirable, he could not rid himself of the hurt so unfortunately produced in him. Nevertheless, as the poet sang, "All men strive and who succeeds?" We cannot blame him for his futile revolt. Even the Olympian Jove was an easy prey to passion. What then could an ordinary mortal like poor Siu Kam do? He laid down his pen, and a mournful expression, as of one who has been called upon to engage in an unfair contest and is absolutely resigned to his outrageous fate, wrapped his countenance, and he began to think himself an interesting martyr on the altar of love.

A knock sounded on the door. "Come in," he said nonchalantly, without turning his face to look at the intruder, who happened to be Wong Tak Cheong, the lawyer. The latter stared at him in wonder—he had never seen him so woebegone before—and called him by name. Siu Kam started and recognizing him said, trying to assume as happy an expression as possible, "Please sit down."

"What's the matter?" asked Tak Cheong, getting ready to wear a sympathetic mien.

"Oh, nothing" was the laconic rejoinder.

"You are not worried over last night's affair, are you?"

"What affair?" asked Siu Kam, startled. "How could he guess what betides me?" he thought peevishly. "My word, he is really a wizard."

"About the pickpocket, you know," said Tak Cheong, a trifle surprised in his turn at this strange lapse of memory.

"Oh, to be sure, I remember it," said Siu Kam, vastly relieved.

He had, in fact, completely forgotten the incident in his preoccupation with an affair so much more absorbing in its character, though such occurrences by no means befell him so often as to merit speedy oblivion.

After he and his three companions had departed from the teahouse, they took a leisurely stroll around the city as a kind of nocturnal exercise calculated to promote sound sleep. In the course of their peregrinations, they entered a lane that led to a main street. It was narrow, dirty, and steep; unlighted by a lamp, its only illumination came from the feeble rays filtering through chinks in closed doors and through partially opened windows. Some hapless persons were sleeping in the lane, huddled up in ragged blankets; once, Siu Kam nearly stepped on a figure lying right in the middle of the road. When about to emerge from this sorry place, Siu Kam, whose mind was somewhere else, was suddenly awakened to reality by an exclamation from Tak Cheong. Spinning round he found, dangling before his incredulous eyes, his purse in a hand, held in the tenacious grip of the lawyer. The hand that held the purse formed part of the person of an unkempt sprig of humanity, who at that moment wore a scared look, plainly regretting his unpropitious action. Siu Kam peered into his pocket and failed to fathom how the magician had contrived to fish the article out as the pocket had all its undisturbed composure intact. A policeman was near at hand, and thereupon they all had to proceed to the station to have the case duly recorded. Siu Kam returned home and promptly forgot about the episode, which normally would have occupied his attention for some time.

"The court will try the case tomorrow," said Tak Cheong, putting on a precise, professional air.

"Yes, so soon," said Siu Kam languidly.

"What the devil is the matter with this chap?" thought Tak Cheong, piqued. "He seems to think that the possible loss of a purse is of no importance whatever." Aloud he said, "I have prepared the evidence thoroughly. The thief is sure to get the maximum amount of rigorous imprisonment. Let me see; how long will that be?"

"As he has not actually stolen anything, perhaps it is just as well if he is let off." Siu Kam uttered this astonishing sentence not because he was inspired by benevolence but in order to get rid of the unwelcome discussion as soon as possible.

"What!" exclaimed Tak Cheong, for a moment losing his becoming gravity. "It does not matter whether he has gotten away with anything or not; he is a criminal all the same. As a matter of fact, if he had really succeeded in his attempt, it would mean that he could not be brought to justice." He eyed Siu Kam askance and thought, "This fellow is dotty. I wonder what has come over him. I hope he has not been ruining his business, for he is a capital friend."

"I had only a few dollars in the purse," said Siu Kam, getting quite bored. "That poor fellow looked as if he was starving. I wish I had given the money to him."

Tak Cheong put on an ironic grin; he seldom smiled except in connection with his profession, and then sarcastically.

"My, my," he said, "are you thinking of becoming a Buddha or what? Why not distribute your property among all the street sleepers in the town? That would at least be more meritorious than giving it to a thief."

Siu Kam blushed in confusion and said, "Well, I feel rather indisposed today and can't concentrate on the case. I shall follow your advice, though."

"That's all right," said Tak Cheong, immediately displaying altruistic interest in his client's welfare. "I have done everything necessary. There's nothing much for you to do. I'll call again tomorrow morning to take you to court. What ails you?"

"I don't know," replied Siu Kam in a hesitating manner. "Perhaps I ate too much last night."

Then, suddenly, he recollected that Tak Cheong had exchanged greetings with the girl and the tall man; strange that he should have been unaware of the importance of this fact. Turning breathlessly to him, he was about to speak hurriedly when the thought struck him that he should not give himself away by a display of undue inquisitiveness. So, composing his features to as expressionless and noncommittal a state as possible, he said carelessly, as if it was just a matter of ordinary polite conversation, "Who was that man who nodded to you last night? I don't remember seeing him before."

"Where did we meet him?" was Tak Cheong's rejoinder, waving his hand to imply that he was on nodding terms with too wide a circle of acquaintance to be able to recollect this one with any degree of ease.

"In the teahouse, you know," said Siu Kam, inwardly praying that the lawyer's excellent memory would not fail him just on this occasion. "There were two men and two girls in the party. You exchanged greetings with one of the girls, I think."

"Oh, I remember," said Tak Cheong airily. "The man's name is Chu Ko San, the son of Chu Weng. The father is one of my most important clients"—he puffed out his chest—"and is a most worthy person. He owns many farms in the New Territories and whole blocks of houses in Kowloon. I collect the rents for him, and he always consults me about his affairs." His tone distinctly indicated that others should follow such exemplary conduct. "However, he is rather weak. His son is a disgraceful libertine. He pampers him. Now, if he were my offspring, it wouldn't be long before he is made to come to his senses." He put on a look of impressive sternness.

"Why, what is wrong with him?" asked Siu Kam incuriously, mentally trying to find a convenient way to put to him another question that was gnawing his vitals out.

"He is a gambling addict and an incurable ne'er-do-well. As the proverb says: 'The fist has already rubbed through the screen.' He has ruined his reputation. The turf and the gambling table are his chief passions. Now there is no harm in an occasional game of cards or buying a sweepstake ticket. But fan-tan, which he plays in the dens of Macao, alone has made his losses total tens of thousands of dollars. The other man who was with him last night is his companion in evil, so I hear. Now that I come to think of it," a ruminative look veiled his eyes, "it was the first time I ever saw him taking out his sister in the company of that man. No decent girl should be seen together with such a person. There was another girl with them who didn't look too good either. He seems to be introducing his sister to all sorts of undesirable people."

"Which one was his sister?" asked Siu Kam with a painful effort to show no interest.

"The one who greeted me, of course," said Tak Cheong. "I don't know the other girl."

"What is her name, Miss Chu? I suppose she is not married."

"No. Her name is—I don't know her personal name. What do you want to know her name for?" said Tak Cheong, raising his eyebrows just a little.

"Just out of ordinary curiosity. This morning's paper mentioned a certain Miss Chu who was going to the South Sea Islands. I was wondering whether it could be your friend," said Siu Kam with a facile mendacity that astonished himself.

"She could not be the person then," said the lawyer, "or else her father would have asked my advice about such a trip. She's a fine girl," he continued, "pleasing in her behavior and modern and progressive in her outlook. She would make an excellent wife for the right man."

"The father, from what you said, must be a person whom one would be proud to meet," remarked Siu Kam after cudgeling his brains desperately to discover a decent way to obtain an introduction to the daughter.

"Certainly," said Tak Cheong without any reluctance. "I think you should cultivate his acquaintance. I am going to see him on some business a week hence. Why not come with me to his house?"

"Well," said Siu Kam, concealing his satisfaction to perfection, "I have hardly any excuse for calling on him."

"One worthy man should know another," enunciated Tak Cheong pompously; "that is reason enough."

"If you think I won't be intruding on him, I shall be pleased to go with you," said Siu Kam politely.

"That settles it," said Tak Cheong. "We had better pay the visit in the evening about six o'clock."

Tak Cheong arose and stalked gravely away. The moment the door was closed behind his visitor, Siu Kam started to walk up and down the room, his mind in a whirl of trepidation, expectation, and exaltation. Joyous smiles broke from him as spontaneously as Aurora disperses the gray clouds of dawn; gone was his lamentable attack of *taedium vitae*—weariness of life—and his despair had deservedly passed into the limbo of oblivion.

"Life," he said aloud, "is a golden reality. It is exceedingly beautiful. I don't know how the Buddhist saint could think that life is so full of sorrow that his greatest wish is to escape the cycle of birth and death. I am not sure that we are ever born again; but if the doctrine of the transmigration of souls is true, I should certainly love to be reborn. Of course," he added as an afterthought, "my next life should be much the same as my present one. It would not do to become a dog or a mosquito. Ha, ha!"

He was full of exuberant vitality the rest of the day, and he worked at his usual tasks right merrily, albeit at intervals almost as regular as clockwork he made a momentary pause to trace in his imagination the elegant and symmetrical figure of the producer of his happiness. So curiously changeable is the human temperament and so reactive to external influence is the mind. Circumstance rides the horse of behavior.

Chapter 4

Macao

Macao, occupied by the Portuguese since 1557, was at the time of this story a superannuated town whose glory, if it ever had any, had long since vanished. Much of the real blood of commerce having ebbed from its veins, it tried to glorify its feeble existence by endeavoring to maintain a reputation as a resort of pleasure, the gambling establishment being its principal ornament. Situated forty miles west of Hong Kong, it could be reached by a small coastal steamer that took more than three hours to perform the journey between the two towns. Standing at the entrance to the spacious estuary of the Chu Kiang or Pearl River, it was surrounded by a belt of brown water, impregnated with the fine earth known as loess. The harbor usually contained some ships, beside a goodly number of the familiar dirty junks, bearing away cargoes of silk, opium, and rice, the exports of the colony. Many historical spots served to remind the visitor of its past, including ruins of forts and churches, and a bust in the botanical gardens commemorated the great Portuguese poet, Camoens, who wrote part of his epic, the Lusiad, at this seaport. Most of its streets were narrow and smelly, though they were not steep like those of Hong Kong.

In the central street of the town, which bubbled a lively, busy scene, soared a hotel of about ten stories, within whose precincts were included a restaurant on the mezzanine and a cabaret on the roof garden. In a bedroom on the third floor sat in earnest conversation two men, one of whom was Chu Ko San, the tall brother of our heroine, Wai Hing. The other was his boon companion, the immaculate Leong Yin Pat, whose jade ring, which bore the figure of a bat, was but the most conspicuous ornament of a smartly dressed person. Because the ideographs for "bat" and "luck" are homonymous, both being pronounced "fu," the bat had become an emblem of prosperity.

The expressions on their faces were deadly serious, for they were engaged in a most momentous discussion; to wit, the attenuated state of their budget, which had suffered deplorably in the course of the past few days on the gaming tables. They had consistently encountered only reverses and now had between them scarcely enough to last one more night. The gambler's conduct is one of the most indubitable proofs of the irrationality of the human mind; though most of his time is consecrated to worry and anxiety and his face is usually a mask of gloom, nevertheless he feels life to be an irksome misery if indulgence in his passion is denied him.

"We ought to have won last night," frowned Ko San, stretching out a hand to grasp a bottle of brandy that was reposing luxuriously on a sideboard at his elbow. "We were winning till a villain with an unlucky squint came along and tried to imitate our stakes. Thereafter our fortune changed rapidly. He was such a bad omen. I thought of giving him a hearty kick." He poured out a tumbler of the intoxicant and drained it off at one gulp as if to banish the evil influence exerted by the stranger he mentioned.

"I noticed it too," Yin Pat assented to his friend's superstitious suggestion. "But what are we going to do now? That is our present problem. How are we to replenish our purses?" His glance distilled a mark of interrogation.

"That is a problem," said Ko San bitterly, "that only the gods can solve."

"We certainly can't wait till it rains gold from heaven," said Yin Pat. "Why not send a telegram to your father?"

"Much good will that do!" retorted Ko San. "Indeed, if he were to know that I am here, it would be fine fun. Last time we almost had a quarrel, and he threatened to disinherit me if I came here anymore.

I bluffed him into believing that I was paying a visit to Canton." He laughed mirthlessly at the recollection.

"Fathers are a nuisance," declared Yin Pat with convincing emphasis. "Luckily mine died a good while ago and left me his property."

He looked at Ko San sympathetically, silently voicing his earnest hope that such a fortunate consummation should likewise befall him pretty soon. He did not mention the fact that what remained of his property after years of extravagance—his wealth was like a one-way street—was difficult to compute, not for its gorgeous proportions, but because he was so hopelessly burdened with an accumulation of debts that he could never be sure what the respective amounts of his assets and liabilities were. His balance sheet would defy the most expert accountant to draw. He had been living on his wits for a long time; so long that he had come to the conclusion that he was a genius in the art of prolonging existence in apparently comfortable circumstances. He knew how to release flattery and capture money.

Ko San was temporarily taken aback by his friend's cynical words and did not make an immediate reply. He had hitherto regarded his venerable parent as an unfailing though sometimes recalcitrant source of revenue but had not considered the profitability of his eventual decease. He did not even know the extent of his possible inheritance as he never bothered his head over business of any sort. His unformulated maxim was to lead a short and merry life. Many gentlemen hold the same enamoring theory; what would happen if they were to live to be centenarians is a moot point. Incidentally, every centenarian, when questioned, invariably avows that he had led an exemplary life, has never known a moment's sickness, presumably not even a cold or a headache, and hasn't done many things that ordinary mortals do. So it can be taken for granted that the merry gentleman never lives to a ripe age at all, for his dissipations are sure to produce a host of ills, not the least of which is ennui induced by satiety. Ko San never pondered the consequences of his conduct; his brain was not constructed for sound reflection.

"Some men are too healthy to perish early," he remarked, evidently referring to his honorable parent. "I confess that I don't regard my father as being really bad. I can't say why; that's how it strikes me. Still, like all these old men, he is full of moral platitudes that are extremely vexatious. Of course, I don't follow his nonsensical precepts. Life would be a perfect bore if I were to behave according to his wishes. A decided bore." He shuddered at the prospect.

"Not the least bit wrong," corroborated Yin Pat. "I laugh when I see a man, especially a young man, who looks as though he has never tasted any real pleasure. Such a one, say I, is an unmitigated idiot."

"Not to spend when one can ..."

"What is the use of money except in giving away in exchange for solid pleasure?" asked Yin Pat, addressing the ceiling. A female voice floated across the corridor; he listened attentively for a moment. "Solid pleasure as in the form of cards, women, wine, etc. What has always seemed to me the most remarkable phenomenon in the world is the miser. He is truly a mystery. The only good thing he ever does is when he dies and bequeaths his horde to a jolly son. It is extremely curious, but out of such bad stock sensible children can be produced."

"What kind of a man was your father?" asked Ko San with the unembarrassed frankness of a pal.

"He was a miser all right," said Yin Pat happily. "I used to have plenty of trouble with him. He would never pay my debts for me. They kept mounting up. When my creditors dunned me, I used to say to them, 'Come and collect your money when you see the doorway of our house stuck with the white paper of mourning.' Extremely witty for a mere boy to say, I think. I was still in my teens then."

"Didn't people report to him your words?" asked Ko San with anxious interest.

"They certainly did. He could do nothing, though. You see, I was an only child, and there was nowhere else for his money to go. To be the sole son has its compensations," said Yin Pat with satisfaction. Then he pursued his discourse in a reminiscent tone. "What a rollicking life I have had! To be sure I spent a lot—more than I could afford perhaps. That's why I am rather hard up now." He flashed an ingenuous smile to show that he was not ashamed of his confession. "But what then? It doesn't matter. I shall soon be all right again. The tide of life must sometimes rise and sometimes retreat. I worry very little."

"You are a very remarkable man," declared Ko San, a flame of enthusiastic admiration kindling in his eyes. "You have long been my ideal."

"Your words are too complimentary," deprecated Yin Pat, pleasure oozing from all his pores nevertheless. "To tell the truth, I have never found a friend like you." And to tell the truth, it was extremely improbable that he could have performed such a feat.

"Our affection is mutual," said Ko San. "I feel that our friendship will last forever." After a short pause, in which he consumed another draught of brandy, he continued, "I see no way of settling our pecuniary difficulties at present. We had better enjoy this evening as much as our limited means will permit and have one more fling on the tables; if our luck does not turn, we'll go home by the boat that leaves here after midnight. What say you?"

"That seems reasonable," said Yin Pat, shrugging his shoulders to denote resignation to the inevitable. "And now, I think, it's time we go for a walk before we have dinner."

The sun, low on the horizon, diffused its lingering mellow radiance over the town as they emerged into the hubbub of the teeming street, pulsing with life in motion. The fokis, or shop assistants, were enjoying their evening rice with a tremendous amount of gusto under the shadow of merchandise; they felt rather pleased that, for a short hour or so, people abounded in the streets but few entered the shops, giving them a breathing spell. The two friends wandered through congested lanes and emerged on the sea front where the boat population was likewise engaged in its well-nigh solitary diurnal enjoyment—eating. The sight was stimulating, and they looked at each other, the same thought silently taking a sweet journey round their minds; they usually took their dinner much later, but now they repaired to a restaurant. An hour later they emerged; the town was now wrapped in gloom, shot with lights, and the crowd was even more numerous, though most of it strolled along at a leisurely pace, enjoying the cool of the evening.

Notwithstanding the fact that there were many gambling saloons, all equally inviting, the two comrades, after casting appraising glances at them from the outside, repaired to their favorite haunt. There, crowded round oblong tables where fan-tan was played, surged the gamesters; the saloon was open to the street, and on the pavement stood a host of onlookers. The play was hot and money flowed. Emotions of hope and fear alternated rhythmically on many a face; some looked as if their lives hung in the balance. Ko San began by winning; being thus put into a high good humor he began to grow reckless. The more he won, the higher became his stakes. Yin Pat was more cautious, but luck was against him from the first; after losing only a few times he had to borrow from Ko San. Thereafter he neither won nor lost to any appreciable extent and became more interested in his friend's play than in his own. After his luck had reached its zenith, Ko San began to lose steadily, just as a stone thrown upward into the air, on attaining the maximum height within its power, descends under the inexorable force of gravity. When a substantial amount had returned into the hands of the banker, Yin Pat advised him to stop for the night, thinking that they could thus afford to pass another agreeable day in the town, but Ko San seemed quite deaf to his friend's suggestion. The sight of the money he had snatched, which for some unknown reason he now regarded as his legitimate and ought-by-rights-to-be-inalienable property, flowing away from him exasperated him exceedingly, and he was resolved to win it back. His own money started to leave him; after some time, in a fit of agonized impetuosity and devoutly hoping for a last chance to retrieve his losses, he put all he had on one big stake on the number three. He could hardly breathe for the suspense and exclaimed excitedly to the banker, "Open the bowl!"

"Wait a moment; the others have not finished laying their stakes yet." He touched the bowl, moving it slightly.

"Open the bowl, I say!" shouted Ko San.

"This is ridiculous," said the banker. But at that time all the stakes were placed and he revealed the collection of beans. After the count was made, the winning number being two, Ko San saw with lightning flashing from his eyes the banker sweep his money away.

"What were you doing with the bowl just now?" demanded Ko San truculently.

"I did not do anything," said the banker with bland politeness.

"Oh yes, you did," said Ko San, his face red with excitement. "You knew I was going to win, so you manipulated the number of beans."

"I think you are drunk," said the banker just as politely. "There are many gentlemen here." He waved his arm round the table to appeal to the other players. "Did any of you see me doing anything amiss?"

"You are a cheat," shouted Ko San without waiting to hear what the others would say.

The outraged banker glared indignantly, and Yin Pat dragged Ko San out of the room as he noticed two men stepping ominously forward, apparently to lay hands on his misbehaved companion.

"I told you to stop playing in time," said Yin Pat when they were safe in the street.

"I am sorry," said Ko San in contrition. "I have lost every dollar. I wonder how we are going to go back."

"Never mind; I still have something left," returned Yin Pat. What he had left was largely made up of the money he had shortly before borrowed from Ko San and that, luckily enough, he had not contrived to lose.

On returning to their hotel they found that it was only eleven o'clock and the boat was not due to sail for another four hours. The electric lifts were still working with extraordinary energy, and there were many people ascending to the cabaret on the roof garden. Yin Pat could not resist the temptation of enjoying a few dances; accordingly, instead of returning to their rooms, they found themselves sitting round a ring enclosing a smooth floor on which lightly glided the feet of the dancers. The hired hostesses, as they deftly followed the steps of their partners who clasped them in a thrilling embrace, chatted and smiled as if they had known them all their lives and looked as if their hearts were full of love for their men.

"What kind of awful stuff is this which you call dancing?" Ko San's father once angrily asked his son. "It was the most indecent exhibition imaginable. When I first saw it—I was dragged thither by curiosity—I nearly fainted. Men and women are clasping one another under the broad glare of the lights and spinning around in such a ludicrous manner. I can conceive of nothing more derogatory to the dignity of man. The very sight of the spectacle is more than enough for me, and the effect of such behavior is demoralizing in the extreme. Of all our modern innovations this dancing is the most undesirable."

Ko San was not in the least disturbed by his father's opinion. "What could one expect from such old-fashioned people as he?" he thought. To him, dancing was all that was romantic and joyous; one had all the delights of making love to a variety of girls without any serious consequences. Moving the legs in this rhythmical way was also good exercise to keep the body fit, and he wanted to be healthy in order to be able to enjoy.

"Good exercise?" burst out his father when this reason was advanced to him. "For every kind of evil there is always some strange excuse. The nervous energy and unholy excitement expended in this form of amusement together with the late hours entailed are more than enough to counterbalance any supposed benefit to health accruing therefrom."

Tonight, however, in his extreme dejection, Ko San did not feel disposed to dance, and he executed a few steps perfunctorily; Yin Pat, though, enjoyed himself thoroughly. After staying on for more than an hour, they repaired to their rooms.

Yin Pat immediately fell asleep after setting his alarm clock so that it might arouse him at the proper minute before they boarded their boat, but Ko San tossed restlessly in bed, a prey to anxiety, trying to hit upon the best means of extracting a fresh supply of dough from his parent. His brain, however, functioned very badly, for he could evolve no plan. He often looked at his watch to see whether it was time to leave the hotel, for the night seemed to him very oppressive and he yearned for the morning.

At a quarter past two he rose and wakened Yin Pat, thus making the latter's alarm clock a superfluity. After collecting their meager appurtenances, they went downstairs and paid their bill; taking their departure from the hotel in rickshaws, they soon reached the steamer. The night was fine, and the bright moon swept the waters softly, weaving her mysterious magic over land and sea and smiling as gently and coolly as if all that she looked upon was at peace. Ko San conceived an antipathy toward the heavenly orb, for it seemed to him that she bore a special sneer for his behoof and impecuniosity.

At three o'clock the vessel silently left the harbor, steaming eastward to Hong Kong. The sea was not rough, though the vessel, being small, rocked to an appreciable extent as it sailed through the darkness, bearing within its bosom its human as well as material freight. Most of the passengers, including Yin Pat, were soon wrapped in slumber. Ko San, attempting to sleep and forget his worries, succeeded so far as to doze off and on in a fitful manner with a goodly series of spectral dreams. When at last he wearily got up and went on deck, the steamer was rapidly approaching the wharf and morning had broken over the green hills in rosy resplendence, arrayed in a garb of oscillating clouds, ethereal in their luminous texture.

Chapter 5

The Meeting

"The weather this evening is extremely fine and bracing," remarked the lawyer, Tak Cheong, to Siu Kam as they were on the point of entering the house of Mr. Chu Weng, the father of Wai Hing. "We are lucky to have chosen today for our little visit. I hope our host is in."

As it so happened, Mr. and Mrs. Chu Weng were enjoying an agreeable confabulation at the time; they were glad nevertheless, if one was entitled to judge from their comportment, to see Tak Cheong and his friend. After the necessary introductions were made and tea, not one whit less indispensable, was placed before the guests, although they had shortly before already imbibed a certain quantity, Tak Cheong entered into a discussion with Mr. Chu Weng concerning the business that had brought him. Mrs. Chu Weng, who, being considerably older than Siu Kam, felt no embarrassment at all before him, began to converse with him on the interesting topic of his mother.

"Ask your mother to drop in and have a chat with us, should she chance to be in our neighborhood," she said with a hospitable smile.

"She will be proud to do so," promised the accommodating Siu Kam with strange confidence.

She then asked him about his mother's name, age, habits, and tastes with charming frankness, and he responded with a certain amount of inward discomfort.

"This is a most well-behaved young man," thought Mrs. Chu Weng. "His family must be exceedingly respectable."

"I hope the daughter is not as inquisitive as the mother" was Siu Kam's reflection. "I wonder where she is."

He looked round the room, not only at the four walls but toward the ceiling, as if he expected her to drop down from that elevation.

Mr. Chu Weng coughed with impressive liberality as his financial discussion with the lawyer came to a close. He possessed a partially bald head, blinking eyes, and a mild mouth.

"He is too gentle to hurt a mosquito," Mrs. Chu Weng was fond of declaring.

She prized this trait of his; it is always very good to have a meek husband. He placed implicit trust in the lawyer and concerned himself as little as possible with business, for he had now reached, as he often said, the autumn of his life and desired to rest his bones. His cough was a manifestation of his relief from the burden of the lawyer's pompous explanations.

"Has Miss Chu gone to the South Sea Islands?" asked Tak Cheong as he stuffed his papers into his pocket.

"No," replied Mr. Chu Weng in huge surprise. "Why do you ask?"

"What can she ever want to do there?" ejaculated his spouse in unison.

"Oh, a person with a name said to have resembled hers sailed for that place a few days ago, according to the papers. I thought it couldn't be she."

Siu Kam was absorbed in contemplation of a delicate porcelain vase on which were painted two winged dragons, the good spirits of the waters, which brought wind and rain. He contemplated these beneficent creatures evidently because they were emblematic of the moral man who could exercise restraint and regulate his feelings to a proper degree of harmony, and he was in dire need of such exemplary behavior. He pretended to be unaware of Tak Cheong's inappropriate inquiry and heartily wished that he had not had occasion to produce such a fiction about the beautiful Wai Hing. He was fearful every second that Tak Cheong might turn to him and put him in an embarrassing position as the man who first discovered the visit of the daughter of the house to those enamoring tropical regions. However, his fears were happily without foundation.

"There she is," remarked Mrs. Chu Weng as a clear voice floated into the room.

Immediately afterward Wai Hing, who had been paying a half-hour's visit to a neighbor, made a graceful entrance into the hall, and the first person on whom her eyes alighted was Siu Kam. For a moment she seemed not very sure where she had encountered him before; then a faint smile, suspiciously suggestive of amusement, curled the corners of her mouth. The lawyer, Tak Cheong, introduced Siu Kam to her.

"I think I have seen Mr. Yuen before," said she serenely.

"Where?" exclaimed both her parents simultaneously.

"In a teahouse with Mr. Wong," she replied with a mischievous gleam in her eyes. She was enjoying herself and no mistake.

Siu Kam gave a barely perceptible start. His astonishment was colossal and would have betrayed itself to a greater extent if not for the influence of the inanimate creatures on the vase, for he was not aware that she had noticed him at all, to say nothing of being able to recognize him. True, he had also seen her only once hitherto, but then he had been forcibly struck by her as with the impact of a thunderbolt and had been thinking of her with scarcely any intermission since then. It could not be that she had been experiencing the same ineffable sensations vis-à-vis him—impossible. The faculty of memory filled him with wonder; daily multitudinous impressions are produced, yet a chance encounter, occurring in the most casual way imaginable, can, after an interval in which it would seem to have vanished completely, be resurrected.

"Are you very fond of teahouses?" pursued Wai Hing.

"Very," murmured Siu Kam rather shamefacedly.

"Why?" came the absurd question.

"I like the jovial atmosphere," answered Siu Kam, taken aback.

"Do you usually stare at the other customers?" she asked with the air of one who is trying to keep up a polite conversation.

"That is a very ridiculous query," interposed Mr. Chu Weng.

"No, I seldom stare at anybody," said Siu Kam in a slightly angry tone; even on his accommodating disposition the stress was beginning to produce too great a strain. "Few people are interesting enough to merit such attention."

Wai Hing was impressed, but she still continued with her most unlovely banter, having never learned the virtue of modest courtesy.

"What kind of people do you consider interesting?"

"One does not analyze one's taste on such a subject," put in Mrs. Chu Weng. "You are really asking most embarrassing questions. Pay no attention to her, Mr. Yuen. She is a bit wrong-headed, like all modern girls."

Yuen Siu Kam smiled and did not know what to say. Wai Hing was hurt by his silence as well as by her mother's slighting reference to herself.

"Being a modern man yourself"—she was singularly obtuse in regard to etiquette—"I should like to know whether you subscribe to my mother's dictum about the young girls of today."

"They seem to me singularly free; too much so in some respects for their own good," said Siu Kam pointedly.

Mrs. Chu Weng laughed. "You are perfectly right." She scrutinized him with benevolent interest.

"Then you would advocate that they should be put under lock and key as in former times," remarked the egregious Wai Hing.

"Not … not exactly," replied Siu Kam. "Though some of them deserve such treatment."

Mr. Chu Weng rocked with mirth; he was so very tickled.

"Obviously, our precious daughter is one of those girls whose liberty has gone to their heads," he observed. "She should be put under strict control."

"Why don't you attempt the interesting experiment?" asked his spouse.

"She is now too big," said Mr. Chu Weng with regret.

"Then you should have taught her better formerly" was the retort.

"What about you?" sneered Mr. Chu Weng, if the faint manifestation round his lips could be regarded as a sneer. "It is the special duty of mothers to take care of daughters."

"I can take care of myself very well," said Wai Hing, tossing her shingled hair. "You two need not quarrel on my account."

"You two!" repeated Mr. Chu Weng with a rueful smile, looking round on the assembled company. "This is her respectful way of addressing her parents."

"Come, come," said the lawyer gravely. "Miss Chu means well. Her words and actions are just the result of high spirits. High spirits breed liveliness. Liveliness breeds a joyful existence. And this is what all people desire," he concluded, pleased with his own logical deduction.

Mr. Chu Weng evidenced surprise. "It never occurred to me that you could be fond of liveliness. You are always quite serious," he remarked.

"I am not a young girl," said the lawyer with great dignity. "Behavior that is appropriate in one person may not be so in another. Nevertheless, my life is a supremely happy one in its own way."

If the lawyer with all his astuteness could only know how little attention the damsel, whose cause he was advocating, was paying to him, his life would have, for the nonce at any rate, deviated a good deal from its normal tenor, so enviably satisfactory, according to his own assertion. His words were to him exceedingly valuable, and inattention on the part of anyone privileged to hold converse with him pricked his vanity. However, Wai Hing assumed an expression that seemed to indicate her due appreciation of the eloquence of her champion; in reality, his voice entered her ears and not her mind.

She was engaged in a most unmaidenly appraisal of Siu Kam, his merits and his eligibility as a suitor. She did not find it difficult to construe his attitude toward her and was secretly very much gratified at her conquest; still, the mere fact that a man loved her did not mean that she should reciprocate in like manner. Though she was addicted to exhilarating discourses on the subject of romance—she and her girlfriends breathed in an atmosphere of amorous fancy—and dreamed of its superb delights, she was yet too shrewd to fall headlong in love with a person of whom she knew nothing. On prima facie evidence she liked Siu Kam; there was nothing wrong with him. When her meditations had reached a gratifying state, she turned on him a pleased smile. Before he could recover from his surprise at this unexpected and unintelligible phenomenon, there entered a corpulent gentleman with his equally corpulent spouse—a well-matched pair. Mr. and Mrs. Chu Weng rapturously greeted the new arrivals; the lawyer rose and gravely signified his intention to take his departure.

"Why not stay to dinner?" Mr. Chu Weng invited.

"Sorry, I have some business to do at home," responded Tak Cheong.

"Please do oblige us by staying," pleaded Mrs. Chu Weng.

"I really cannot," said Tak Cheong, impervious to her appeal.

"At any rate, your friend need not go back with you," remarked Mrs. Chu Weng. "You must allow us a little more of your company," she said, addressing Siu Kam.

"I—am sorry …," began the embarrassed Siu Kam.

"Please do pass an hour or two more," said Wai Hing, flashing eloquent eyes.

The accommodating Siu Kam could not possibly resist such an invitation and dumbly assented. Tak Cheong raised his eyebrows at Wai Hing's words but said nothing and solemnly waved farewell to the assembled company. Probably because her parents were preoccupied with the new arrivals, Wai Hing suggested to Siu Kam that they adjourn to another hall to play a game of ping-pong while the meal was still in the course of preparation. He was an indifferent player; however, enthusiasm made up for lack of skill, and he hit away as if wielding a wooden bat was his conception of an ideal life.

More than once he was on the point of blurting out his love when she gave him an especially sweet smile, which he was tempted to believe distinctly conveyed an invitation to him to proclaim himself. He checked his impulses in time and mercilessly knocked the poor celluloid ball into the net or sent it spinning right off the table to come into violent collision with the wall. Excitement gripped him as strongly as a spider holds a fly caught in its web, though he did his best not to betray it. The dragon influence had not lost all its potency for good.

"How do you like Hong Kong?" asked Siu Kam after beating his brain a good deal to find a suitable topic of conversation.

"I suppose I like it," she replied. "In any case my acquaintance with other parts of the world is so limited that I can't say for certain that I wouldn't find other places more satisfying. Although women nowadays have a good deal of freedom, I still find it impossible to travel wherever I like, to visit strange countries as I long to do."

He looked a bit foolish, as if he had received a snub. She noticed his crestfallen face and recollected their earlier discussion about modern girls. When she uttered her last remark it was not her intention to administer any rebuke to him, and finding that he was now a subject of great interest to her, she was eager not to repel him in any way.

"It seems strange that we have not met each other before," she said wistfully, "although we have both lived so long in the same city. I wish we had been acquainted earlier."

"Not so strange perhaps," he observed, brightening up at her words with the instantaneous response of an electric lamp at the touch of a switch. "After all, there is a big population here, and one can't be expected to come across everybody. Nevertheless, I am extremely sorry I did not know you from childhood."

She assumed an entrancing expression, evidently meant for his sole behoof, and said softly, "How strange fate is!"

"Very!" he corroborated.

"Do you believe in fate?"

He was taken aback and was at a momentary loss to give an answer. Then he solemnly observed, "Undoubtedly fate rules our lives whether we like it or not. I find that what I do for myself is so little compared to what happens to me willy-nilly that I am forced to become a fatalist. I don't know whether this is a noble or ignoble attitude."

"It's quite reasonable. I also believe in fate, especially on those occasions when I can't get what I want."

They laughed in unison; it was a refreshing sight.

"Marriage in particular …" He hesitated; he had given vent to the words without any premeditation and now felt abashed.

"What about it?" she asked inquisitively.

"Is determined by fate," he concluded lamely. She was silent; he became eloquent.

"You know, our ancestors were particularly fatalistic. Of course, their attitude was too extreme. We have only a general belief that our life is influenced by destiny and so feel a bit more resigned when evil befalls us. They, on the contrary, tried to know their lot beforehand and act accordingly. They made liberal use of a book published annually, the Astronomical Almanac, that told them what to do and to avoid and when. Before a couple could get engaged …" He paused, apparently to pick up the ball, which he had knocked on to the floor. "It had to be consulted and their horoscopes compared to see whether it would be desirable for them to marry. Can you think of any worse nonsense?"

An emphatic shake of her head from side to side was the response.

"Our former superstitions were most remarkable," he continued with some heat, engendered by a combination of rising oratorical fervor and the expenditure of physical energy in the course of the game. "One of the strangest beliefs was that of feng shui (the geomantic science of wind and water). The nature of the landscape was supposed to exert great influence on the fortunes of people. If a person built a house, geomancers had to be consulted about its favorable location. If a man had a bad son, it was commonly remarked that his ancestors were buried in the wrong place. Preposterous!"

"You are quite right" was the gratifying answer.

"Such absurdities unfortunately still exist."

They both simultaneously shook their heads at this lamentable state of affairs, and it did not take a seer to know that they were making splendid progress.

"All my life I have been the subject of censure by the old women. Whatever I do seems to be automatically wrong … The best thing is to ignore them."

"That's just my attitude. Luckily, they are now powerless to exert any control over us. I am glad I wasn't born in the last century."

They sat down, quite exhausted from their arduous exercise, but the unconscionable dinner still existed only in the pots and pans.

"Are you fond of going out and seeing things?" he asked, mopping his face.

"That is one of the habits that have drawn upon me the greatest amount of criticism. I don't know how it is possible to stay inside the house even for a day."

"Do you wish to go for a tour round the New Territories?"

She considered the proposal with a reflective eye and said laconically, "When?"

"Any time you like. This weekend, say. The weather nowadays is very fine. The scenery is superb."

"Are you a poet?" she asked with glowing eyes.

"No, I seldom even read poetry," he returned. He thought to himself, "She is given to asking such embarrassing questions. Talking to her is really no joke."

"Poetry seems mighty romantic, but I can't appreciate it," she observed lugubriously.

"Few people do," he said consolingly. "You haven't told me yet whether you agree to take the ramble."

"Oh! I'll go all right. It'll be enjoyable. Your parents won't object?"

"Why should they? In any case it doesn't matter. I don't want them to think ill of me, to think that I am spoiling you."

"Nobody can spoil me," she said spiritedly.

"Oh!"

Dinner was announced. He was rather taciturn and was too polite to eat much, in spite of the almost maternal entreaties of Mrs. Chu Weng. He never felt it easy to take a meal at another person's house, especially when that person was a comparative stranger and etiquette and formality were almost compulsory; on such occasions eating ceased to be a natural occurrence and a pleasure and attained the rank of a convention and a misery. He could not be prevailed upon to take more than one bowl of rice and was happier to leave the table than most men would be to sit down to it.

After an additional half-hour's stay, he rose to take his departure.

"Come again," said Mr. Chu Weng politely.

"I shall," promised Siu Kam.

"Drop in as often as possible, and don't stand on ceremony," said Mrs. Chu Weng effusively.

"I'll make good use of the privilege," smiled Siu Kam.

Wai Hing followed him to the front door to see him off, and they conversed for another five minutes before he tore himself away.

"Au revoir!" he said.

"I hope no accident will hinder you from coming a few days hence. Au revoir!"

Chapter 6

The Ne'er-Do-Well

Ko San, the profligate brother of Wai Hing, groaned. He stalked up and down the hall in a state of perturbation and acute misery, unable to sit still, tortured by dark forebodings and a general sense of helpless frustration. He had not left home for two days, two long, dreary days, which seemed to him an eternity of vacancy. How had he passed the time? Monks can spend years on end in monasteries, practically consigned to utter inaction—the Indian Buddhist patriarch, Bodhidharma, arriving in China in the sixth century, is reputed to have sat in a cell for nine years, staring at the wall. Scholars can pore over tome after ponderous tome in their libraries without feeling the need for fresh air. Women in former ages could be happy pottering about the house, engaged in a variety of chores. Ko San was neither a monk nor a scholar nor a woman. He knew of only one way to make the days flow in easy, unconscious succession—the active pursuit of pleasure. Unfortunately, in this unreasonable world, his kind of joyous life did not depend for its success on himself, but on ridiculous, oblong pieces of paper that possessed a magic significance in civilized society. This paper of mystic might was out of his reach; thus, was he forced to endure an abysmal existence for fifty hours.

He banged his fist on the table in his fury and felt that life was most unfair to him. What had he done to deserve such a disgraceful fate? Really, he was fed up with everything. His fury abated, and pity for his unmerited misfortune clung like a dewy tendril to his heart. He almost wept. Poor fellow! Born in such a ruthless world! Then his anger flared up again—anger against his father. His friend, Leong Pat, was right in his view of the irrational conduct of parents and their inconsiderate attitude toward their offspring. What were parents made for? They should find their greatest happiness in sacrificing themselves for their sons. When they themselves were past the age of youthful enjoyment, they should find a high sort of vicarious pleasure in seeing their children sport and spend. If they were not blessed with enough grace to quit the world in good time, then at least they should have the decency to make over to their children a sizable portion of their property, if not all of it.

He remembered the case of two brothers with whom he was slightly acquainted. Years ago, their father contracted a very serious disease; thinking that he was about to die, he divided his property between them so that there need be no danger of a contested will after his decease. Unluckily, he made an amazing recovery and wished to have his property back. Both his sons refused to return what had been legally transferred to them; the old man, after dragging out an embittered, impoverished existence for some years, for his sons gave him only a diminutive income, died unlamented. Now, the older generation up to that day condemned the behavior of the two miscreants, as they were termed; to him, they were doing just the right thing. Why should the old man have recovered from his almost mortal disease? He had no business to commit such a preposterous and inconvenient outrage, but then these old folks were always so inexplicably perverse.

A step sounded in the adjacent hall; that must be his father. He must have it out with him, once and for all; his face became frightfully stern, and he compressed his lips tightly with the light of battle glinting in his eyes. He leaned against a chair and with arms akimbo waited for his coming.

Mr. Chu Weng, who was quite unconscious of the beneficent edification in store for him, sauntered into the hall with his customary air of freedom from all worry, bearing the symbol of his ease; to wit, a pipe, which, as long as a walking stick, possessed a peculiar appearance, with its twists and a bowl carved with the figure of a dragon. Whenever he sat down smoking this pipe, holding it firmly by the middle of the stem, he looked patriarchal with the dignity and ease of an immortal.

"Leisure, lasting a whole day, makes a man an immortal for that day," runs the proverb. He was an enviable man; but the jealousy of the gods having been aroused at the sight of one who aspired to live like them, he was consequently destined to have a curse sufficiently potent to shake his peace thrust upon him.

He entered the room with his eyes on the ground, and so he failed to notice his son's disagreeable visage. Going straight up to a round glass aquarium, wherein swam a number of goldfish amid a scattered array of seaweed, he stood immobile, absorbed in the pleasant spectacle, which filled him with a soothing delight such as one gets from the contemplation of whatever possesses serene, mellow beauty: the evening star, a bird roosting on a leafy twig, a soaring pagoda, or an ancient ornament of jade. Silently glided the innocent fishes, and silently watched Mr. Chu Weng. Finally, he turned round with a sigh and took from his pocket a pouch, from which he extracted a pinch of tobacco. With the left hand he drew back his pipe so that while the mouthpiece was behind his shoulder, the bowl, which he proceeded to stuff with the tobacco held between the fingers of his right hand, reposed conveniently under his double chin. Before the fragrant weed was safely lodged in its last resting place, he raised his head and saw the strange gleam in the eyes of his son. His faculties became temporarily congealed; then, recollecting himself, he struck a match with trembling fingers and took one whiff at the pipe.

"What's the matter?" he asked mechanically. No reply saluted his ears, and he felt dazed. "What have you been doing?" He stared at Ko San's physiognomy with a speculative interest.

"Nothing," almost shouted that unaccountable individual.

In a state of extreme perplexity Mr. Chu Weng asked, "Why do you stand there like a log of wood?"

The tall Ko San turned away and walked toward the window. "To tell you the truth," said he, without looking at his father, "I need money very sorely."

"You received a large sum only ten days ago. You couldn't have spent it all so quickly."

"I lent more than half to a friend."

"When did he borrow from you?"

"A week ago. He was supposed to repay me yesterday. Unfortunately, when I asked him about it, he said he couldn't raise the necessary amount. He was not sure when he would be able to do so but promised to return me the money some day. He was evidently suffering such poverty that I hadn't the rudeness to press him for it. He's an honest man, though, and he will not cheat me," said Ko San.

"Your help to your friend in distress is honorable. However, you should bear the consequences of your action, not me. I haven't any spare money now. You had better wait for him to repay you," said Mr. Chu Weng, knocking out the ashes from his pipe slowly.

"He may take a long time to do so," exclaimed Ko San, his eyes flashing. "In the meantime ..."

"It would be excellent for you to spend nothing at all for some time," said Mr. Chu Weng. "It's high time you learn to be more economical. You have been squandering more money than I can afford. You seem to regard money as sand."

"I do not hold any such opinion," retorted Ko San bitterly, "though I certainly don't think that a one-cent coin is as big as a cartwheel, an attitude that is evidently yours."

"You would probably be of the same mind if you had to work for your money. In fact, I consider that you have lived long enough shaking your legs. You had better start to earn your living."

Ko San trembled in every limb and was absolutely bereft of speech for a few minutes, never having heard his parent speak thus before.

"Ha!" he finally burst out ferociously. "And what kind of work do you yourself do? Sitting still and entrusting your property to a rascally lawyer, that's all. You say I should work. Very well then; I'll work. Let me manage all our family affairs."

"I have occupied a sufficient length of my life with business," retorted Mr. Chu Weng. "I was not born like you to be a burden to my parents. I do not employ any rascally lawyer. If you are referring to Wong Tak Cheong, he is a good man. As for allowing you to handle my property, I might as well say farewell to it at once."

Ko San cast on him a venomous look.

"You need not glare at me as if you were going to eat me. Every word of what I say is true," continued Mr. Chu Weng. "And, finally, I confess that I don't believe in the least your story about your lending to your friend."

"Do you mean I would tell you a lie?" burst out Ko San.

"It would certainly not be the first time you did so," said Mr. Chu Weng deliberately. "Why were you absent from home for almost a week?"

"I told you already that I went to Canton to see a friend," replied Ko San.

"You seem to have a multitude of friends. I was told by a man whose trustworthiness is above suspicion that he saw you in Macao five days ago. I have no doubt you have lost all your money at the gaming tables again," said Mr. Chu Weng.

"Whoever told you that was a liar!" shouted Ko San.

"All the same I prefer to believe him," retorted his venerable parent. "And you won't get out of me any more money to squander."

"I now realize what kind of a father you are," said Ko San banging his fist on the table. "Your treatment of me is outrageous! It would be a blessing if you were dead!"

"How dare you …"

"You are a heartless dotard. You are a rotter through and through and deserve a violent end."

Anger swelled the breast of Mr. Chu Weng, and promptly taking a step forward, he endeavored to bring down his pipe on the head of his unnatural son, who, before it could come into active contact with his valuable property, shot out his hand and, wrenching it away, tossed it out of the most convenient exit, namely, the window. Mr. Chu Weng, thus balked, rushed forward, and in another moment probably a sanguinary scuffle would have ensued if providence had not intervened in the person of the gardener. In most quarrels there is a spectator present to act as intermediary in separating the combatants, and it is probable that an encounter conducted in front of friends is seldom fundamentally serious. The antagonists, that is to say, are not anxious to come to real grips with one another. A fellow bent on a genuine tussle would seek a secret spot to fall foul of his enemy, and this kind of quarrel often terminates in a bloody crime. In the present case, father and son were not aware that there was any witness to their contest. However, as they were shouting vociferously in a house that was not exactly an anchorite's den, they doubtless expected someone to come to the rescue, though they were both aware that Mrs. Chu Weng as well as Wai Hing had gone out early, each on her respective errand, which, not being of any particular importance, need not be specifically chronicled.

The gardener, whose name was Liu Ho Fook, a stocky man still under thirty but possessed of a face so apathetic and stoical that he might well seem to a hasty observer to be an incarnation of the wisdom of the ages, was tending some pots of dahlias and heliotropes in front of the house when he heard the voices of his employer and the latter's son raised to an unusual pitch. Snatches of their words floated out to him, and he became dimly cognizant of the cause of the unseemly altercation.

Though curiosity was one of the characteristics utterly alien to his nature, still, as the quarrel progressed and threatened to become more serious, he drew nearer the door of the hall, the only explanation for his behavior being that a contest of any shape and variety seems to exert a kind of centripetal force over mankind in general. He hid behind the door waiting for the sounds to cease and occasionally peered through the longitudinal slit that separated the door from its post. As soon as he saw Mr. Chu Weng making for Ko San, he precipitately bounded into the room and thrust his body between them with the result—by no means an exceptional remuneration for such gallantry—that he received two capable blows, one on his face from the father and the other on his back from the son. He pushed the older man away and thus tore them asunder.

"Please calm yourself, sir," said Ho Fook, rubbing his anterior and posterior anatomy alternately and addressing Mr. Chu Weng. "Forgive the young master; a son is a son."

Mr. Chu Weng did not wait to hear any more of Ho Fook's pleadings but retired to another apartment, where he sat brooding over the monstrous character of modern youth. Turning round to retail some equally appropriate remarks to Ko San, the gardener found his expression so forbidding that he desisted from his benevolent intention and retreated without more ado to his work. Moving to a part of the garden near the road, he was proceeding to inspect some dwarf trees, which, with their curly branches covered with dark-green foliage, elicited admiration from many a visitor, when the immaculate Leong Yin Pat sauntered in with his habitual debonair jollity.

"Do you know if Mr. Chu Ko San is in?" asked Yin Pat after nodding to Ho Fook.

"Yes, he is," replied the gardener. He spoke slowly, as was his wont, and with a stolidity that characterized his general appearance and behavior. He was never known to laugh; even a grin was rarely visible on his wooden countenance. He condensed in himself the bleak misery and weighty burden of generations of ancestors bound to the soil. His state of mind was one of contentment and resignation, induced not by any conscious philosophizing but by life's overwhelming stress. Many miseries, chiefly traceable to extreme penury, had systematically alighted on him; the anguish had corroded into his soul. Bandits had massacred most of his family in his native village; owing to the ignorant manipulation of an ancient crone, a friendly neighbor who volunteered to assist in the delivery, his young wife had died in attempting to give birth to a still-born child; he had been tossed from one laborious job to another, subsisting on starvation wages (he came to his present work only a year ago, and it was the best he had done so far); and harsh treatment on the part of many a man aggravated his sorrows. Sages might chant panegyrics in honor of poverty; they could be happy, for they have access to mental pabulum. Wholly illiterate as he was, Ho Fook had no such consolation; neither was he a subtle sophist, well able to weave a web of plausible ideas to buttress up his ego. He was beaten by life, and he submitted to defeat as instinctively and inevitably as a crushed worm. He worked hard, not because he found toil inspiring or because he was unduly energetic, but simply because he did not know how else to pass the time. To him, happiness was a sacred dispensation, specially reserved for superior beings who lived on a wondrous plane; the fairies enjoyed it to the full, and mortals, excepting him and those of his ilk, to a lesser extent.

"These dwarf trees are a fine sight," said Yin Pat smilingly. "Indeed, you keep the garden very well."

"Thank you for your kind words, sir," said Ho Fook without moving a muscle of his face.

"You must be a happy man," declared Yin Pat. "You are doing pleasant work and doubtless earn enough to keep your family. Are you married?"

"My wife is dead," returned Ho Fook after a momentary pause.

"Oh, I am sorry," said Yin Pat. "I had better enter now. Is any member of the family in besides Mr. Chu Ko San? Are there any visitors?"

"No visitors so far today," answered Ho Fook. "The master is in; both the mistress and Miss Chu are out. Perhaps if they had stayed at home ..."

"Why! What has happened?" questioned Yin Pat as the gardener paused uneasily.

"Nothing much. The master and Mr. Chu Ko San had a quarrel just now. I dare say it did not mean anything."

Leong Yin Pat's curiosity was immediately aroused, and feeling that his friend could not have emerged profitably from the struggle—this boded no good for his own interests—he rapidly thought what he should do under the circumstances.

"What was the cause of the quarrel?" he queried.

"I don't really know," replied Ho Fook, "and it would be extremely impertinent of me to poke into their affairs. Still, for your information, I think that Mr. Chu Weng was refusing to give money to his son. All quarrels are very sad, especially those between father and son."

Yin Pat seemed reluctant to enter the house now; sitting himself leisurely on a stool, which lay there on the grass conveniently, he proceeded to watch Ho Fook at work, offering him various suggestions on the cultivation of flowers—displaying a knowledge that astonished the gardener—and praising him at suitable intervals. In the course of the conversation, he managed to extract from him a good deal of personal information; Ho Fook never before had found a more affable gentleman nor one so interested in his life. He gradually warmed up and in spite of his natural taciturnity related one or two anecdotes about his experiences to date, which were listened to sympathetically by Yin Pat. Among his interesting habits what appealed to the latter most of all was his propensity for thrift; little as his earnings were, he yet managed to lay aside a certain proportion for future use, for he might remarry or contract a serious illness. In any case, as he said, there was no need for him to spend so much now, and he would, if he did not meet a premature death, certainly grow too old to work.

"I have at present seven hundred fifty dollars," he revealed. "That is all my property in the world, all I have got after working for I don't know how many years."

"You are very lucky to have saved so much," said Yin Pat. "Some people who earn more than you don't save anything. You are a worthy character."

Ho Fook felt grateful for this commendation.

"Your kind words will always remain in my memory," he declared.

"What use do you make of the money now?" asked the immaculate Leong Yin Pat, taking out a handkerchief to wipe his face as it was getting hot.

"No particular use," returned Ho Fook surprised. "I am just keeping it."

"Where do you deposit it?" queried Yin Pat nonchalantly.

"Why, I keep it in a secret place," was Ho Fook's response. "I put it all in a tin, which I bury in a corner of the garden, because," he said apologetically, "someone may try to steal it."

Leong Yin Pat looked slightly dazed. "You have a most wasteful method of saving money. It is lying idle. Besides, it's still not safe. A clever thief may find out its hiding place, and it doesn't require more than a few seconds to dig it up and take it away."

"What else can I do with it?" asked Ho Fook, mystified.

"Why not keep it in a bank?" observed Yin Pat, making a plunging motion with his right hand to give meaning to his words.

"Does a bank keep people's money?" Ho Pock's mystification was complete.

Yin Pat explained the uses of a bank with patience and clarity. "You will earn interest on your deposit. All you have to do is to place it there. It will also be perfectly safe, and you can get it back together with what it has earned whenever you like."

"The bank is a very remarkable institution," declared the gardener in a tone of admiring awe. Then he added lugubriously, "But will it take such a small sum as mine?"

Leong Yin Pat considered the problem for a second. "That's the trouble," he regretfully uttered. "I never thought of it before. The bank, curse it, won't bother over small sums."

Ho Fook evidenced profound chagrin.

"However," said Yin Pat consolingly, "there is a way out if you don't mind it. I have an account in a big bank. I can keep the money for you in my name. Of course," he laughed jocularly, "provided you trust me."

Ho Fook was lost in momentary reflection. He wanted to secure all the benevolent services of the angelic bank; he debated with himself for a while about the advisability of delivering his money over to Leong Yin Pat. His hesitation was very faint; he took Leong Yin Pat for an opulent gentleman without misgiving, a person who would certainly not cheat him of a sum that, however important it was to Ho Fook, must appear quite paltry to him. Besides, the same superior man was endowed with a most magnanimous character, as could easily be gauged from his conversation and behavior. Not to put his trust in him would be to insult him.

"You are very good, sir," observed Ho Fook gratefully. "It goes without saying that I trust you. I must be very presumptuous to do otherwise. But do you really feel that you won't inconvenience yourself on my behalf?"

"Not in the least," asseverated Yin Pat. "I never saw a more virtuous man than you before. I'll be only too glad to help you in any way." A charming smile of generosity sat on his lips.

"I'll go and get the money for you this instant," exclaimed Ho Fook, rising up with unusual alacrity.

Leaving Yin Pat, he trotted to a part of the garden at the back of the house and soon returned, grasping a rusty tin. The former took it from him with an air of slight boredom, opened it, and removed the notes, which, after counting them with a negligent rapidity astonishing to Ho Fook, he stuffed into a capacious purse.

"It will be quite safe," observed Yin Pat patronizingly. "I'll put it in the bank directly when I go home together with mine."

"Thank you very much." Ho Fook was profoundly touched.

"Now I had better go in and see Mr. Chu Ko San," said Yin Pat courteously.

Thereupon he sauntered into the house with rapid strides, smiling to himself the whole time. He found his friend seated in a dejected attitude; assuming a sympathetic mien, he extracted from him the entire history of the cause of his misery. He cheered him as best he could, and his friendly behavior might well serve for an object lesson to unsocial persons.

"There's no need to feel depressed," asserted Yin Pat. "Things will be sure to improve later on. The old man will gradually come round, without a doubt."

Ko San replied with a sound between a snort and a groan and buried his face in his hands. He was possessed with half a desire to murder his venerable parent and half a desire to commit suicide. His face was red, and his lips twitched feverishly.

"Come," proceeded Yin Pat genially, "don't take it to heart so much. Treat the experience lightly. As is commonly expressed:

'Transform the great affair into a small affair; then transform the small affair into no affair.' What do you say to our going to the club?"

Ko San for the first time in his life experienced singularly little inclination to visit that place, for he did not feel it comfortable to brush elbows with his acquaintances in his distressing condition; still, under the persuasion of the magnetic Leong Yin Pat, he reluctantly went out with him. As they passed the gardener, Ho Fook, who looked up with a respectful mien, Yin Pat rewarded him with a munificent smile while his hand instinctively crept toward his pocket.

"What a fine gentleman!" said Ho Fook to himself, gazing after the retreating figure of Leong Yin Pat. "He is a chi-lin (unicorn) among animals, a feng-huang (phoenix) among birds! As for the young master," he wiped his face with a grimy palm while he paused to think of the morning's quarrel, "I really pity him. I wonder why he needs money so badly. If I had only a tithe of what he spends, I should consider myself lucky. And yet he is evidently miserable. This is strange, very!"

Chapter 7

The Tour

The golden light, shooting mildly and serenely from a blue sky, bubbling with agglomerations of white clouds from whose shapeless folds, shreds of a fluffy delicacy, were continually creeping blithely away, covered the world with its happy smiles. It was ten in the morning, a delicious hour when one has definitely shaken off the uneasiness of awakening and not yet felt the ill feeling of fatigue due to appear as the day advances.

"I awoke very early," said Siu Kam in answer to a question Wai Hing had just asked him. They were going for a ride round the New Territories.

"How early?" Wai Hing wanted to know, apparently for the sake of talking and not because the information was important.

They turned a corner, and her house, from which they had started, vanished abruptly from sight.

"Oh, six o'clock, nearer five, I should say," replied Siu Kam, casting a quick look at her and then directing his eyes toward the road in front.

He was driving the car, and she was sitting by his side cool as a cucumber. There was nothing worth noticing in her appearance, except that to a careful eye well acquainted with her she seemed better groomed than usual; perhaps this was in honor of her companion. Very fine she looked, and a man of stronger heart than Siu Kam's might well quake a little.

"Why did you wake up at such an unearthly hour?" continued Wai Hing, pleased for some reason not difficult to divine.

"Well, the whole of last night I thought of you, and somehow I had to get up as soon as possible."

"Really!" Her voice contained a thrilling quality. "I suppose it's ridiculous. I dare say you didn't have such an experience."

She looked pained and reproachful but kept her mouth shut.

They raced smoothly along Nathan Road, which was broad, level, clean, and less crowded than the streets on the island. Wai Hing looked at the glittering shops and the hoardings outside the cinemas. Advertisements saluted her eyes on every side.

"What is the idea of so much advertising?" she remarked with evident distaste. "It is quite enough to get on one's nerves. You find it everywhere. The newspaper, screen, radio, house, and street all fairly blaze with it."

"After all, people have to sell their goods, you know," said Siu Kam.

"They could very well confine it to newspapers only, or better still, to some magazines devoted purely to descriptions of goods. Then, if we want to buy anything, we could just look into those journals."

"I am afraid nobody would take the trouble to look into such catalogs."

"I wonder whether people really believe in the claims of advertisements. One could be perfect mentally and physically without any trouble at all if what they say were true. Medicines that could cure every disease in three days or money refunded; the sure method to reduce from 250 pounds to perfect slimness in the twinkling of an eye; how to grow a thick head of hair though perfectly bald; the easy way to get a lovely, soft skin, sparkling teeth, or lips that men love to kiss." She paused abruptly and looked out of the window, confusion all over her. Obviously, she had made an unfortunate slip of the tongue.

"Carry on with your comments," encouraged Siu Kam, turning on her a swift smile; then seeing her blush, he assumed a serious mien and sounded the horn, though there was only one solitary pedestrian, an old man, who was already so near the edge of the road that he couldn't possibly take another step to the left without tumbling into the drain. "They are mighty interesting."

Evidently she didn't agree with this tribute to her conversational powers, for she maintained a horrible silence.

"I was once lured into subscribing to a course that would teach me how to astonish my friends by playing the violin like a master," continued Siu Kam after waiting in vain for his companion to speak.

"And did you astonish anybody?" politely asked Wai Hing; by this time, she had resumed her usual coolness.

"I astonished myself all right," he replied happily. "When I received the instrument and the instructions I didn't even know how to begin. I managed to produce such an agonizing screech that my mother begged me, if I valued her life, not to continue with it, as her nerves were all frayed. Ha, ha!"

Wai Hing laughed in unison.

"I also once," she confessed, "tried to learn how to make artificial flowers. 'Earn while you learn,' ran the advertisement that I saw in a magazine. I was anxious to earn a little pocket money to show I was quite clever."

"And how much did you earn?"

"Not the ghost of a cent" was the unabashed reply. "First, I did not know where to sell them; secondly, not even my friends could be induced to accept them as presents. They were so queer."

"No wonder you don't like advertisements," he said banteringly.

They left the modern Kowloon behind them and came to Kowloon City, an old town—or rather village, in spite of the name—surrounded by a wall. It consisted of a mass of dilapidated houses separated by filthy, narrow lanes that emitted a frightful stench. Its inhabitants, the peasants, seemed to be quite happy and tilled their green fields assiduously. There was nothing interesting about the place except its antiquity and a legend, according to which it was once the resting place of an emperor. When the last ruler of the Sung Dynasty fled before the Mongols in the twelfth century, he came to that spot and fixed his abode on a hill that dominated the town. Thence he embarked and made a last stand against the pursuing barbarians, fighting a naval battle at the mouth of the Canton or Pearl River. The day was lost, the fleet was destroyed, and the hapless emperor, who was only a boy, perished in the waves. One hundred thousand men lost their lives. The rock where the emperor was supposed to have pitched his camp bore an inscription, and it was called, in the local vernacular, "Sung Wong Toi" or "Sung Emperor's Platform."

Our excursionists did not alight at the village but went past it and, after a short time, found themselves speeding along a country road in the direction of Shatin.

"One of the most lamentable things about the ancient Chinese," remarked Siu Kam with the contemplative look of an inspired critic, "was the lack of sanitation in their towns and villages. Whatever beauty and interest a place like the old village we have just left may contain is positively spoiled by its frightful squalor. And yet we are told by the Venetian, Marco Polo, who came to China in the twelfth century … I suppose you have heard of him?"

"Oh yes, I read of him in school," replied Wai Hing demurely, implying that her companion's pedagogic discourse reminded her of days long since vanished and that she was by no means interested in such solemn stuff.

"Well," continued Siu Kam, obtuse to her innuendo, "that admirable traveler said that in the city of Hangchow every man took a bath daily. He recorded it with apparent surprise, from which we may conclude that regular baths were quite rare in Europe in the Middle Ages. Thus the inevitable conclusion follows," the logician radiated through his visage, "that the Chinese were careful about personal cleanliness. Why then did they not know that towns and villages should likewise be kept clean?"

Wai Hing shook her head mutely to indicate that the intriguing problem completely floored her.

"People are so contradictory in their habits," resumed the prosy Siu Kam, answering the question himself.

They climbed up a steep and narrow road bounded on one side by a granite hill covered with red sand; on the other side they looked down on a hamlet far below the level where they were. The small brick houses were bordered with cultivated fields. Away in the distance gleamed the sea, dotted with vessels. They soon came to Shatin, where rice was grown in abundance and which was situated by Tide Cove, a pretty creek. They stopped near the shore and gazed at the enchanting sea; on the opposite side green hills rose from the water's edge. With the sea constantly in view, they raced along and soon arrived at Taipo Market, the name of a village where a fair was held every few days. It so chanced that this was one of the days, and the concourse of people at the fair was immense. The streets were narrow, and the smell wasn't too pleasant. There wasn't much to see at the place, and they soon left it.

By this time it was midday. Siu Kam's heart progressed with the journey. His passion became more and more uncontrollable. He felt that he must declare it or he would burst. But he also felt that it was a step fraught with uncertain consequences; to tell a girl that he loved her after knowing her only a few days might well be regarded as a highly dangerous proceeding. Supposing she spurned him ... Supposing she were to misconstrue his exceedingly honorable intentions and storm out of the car and, like the virtuous, insulted heroines of romances, start to walk back, leaving him a disconsolate villain. Fine fun it would be! He was not an adept in the complicated and refined art of love making; indeed, it was the first time in his life that he wished to say any word to a girl that savored of such. Unconsciously, he gave a slight groan.

"What's the matter?" asked Wai Hing in surprise.

"Oh nothing!" he quickly exclaimed.

She gave him a queer look but did not utter any word. He continued with his reflections. Of course, he might wait a good while longer before committing himself, might get really intimate with her first. But, strangely enough, he had a feeling that he was already so intimate with her that further interaction could not make it any more so. He seemed to know her thoroughly, as if he had associated with her all her life; he could sense no barrier between them. An odd consciousness! On her part ... He could not tell what her attitude toward him was. He had always scoffed at telepathy but now wished it glorious success and that he was versed in its mysteries. Then there would be no need for all this tormenting conjecture. After all, though they had known each other only a short time, they were already on very friendly terms. Why should a girl conduct herself toward him so sweetly unless ... unless she liked him at least. In any case, he could not bear the pain of keeping his adoration to himself any longer. Better make one sublime declaration! Risk the outcome. If the worse came to the worst ... He dared not linger over this idea. Finally, after working himself up to a torturing degree of heat, aided doubtless by the heat of the sun, he decided to take the plunge.

"I never loved any girl before," he said, talking in the strain of an autobiography.

"How interesting!" murmured Wai Hing, turning her face toward him; she was evidently cogitating some problem of her own. Then all of a sudden as the full nature of his revelation flashed on her, she added rather breathlessly, "Before what?"

"Before I met you," he replied promptly.

"Oh!" she exclaimed as if he had struck her a forceful blow.

"Yes, really and truly," he declared with unparalleled earnestness. "The very first moment I saw you I thought you were wonderful!"

"Indeed!" she murmured, not knowing what else to say.

"Do you doubt my sincerity?" he asked in agonized accents.

"Of course not! I feel very flattered by your good opinion."

"You are a paragon of beauty—a glorious star—a fairy damsel."

She laughed merrily; he looked pained.

"I can't imagine myself any of the beings you so generously identify me with," she explained.

"You are too modest."

"Most people would say that I am not."

"They know nothing about the real you," he said, in tones implying that he was alone in enviable possession of her secrets. "I have met a great many girls …"

"How many?"

"I don't mean I was acquainted with them; I only saw them. The number is therefore countless. But you surpass all of them."

"I never felt so pleased in my life."

"I am a very ordinary man …" he began.

"No, you are wonderful," she murmured.

"Then you will not think it fantastic if I were to ask you to marry me," he said, scanning her face.

"No; I wouldn't deem it such." She dropped the words slowly, beginning to feel uncomfortable.

"Will you marry me, Wai Hing?" He uttered the tremendous words to his own immense astonishment.

"Wait a moment!" she exclaimed, putting up a hand before her face as if blinded by lightning. "Not so fast. I didn't say I was ready to marry you. We have known each other such a short time only."

An anguished expression swept over his visage. "I feel as though I had known you from your birth."

"Curious though it seems, now that I come to think of it, I too feel that we are old friends."

"Then you care for me?"

"I like you immensely, but I am not sure that I love you," she whispered. This was evidently nothing more than a maidenly subterfuge.

"What's the difference?" he asked with obvious joy and assumed ignorance.

"I mean that I can't tell whether I want to marry you or not."

"If you don't, I'll kill myself," he firmly asseverated with the air of a doomed hero.

"You are very persistent," she told him with a liquid look. "And as it's a pity that a charming person like you should cease to live for such a trifling cause, I think I'll marry you."

"This is—this is the most marvelous moment in my life!" he almost shouted. "Do you mind if I kiss you?" And he brought the car to a sudden halt.

She turned her face away in embarrassment. Nothing daunted, without waiting for any verbal permission, he performed the symbolic rite. Unfortunately, this being his first taste of the mystery, his technique was imperfect, basing our judgment on the Hollywood standard; probably, one hopes so at any rate, he would improve later on. However, it would be highly censurable to expatiate on a fault that might be damaging to his character as a hero, and so the less said about it the better.

The happy couple proceeded in perfect bliss on their journey, passing through scenes of superb beauty that appeared even more entrancing to their eyes than they actually were. Soon they entered Fanling, the name meaning "Chalk Ridge," a pleasant district of country houses. Then they turned westward, and fields and villages flashed past them as they rode in silence absorbed in their own thoughts. The farmers were busy in their wet rice fields and seemed to have no worries as they bent over their tasks with their trousers pulled up above their knees. The red bauhinia was in splendid bloom, and an air of joyousness pervaded the entire countryside. In the distance green hills stood silhouetted against a blue sky.

After some time Wai Hing awoke from her reverie and remarked, "What a beautiful scene! How peaceful!"

At that moment Siu Kam suddenly swerved the car to avoid running over a hen that was scurrying across the highway.

"The countryside is undoubtedly a delightful place," said that city gentleman, "though it has its inconveniences and vexations, mishaps, and tragedies. It might be pleasant to go for a walk or drive through it occasionally as a relief from the urban crowds, but it is another matter altogether to dwell amid rustic surroundings the whole year round."

"I suppose so," Wai Hing remarked slowly. "It would be such a bore living on a farm. I wouldn't care very much to rise up early every morning to the crow of the cock and then proceed to feed the fowl or till the land."

"You are an incorrigible town dweller," laughed Siu Kam. "You wouldn't like to live on a mountain, let the Tao work through you, and eventually become an immortal, world you?" he added quizzically.

"I certainly wouldn't," retorted Wai Hing. "I don't see any fun in being an immortal. Furthermore, in spite of their recorded deeds, I don't believe there have ever been such beings."

"You are a skeptic," Siu Kam asserted in the same bantering tone, a tone quite unusual with him. "Poets have sung rapturously of the country life," he continued musingly, "but their enthusiasm is not to be taken as evidence of the soundness of their views. In the old days, most people had perforce to live by the land, but nowadays it need not be so. As science advances and transport grows more and more rapid and industrialization gains momentum, people could all dwell in sizeable towns with all modern conveniences and amenities. Living in isolated farmhouses or wretched villages is to lead at best a narrow life and hitherto a squalid one."

"But how can farmers live away from their farms with no one taking care of them?" asked Wai Hing.

"That is not a difficult problem to solve," said Siu Kam airily. "They can take turns in performing the duties of watchmen."

"You seem to be a revolutionary with strange ideas," observed Wai Hing with an incredulous smile.

"I am nothing of the sort," said Siu Kam, astonished. "This particular idea just came into my head. I must confess that I am not at all enamored of the life of the peasant with its frightfully limited range of interests and its miseries. Look at those water wheels grinding and water buffaloes plodding," he pointed; "incessant toil of man and beast."

"I quite agree with you," said Wai Hing sweetly.

"Not liking to live in a sordid village," pursued Siu Kam, "need not imply, of course, lack of appreciation of the beauty of the countryside. Far from it. I enjoy natural scenery."

In course of time they arrived at Castle Peak. They alighted from their vehicle and climbed up some steps to a restaurant, where they ordered lunch.

"I am famished," averred Wai Hing.

"A journey always makes a person feel hungry," said Siu Kam in a sympathetic tone. "What would you like to eat?"

"What have they got?"

They studied the menu item by item.

"Braised mushroom with bamboo shoots would be fine," said Wai Hing. "Diced chicken with walnuts."

"What about some fish?" asked Siu Kam. "Say, baked garoupa in sweet and sour sauce."

"Good," agreed Wai Hing.

Siu Kam gave the order to the waiter and after inquiring from Wai Hing asked for iced tea to be brought first.

Still with his mind on food, Siu Kam said, "I presume you prefer our Cantonese cuisine to any others."

"Of course," replied Wai Hing. "I suppose," she added, "that's because we have been brought up on it, though, objectively speaking, I can't imagine anything better."

"Cantonese food," remarked Siu Kam, "is of all the varieties of Chinese cuisine the best known in the West. That of course," he added judicially, "is probably due to the fact that the Chinese who set up restaurants there have been mainly Cantonese."

"I also like Shanghai food," said Wai Hing. "Its sweetish taste is delicious. Chicken in sesame sauce is a favorite of mine."

"For my part, of the cuisine of other provinces I plump for the Szechuan," said Siu Kam. "I like its pungent flavor and its roast duck."

"You are welcome to your preference," smiled Wai Hing.

"Every people has its own style of cookery," observed Siu Kam ruminatively, "and it is strange what people eat. The appeal of a particular style is, I should think, purely a matter of training. What one learns to take in childhood is what one considers best all one's life. There is no objective standard for considering this dish delicious and that appalling."

Their meal arrived, and they fell to it with gusto. While enjoying a dessert of watermelon and longan, they looked down at the bay below with its emerald-green water scintillating in the sunlight.

Siu Kam felt he was never happier in all his life, and he did not hesitate to express the sentiment.

"Life is good," agreed Wai Hing.

"I can sit here for hours amid all this peaceful, beautiful scenery," said Siu Kam. It is doubtful, however, whether he would have been quite so enchanted with the surroundings if he were hungry instead of sitting in a restaurant where he had just partaken of a satisfying repast.

"The air is certainly soothing," said Wai Hing. She pointed to a glass aquarium. "Look at those goldfish. They swim so serenely, as though there were no trouble on earth. Sometimes I wish I were a fish gliding in a stream or a bird floating on the breeze."

"You would make a charming denizen of the air or the water," smiled Siu Kam. "But what possible trouble could have entered your experience to make you entertain such fancies? I should have thought that your life has been one of pure happiness."

"No person can be happy all the time," asserted Wai Hing. "It is doubtful whether anybody can truly say that his share of pleasure has been more than that of sorrow. If he believes that, he must be possessed of an extraordinarily sanguine temperament."

"I suppose you are right," said Siu Kam wistfully. "The human frame would seem not suited to perpetual bliss. When one has no pain of any sort, one starts yearning for what is unattainable, thus making oneself miserable. Again, when one has a certain enjoyment for some time, one starts suffering from satiety. In fact, one is never satisfied. What a tragedy!"

"Just so," remarked Wai Hing. "We suffer all sorts of woes from birth onward. Some are physical, like those due to illness, and others are of mental origin, as, for example, disappointment at the loss of something."

"True," assented Siu Kam. "Furthermore, another classification of pain is according to the cause. A good deal of distress comes from nature, like earthquakes and typhoons, but the greater part is due to man himself. Rivalry, jealousy, malice, acquisitiveness, and other passions lead him to inflict misery on one another and even to murder. It's strange that people should be like that. According to Confucian theory, man was originally good. This is doubtful when one considers the amount of evil and consequent misery in the world."

"Have you thought deeply on this subject?" smiled Wai Hing. "Have you had a miserable life?"

"I can't say that my reflection over this theme has been unduly excessive," said Siu Kam heavily. "Neither has my life been on the whole unhappy—so far. No proper judgment can be passed on a person's life until it is ended. However, I am not too optimistic over what the future holds, seeing that life, generally speaking, tends toward misery."

With this lugubrious sentiment, he fell silent. Shortly thereafter, they arose and proceeded toward their vehicle and drove away. Journeying along the southern coast of the New Territories with the clear blue sea in full view, they sped on, enjoying the drive. Wai Hing gazed intently at a whole fleet of fishing junks come in with their sails glinting in the sunlight.

They talked intermittently; for the most part, Siu Kam was intent on the road ahead and Wai Hing was absorbed in her thoughts. In course of time, they passed through Laichikok, Shumshuipo, and Mongkok and thence came to Wai Hing's home; Siu Kam did not stop for long, but after fixing a date for their next meeting, he sped home thoroughly satisfied with the day's outing and never happier in his life.

Chapter 8

Opposition

Mrs. Yuen Ko, the mother of Siu Kam, was a strict adherent of tradition, which to her represented an infallible and sanctified canon of truth to be accepted without any question or murmur, however harsh it might occasionally appear; any new idea spelled anathema. What she particularly prized and practiced was allegiance to the ancient code of behavior governing the various social relationships, the duties vis-à-vis relatives and friends. Justice, according to her, must be maintained, and as she waxed older, her sternness correspondingly increased. Conceiving it to be the duty of a wife to submit to her husband, she had always been a model in that respect, although Mr. Yuen Ko could, without great difficulty, have been reduced to a satisfactory degree of obedience to her.

She had brought up her children with rigorous discipline, endeavoring to maintain an iron control over them; still, she loved them intensely and was genuinely devoted to their welfare. Her children, including Siu Kam, Silver Moon, a girl of eighteen, and Siu Yip, a boy of fifteen, had responded to her treatment with facility; they were all well behaved and, in fact, desirable in every respect. Whenever she and her friends were engaged in discussion about children—a pastime very much to their taste—she would refer triumphantly to hers as inimitable specimens and finally wind up with a recital of their merits, which elicited the hearty, though secretly envious, admiration of her listeners, who would remark that heaven was specially gracious to her in bestowing on her such wonderful offspring. Now even her youngest child had almost reached maturity; none of the three had ever given her any trouble, and there was no reason why she should expect it. She therefore possessed the deepest satisfaction with life.

The statement above unfortunately needs to be amended, if absolute veracity is to be observed. She did have one cause for worry—the reluctance of her eldest son, Siu Kam, to provide her with a suitable daughter-in-law. There is always a fly in the ointment, and this was a most unwelcome defect in an otherwise excellent son; however, it was not too severe for her to endure, and she grew resigned to it. Imagine her surprise when a kindly acquaintance told her blissfully that Siu Kam was carrying on with a certain girl, whose home he was in the habit of frequenting; why, the kindly acquaintance continued with a pleasurable twinkle in her eyes, they were going about openly in the town. She refrained from giving any specific details about the girl, only mentioning that her demeanor savored of the very bold and that she did not bear the remotest resemblance to the retiring and shy Silver Moon. In conclusion, she congratulated her on her precious acquisition and said that her incomparable son had now chosen for her a praiseworthy daughter-in-law. She stressed the word "chosen" with malicious emphasis and tripped away serenely.

For some minutes after the departure of the visitor, Mrs. Yuen Ko could not speak a word; her world was tumbling about her ears. So that was the reason why her son so obdurately refused to consider matrimony, not because he was peculiarly shy of women, as she had hitherto fondly imagined, but because he was running after a revolting and disgraceful hussy. She never imagined that he could be given to such duplicity. How could she commend her children to her friends again? They were now probably laughing at her, twisting their waists and holding their bellies in their excessive mirth. At this agonizing reflection she arose and rushed into the library to find her husband, who was reclining on a long chair, reading the religious romance *Travels to the West*. He was smiling at one of the exploits of the supernatural monkey, Sun Hou-tzu, and the gullibility of the immortal pig, Chu Pa-chieh, when he heard the door violently burst open and saw his wife come rushing in. Naturally assuming that some horrid catastrophe had occurred, for in all the years of their connubial union, he had never beheld her like this before, he dropped the book and stared at her with

86

fixed eyes, which, even in their normal state, were quite remarkable for their protruding appearance and now looked grotesque.

"Siu Kam …," panted Mrs. Yuen Ko.

"What's the matter?" murmured Mr. Yuen Ko, visions of a mangled corpse, bespattered with grime and blood, swaying dramatically in his head.

"He's going about with a … a girl," sobbed Mrs. Yuen Ko, collapsing in a nerveless heap on the floor and burying her face in her hands.

Mr. Yuen Ko opened and closed his mouth several times like a fish just drawn out of the water and finally clenched his fist and exclaimed, "How dare he behave like this? Where is he? The wretch!"

"I don't know," replied Mrs. Yuen Ko, blowing her nose.

"You don't seem to know anything," exclaimed Mr. Yuen Ko irritably. "Why do you believe that he has a girl, huh?"

Between pitiable spasms, Mrs. Yuen Ko revealed the source of her information and what little had been told her about the culpable character of their son's infatuation, adding her conviction that she was no good and that she was, if not actually a sing-song girl, at best very little different from one.

"We'll find out when he comes home," said Mr. Yuen Ko, resuming his calmness and his book; unfortunately, the adventures of the four pilgrims across wild lands on their way to India to bring back the Buddhist canon had lost their appeal, and he turned over the pages listlessly.

That day, as luck would have it, Siu Kam returned home earlier than usual, there being little work for him to do in his office. Entering the sitting room with a heart as destitute of all anxiety as the Kwangtung winter is of ice, he found both his parents seated with grim, determined faces, very unlike their customary selves. Unable to divine the cause of the phenomenon, he thought it best to refrain from asking any questions that might not bring about a more genial atmosphere; strangely enough, he did not by any chance connect it with himself. After an uneasy silence, wherein they riveted their eyes on him in a most unaccountably threatening fashion, he feebly murmured his hope that they both had had a pleasant day.

"Very pleasant," said Mr. Yuen Ko with unnecessary emphasis. "I dare say yours was more pleasant."

With a sudden sinking sensation about the region of the diaphragm Siu Kam became aware of the battery that had produced the electrical disturbance in the atmosphere. He had refrained from recounting to his parents his association with the lovely Wai Hing, not because he anticipated trouble in such an eventuality, but because, with his procrastinatory propensities, he thought he could very well defer the information to a more convenient date. As they had always been so desirous for him to enter into the matrimonial state and perpetuate their honorable line, it had seemed to him singularly improbable that they would offer any opposition to his laudable choice, though he was perfectly aware that they were conservative and his behavior would not be regarded as falling in with the very best tradition. The excellent proverb says: "The superior man understands with one word; the fleet steed with one touch of a whip." As Siu Kam—it would be an insult to harbor any other notion—evidently belonged to that blessed division of humanity referred to in the first half of the maxim, he wished that he was far away from the impending scene; as far away, shall we say, as the lotus eaters from their island home, "far beyond the wave." He moved his legs restlessly and as usual tried to seek comfort by looking at some inspiring object that might chance to fall within his purview. What he now found was a picture on the wall representing Pan Ku ardently shaping the universe out of chaos with a colossal adz.

"Has anything special happened to you recently?" asked Mrs. Yuen Ko.

"Eh, nothing," murmured Siu Kam, removing his eyes for an instant from the benefactor of humanity.

"Very disappointed to hear this," said Mrs. Yuen Ko. "You have appeared much more cheerful these days, so I thought you had discovered some new source of happiness."

"Eh, not exactly." Siu Kam modulated his tongue with extreme difficulty.

"Come," said Mr. Yuen Ko sternly, "we have been told that you are rambling about the town with a girl. Is this true?"

"Ah ... aw ..."

"Yes or no?" demanded Mr. Yuen Ko impatiently.

"Well, you see ...," began Siu Kam, his face a perfect crimson.

"Answer this question at once," thundered Mr. Yuen Ko. "Yes or no?"

"Yes!" said Siu Kam, driven to a one-word reply like a culprit on the dock subjected to a ruthless interrogation by a member of that professional body of pundits privileged to regard their victims as mechanical contrivances, designed to answer questions with precision and endowed with no feelings or irresolutions.

"Yes!" shouted Mr. Yuen Ko. "And you have the effrontery to tell me that. You have disgraced the honorable reputation of your family, which has never been tarnished before. I wish I had wrung your neck while you were a baby. A fine son you are!"

"And to think that we have lavished all our care on you for nothing," said Mrs. Yuen Ko, putting her blue handkerchief into active service. "I wish I had never borne you. So much misery I had to undergo for your sake."

At the recollection of her maternal toil and wasted tenderness, she burst into a cataract of sobs. What with fear at his father's rage and, still more, pity for the suffering he had brought on his mother, Siu Kam was in a perfect pit of agony, cursing himself for all the trouble he had caused and really wishing that he had never emerged into life. He was now in for an unenviable time and no mistake.

"There is no need to get so angry," he said placatingly. "She is of good family."

"Indeed!" exclaimed Mr. Yuen Ko. "What good family would allow their daughter to gad about with a man?"

"Nowadays people don't behave in exactly the same way as they did."

"That is the usual excuse for all kinds of evil," averred Mr. Yuen Ko.

"Why didn't you tell us what you had in mind," said Mrs. Yuen Ko, "instead of trying to deceive us? You could have very well told us your real intentions. There was no need for you to pretend that you didn't want to marry."

"I never deliberately bluffed you. I met her only recently."

"Is that so?" came from Mr. Yuen Ko in not the most gracious of tones. "And may I ask who she is?"

"Yes," said Mrs. Yuen Ko, chiming in with appropriate emphasis. "Who is this fairy that has wrought such a wonderful transformation in you?"

Siu Kam frowned slightly at this sarcastic reference and concisely revealed her identity, taking good care to vindicate her character and stress the highly respectable standing of her parents.

"I don't like her father," staunchly asserted Mr. Yuen Ko, flicking his sleeve to give point to his words. "How could he allow his daughter to behave thus? I shall not be surprised if he is secretly a pimp."

"And I am extremely averse to meeting a woman like her mother," said Mrs. Yuen Ko with equal force. "There is no doubt that she has pricked on her daughter to run after you."

Siu Kam, in spite of his ingrained filial piety, flushed angrily and turned his visage toward Pan Ku, wondering why, when he evolved heaven and earth, he did not invest man with perfect reason. Then he remembered that it was owing to the dissolution of his body that specific objects arose: from his hair, flesh, blood, and sweat came the plants, the soil, the streams, and the rain respectively, while the ancestors of humanity were the parasites that thronged his corporeal frame. How could such sickening things as parasites engender a fine posterity? He also knew that nowadays people believed that man's ancestors were apes, which, he thought, could not be much more admirable than parasites. He sighed.

"Thinking of hurrying to see her, I suppose," said Mr. Yuen Ko, hearing the sigh. "I think with your madness your business must now be on the verge of ruin."

"It isn't," said Siu Kam.

"I command you to give her up," said Mr. Yuen Ko with ungraceful violence.

"I won't," retorted Siu Kam. "I don't see what is wrong with her and why what other men's sons can do I can't. If you were to know her better, you'd be convinced of your injustice. I have never opposed you in anything before; unfortunately, I have to do so this time."

Mr. Yuen Ko looked at Mrs. Yuen Ko, and Mrs. Yuen Ko looked at Mr. Yuen Ko. Both suffered from a temporary attack of paralysis and tried to obtain comfort in each other's faces.

"Injustice is a thing I loathe," continued Siu Kam violently. "I am old enough to know what I like. I resent your interference."

To give force to his words, he stared ferociously at the picture on the wall. A light breeze shook it, and Pan Ku seemed to make a pause in his cosmic labors to nod his hearty approval.

"You are talking nonsense," said Mr. Yuen Ko, recovering his faculties. "Injustice is a word that can't be applied to parents. Unless your unworthy infatuation has completely deranged your mind, you must feel that our actions are prompted by our sincere interest in your welfare."

"I am very doubtful of that," maintained Siu Kam stoutly. "So far as I can make out, you are purposely trying to make me wretched for life."

"You are certainly behaving in a manner very different from that of the twenty-four classical examples of filial piety," sobbed Mrs. Yuen Ko. "They would never have dreamed of accusing their parents of cruelty."

Silver Moon, whose character was exceedingly gentle and inoffensive, stood in one corner of the room, the picture of a damsel in distress, but her distress was not such as required the officious services of a valorous and accomplished knight. She found all her happiness in the home, in peace and seclusion, in needlework and family affection. The essence of all that was soft and serene resided in her person, from her languid eyes and rounded chin to her slow movements and timid voice. Her equable mind was never vexed by any torturing doubts or desires: jade and pearl, not gold and diamond, best illustrated her nature. Her friends regarded her as a dull, spiritless nonentity, and she certainly was not brilliant intellectually, if by that is meant the ability of a girl to give a witty repartee or exude fashionable smartness. She was not likely to become an ardent feminist, and it was inconceivable that she would ever have the courage to deliver a harangue on the rights of women. As a matter of fact, she was so very timid that she seldom stepped into the street and grew up from childhood under the close protection of parental wings, from which she never dreamed of escaping. Altercations of any sort were highly displeasing to her. After recovering from her first surprise at the cause of the conflict between her brother and her parents, she listened silently in an attitude of sorrow.

"I think Elder Brother did not mean to speak rudely," said Silver Moon in a faltering voice.

"What makes you hold that belief?" asked Mrs. Yuen Ko unpleasantly, turning on her a resentful face.

"He has always been a dutiful son," advanced Silver Moon hastily, in blushing confusion.

"He is no longer so," declared Mrs. Yuen Ko sternly. "He has been corrupted by a shameless hussy."

"We haven't seen her at all," pleaded Silver Moon in a most melodious tone. "Would it not be better if, instead of condemning her straightaway, we ask Elder Brother to introduce her to us so that we can judge her merits more properly? She must be quite desirable or else he would not have come to like her."

"Your words are ridiculous!" cried Mrs. Yuen Ko angrily. "She can never be a good person, and that's the end of it."

"After all," persisted Silver Moon, "Elder Brother is quite sensible."

"I don't care whether he is sensible or not," returned Mrs. Yuen Ko violently. "In any case the mere fact that he first picked her, and not we, makes her odious. I refuse to have anything to do with her." After a short pause to take breath, she added suspiciously, "Why are you so earnest in defending him? You are not thinking of following his beautiful example and choosing your own husband, I suppose?"

This indelicate remark completely crushed Silver Moon and reduced her to blushes and trepidations.

"Whether you want to have anything to do with her or not," averred Siu Kam, who had been staring gloomily at the inspiring Pan Ku, "I am more or less engaged to her already."

"What!" shot forth from Mr. Yuen Ko, his protruding eyes on the point of popping out.

"We have promised to marry each other, and it amounts to an engagement."

Mr. Yuen Ko arose from his chair and shouted, "Outrageous boldness!"

Mrs. Yuen Ko raised her eyes aloft and shrieked, "Heavens!"

Silver Moon clasped her fragile hands and murmured, "Such rapid work!"

"That I ever lived to see this day!" exclaimed Mr. Yuen Ko as he stormed out of the room.

Mrs. Yuen Ko repeated the identical words in a parroty voice and likewise vanished from the scene.

Siu Kam sank into a state of abysmal misery, while Silver Moon seated herself opposite him with a look on her face compounded of sympathy and wonder, the latter feeling in the ascendant: she was plainly marveling at the queer conduct of her erstwhile unromantic brother.

"What is she like?" asked Silver Moon in a soft voice.

Siu Kam vouchsafed only a dismal groan.

"Is she beautiful?" continued Silver Moon.

No answer.

"When did you first meet her?"

94

Profound silence.

"Well," said Silver Moon resignedly, "clearly you think her too precious to talk about. I have a feeling that she is probably very wicked."

"What do you mean?" cried Siu Kam. "She is as good as any girl alive."

"You acted very foolishly," said Silver Moon, looking extremely wise herself. "After you decided you wanted her, you should have told us to request her hand for you in a formal manner through the medium of a go-between."

"I hate go-betweens," Siu Kam protested vigorously.

"And you shouldn't have gone about with her so that all our friends could notice it and pass remarks," continued his adviser.

"They had better keep their tongues inside their heads." He clenched his fists as if he saw enemies all round him.

"Unfortunately they won't. Why, people find it one of the chief pleasures of life to talk about others, especially their misdeeds," stated Silver Moon with delightful insight.

"What shall I do now?" asked Siu Kam of himself, though he spoke in a loud voice. "I never imagined I would tumble into this mess."

"Do you really want her?" Silver Moon gazed at him questioningly.

"Of course" came the forcible retort. "Otherwise what was the quarrel about?"

"Then marry her," said Silver Moon graciously.

"I shall certainly do that," affirmed Siu Kam with impatience. "But what about our parents? I don't want to live on terms of enmity with them forever."

"Most probably in the course of time they will come to accept the inevitable," observed Silver Moon sagaciously.

"You really think so?" asked Siu Kam in an earnest tone.

"Yes, provided, of course, she turns out to be truly good," replied Silver Moon with a trace of doubt in her soft eyes.

"I am tired of saying that she is good!" exclaimed the exasperated lover.

"How did you come to like her so much?" questioned Silver Moon with great interest.

"Well, I don't know."

"They say that marriage is made in heaven. Doubtless you were both destined for each other." She offered her own explanation in lieu of receiving one. "That's why you are so fond of her."

The well-pleased gentleman did not contradict this assertion.

"How does she dress?" queried Silver Moon inquisitively.

He gave a vague answer. "Oh, like other girls."

"How long does she keep her hair?" pursued his questioner, undaunted by the meager nature of the information.

"Down to the neck," said Siu Kam, dimly remembering that in their ride her hair flew about above her shoulders.

"She is very lively, isn't she?"

"She is certainly never dull."

"I hope she is not proud."

"She isn't."

"Is she fond of domestic work?"

"Well, I have never ..."

"Seen her do any. That is not going to endear her to the old folks. What does she do?"

"She enjoys herself in various ways."

"That will not make her any more pleasing either. What kind of food does she like to eat?"

"She doesn't eat much."

"She must be quite slim then."

"Yes, and beautiful."

"I wonder ..."

"What is it?" asked Siu Kam as his sister hesitated.

"I wonder whether she can be perfectly good. A girl who is willing to wander about with a man ..."

Siu Kam jumped from his chair in such excitement that it overturned with a crash.

"How many times have I got to say that she ..."

"It must be glorious for a girl to have a man to adore her to such an extent," murmured Silver Moon wistfully. "I am dying to meet her."

Chapter 9

The Typhoon

Rain fell with melancholy sounds on the deserted streets of the city, mantled in the gloom of night. Pattering with soft persistence against the roof, it awoke Siu Kam, who shivered, opened his sleepy eyes for a transitory second, and promptly closed them again. An agonizing dream, wherein he crashed from a cliff into a valley of prehistoric monsters, effectively destroyed his slumber; he leaned on his elbow and gazed into the darkness outside. He lay back on his pillow and listened to the splashing sounds while his mind wandered hither and thither over a variety of subjects, ranging from the rain to business, from his life in the near future to Wai Hing. He even pondered the problem of immortality, only to dismiss it with a sigh as one invested with the attribute of insolubility. Returning to the rain, he thought how such an inconvenient thing, specially to be regretted in the daytime when it interfered with one's work or pleasure, was yet a blessing, one of nature's most invaluable gifts to man. Severe droughts in the various provinces of China, causing failure of the crops, often resulted in millions of people perishing. He shuddered as he pondered famines, which compelled men to feed on barks, roots, and leaves. Then he tried to picture to himself the course of the water, which was now descending as rain; it stole from the sea as vapor, formed a beautiful cloud, and now was returning to whence it came.

A wind sprang gradually to life, and from a sibilant murmur it grew in intensity to a deafening roar. When it was still not very strong Siu Kam arose and closed the window, for the furniture in his room vibrated to an ever-increasing extent, and the framed pictures on the walls were in danger of darting from their hooks. But now even the securely bolted window trembled under the impact of the tremendous force, threatening to give way altogether, and he had to jump out of his bed once again and spend a good long while barricading it. Pandemonium seemed to fill the sky. He lay still, intently listening to the seething, vociferous fury and wondering how long the typhoon would last. As he thought of the possible damage it might bring in its train, he reviewed in his mind all that he knew of this terrible phenomenon of the South China Sea. Its onset is always more or less a calamity, always dreaded. Summer is its season, and the presence of moisture in the atmosphere is necessary to its occurrence. The Chinese cherished a traditional belief that, when thunder sounds and lightning flashes, typhoons will not follow. Siu Kam, after cudgeling his brains a good deal, recollected that he had seen the heavens gleam with lightning near the north as, after his visit to Wai Hing, he was leaning over the railings of the launch that was transporting him across the ferry shortly after the sun had ended its diurnal journey. He was not usually given to observations of the state of the sky, as the earth around him was, he found, expansive enough to occupy his attention, but that evening he felt specially exhilarated and let his eyes roam over everything, from the obscurely illuminated shops to the scintillating appearance of the city and from the gloomy clouds to the rippling waves. Evidently, the traditional belief about lightning was unreliable.

The typhoon increased in fury. It travelled from the south at a terrific speed, reaching over 150 miles an hour. Its motion was a vortex, whirling round and round in a direction opposite to that taken by the hands of a clock. Houses shivered, and trees were torn up by the roots. Behind firmly shut doors people slept uneasily, while the unfortunate homeless ones whose beds were the pavements pressed closer against the walls. Big holes appeared in the roads, and furniture was blown out of the houses; rocks rolled down the hills and smashed the buildings at the base. The vessels that thronged the harbor tossed and heaved; boats capsized, and even ocean liners were dashed aground and severely damaged. The wreck of an entire fishing fleet took a toll of several lives. The forces of evil, yelling anger and destruction, spun wildly over the earth.

Wai Hing, like Siu Kam, had awakened to the sound of the falling rain, though her thoughts were not characterized by the deadly seriousness and gloom of his. Indeed, she could not be said to have any connected train of ideas; instead, vague, gossamery fancies floated through her mind in her semiconscious state. The typhoon was of no interest to her and scarcely tinged her meandering reverie. She felt pleased that it should have occurred at night and hoped that it would pass away by the time morning broke. Suddenly, a loud explosion somewhere in the house made her start up in confusion; she arose and emerged from her room without any clear conception as to what she expected to see. Peering up the dimly lighted corridor she noticed her parents with their heads elevated toward the roof, through which a hole had been punched by the wind. She was hurrying toward the spot when a window suddenly broke from its hinges and, flying straight against Mr. Chu Weng, laid him prostrate on the wooden floor. Wai Hing and her mother quickly lifted him up and, with great difficulty, managed to put him on his bed, where he lay unconscious and deathly pale, breathing in a labored manner. Meanwhile, the wind drove through the house with ferocious violence, sweeping chairs and tables together and smashing vases and mirrors with howls of nerve-wracking intensity. The unfortunate Mr. Chu Weng was eventually revived, but finding that he suffered from a tender pain in his right leg, he was unable to move.

The typhoon gradually whimpered away as day arrived, leaving behind it all the havoc it had wrought. The loss in life and property was great; many houses had been totally destroyed, and the city presented a desolate spectacle. Siu Kam, as he hurried along on his way to Wai Hing's residence, was dismayed to find that there were streets that were not merely wet from the rain but badly flooded as a result of the bursting of water pipes beneath the ground while others were blocked with heaps of debris. The queerest sight that greeted his eyes was a heavy iron safe that had actually been blown right out of a room situated on the fourth story of an apartment house; its fall produced a deep cavity in the road. He instinctively lifted up his hand toward his head, evidently wondering what would have happened if that ponderous article had come into contact with his cranium; shattered the latter would have been without a doubt. In the harbor he saw the planks of wrecked junks floating on the water, their erstwhile owners standing on the shore and loudly lamenting their losses.

When he reached the house of Wai Hing, the first thing that riveted his attention was the sorry nature of the garden, which had indeed ceased to resemble one, as the plants were well-nigh invisible and the pots were masses of fragments, scattered everywhere.

"Good heavens!" involuntarily exclaimed Siu Kam. "What have we here?"

Ho Fook, the gardener, stood amid the wreckage, surveying the scene with a rueful face. He had passed a most unenviable night, for the hut in which he lived actually rocked to such an extent that it was in peril of imminent collapse; but mercifully, although it had sustained severe casualties in diverse places, it still remained intact and habitable. His own person, a much more valuable commodity, was untouched by any injuries beyond minor abrasions. In thanksgiving for his miraculous escape, he had conscientiously prayed to his patron deity, before whom the incense sticks he burned were still smoking.

"Well, Ho Fook," said Siu Kam, who, being a frequenter of the house, had naturally come to know him, "you have a hard spell of work before you. What a typhoon we had last night!"

"Terrible!" responded Ho Fook.

"It has caused extensive damage," continued Siu Kam as he prepared to enter the house.

He found Wai Hing alone in the sitting room, a faraway, solemn look in her eyes in place of her usual gaiety.

"Why so serious?" asked Siu Kam, glad to find her all unhurt.

"I was thinking how destructive nature could be," she replied in a grave tone.

"Ah! I see the typhoon has made you a philosopher. How did you pass the night?"

"In a most wretched manner."

"Nothing was amiss, I hope."

"Unfortunately, Father was rather seriously wounded. His right leg was fractured. We did not know it at the time; we thought he had received only a shock. Now it seems he may not be able to walk for months, according to the doctor, who has just been here."

"Very regrettable."

"I hope he doesn't become a cripple for life. At his age, a broken bone is no joke."

"I dare say it's not so bad as all that."

"We'll have to see."

"The typhoon has wrought havoc in not a few houses. Your garden is in a sorry mess. I never saw such a woebegone figure as Ho Fook's. He will have plenty to do."

"The garden is a small matter," remarked Wai Hing resignedly.

"Yes, of course," hastily agreed Siu Kam. "It's highly unfortunate that Hong Kong is subject to typhoons. However, most countries appear to be afflicted with some natural calamity or other. There are volcanoes, earthquakes, floods, drought, landslides, and whatnot. I don't know which is worse."

"They are all equally bad," firmly asserted Wai Hing. "I hope I never come across any of them."

"It has always been my view," said Siu Kam with an air of philosophical profundity, "that life is experience. All experience, good or bad, should be welcome. After all, nothing lasts. An hour of misery or a day of happiness soon comes to an end, but the memory of the experience remains, and the more diversified the experience the richer the memory becomes."

"Is that so?" queried Wai Hing without any enthusiasm. "Pleasure and pain may pass away, but a minute of intense pain is not at all an experience to be cherished. I would wish to have only happiness. Incidentally," continued Wai Hing mischievously, "since you seem to like misery, next time if you hear of a pestilence raging somewhere you should make a beeline for the place."

"I don't mean," said Siu Kam with a pained look, "that one should deliberately go and seek trouble. That is undesirable. But if trouble comes, one should take it as an experience that need not be too strongly deplored. In this way one can have a greater measure of happiness."

This paradoxical statement left Wai Hing cold. "Trouble is trouble and happiness is happiness," she maintained. "I don't find any joy in calamity."

Siu Kam fell silent.

Just then a visitor entered the hall; to wit, Leong Yin Pat, who had come in search of his bosom friend, Chu Ko San. On being told by Wai Hing that her brother had gone out, he did not thereupon take his departure but, observing the mess in the house, commiserated with her on the havoc caused by the typhoon. He looked at Siu Kam curiously, and Wai Hing made the requisite introductions.

"I hope," remarked Yin Pat pleasantly, addressing himself to Siu Kam, "that you have not sustained any damage to your home."

"Fortunately none," answered Siu Kam.

"Hong Kong is a beautiful place, but I suppose, to make up for this, it has to be marred by typhoons," said Yin Pat regretfully.

"Mr. Yuen thinks that it is good to have a typhoon to make life more interesting," remarked Wai Hing maliciously.

"Indeed," said Yin Pat with just a slight surprise in his affable voice. "I never considered this aspect of the matter before. What an appealing point of view! I must remember this."

Siu Kam felt uncomfortable. He said deprecatingly, "I only suggested that an occasional trouble might serve to heighten our awareness of our joys."

"Quite true," said Yin Pat. "If we ate sharks' fins and birds' nests all the time we would find them insipid; we need to take salted vegetables too to make us appreciate good food."

Wai Hing smiled at the illustration.

"What line of business are you in?" inquired Yin Pat of Siu Kam, turning away from the subject of typhoons.

"I operate a textile factory," replied Siu Kam.

"How interesting!" observed Yin Pat enthusiastically. "Cloth is such an essential material. Imagine how we would look without clothing!" He racked his brain to continue the conversation. "Talking of clothing, every race wears it, though the fashions are multifarious. It is curious that people should have thought up such strange forms of dress."

"True," said Siu Kam laconically

"I was in Malaya some years back, and I was captivated by the sarongs that were worn by both men and women."

"The girls in sarongs must be delightful," remarked Wai Hing.

"I should think any man would be enchanted by them," said Yin Pat. "What a simple yet sexy form of dress!"

"It does look ornamental," said Siu Kam.

"But if one doesn't know how to wear it or if one is careless in tying it up properly and it were to drop down, it would be most embarrassing," remarked Wai Hing unabashedly.

There was no answer to that one, and none was forthcoming.

"People have queer habits," remarked Yin Pat. "The natives there eat with their hands."

"They don't seem to care for cleanliness," said Wai Hing.

"That's not quite correct," said Yin Pat smilingly. "They wash their hands regularly before every meal. They bathe much more often than we, though this is as much to cool down on account of the heat as for cleanliness."

"Talking of heat," said Wai Hing, "I presume you found the tropical climate unpleasant."

"The perennial heat was certainly not what one would wish, but it was not intolerable. It was not extremely hot. Though cool weather is more comfortable than hot, the cold winters of snow and ice of so-called temperate lands are no better than the heat of the tropics. Hong Kong has a wonderful climate, not too hot in summer or too cold in winter."

"We are certainly lucky," agreed Siu Kam.

"We would be luckier if we didn't have typhoons," said Wai Hing lugubriously.

"Of course," Yin Pat readily concurred. "However, every land has its natural calamities. There are no typhoons in Malaya, but though I never saw any, parts of the country are said to be subject to floods. These can wreak tremendous havoc. When the rain falls continuously for days on end then the low-lying towns and villages on the banks of swollen rivers are covered in several feet of water. Houses are submerged, property is ruined, and sometimes human beings are drowned. Even when the flood is on a small scale it is disturbing; traffic becomes difficult, the residents are stranded, and household goods are damaged."

"Yes," said Siu Kam, "every country has its natural calamities."

Yin Pat looked at his watch.

"I must make a move now," he remarked. "I have to visit a friend."

He took his departure, and shortly afterward Siu Kam also left Wai Hing. As he proceeded to his office he was still in somber mood.

Chapter 10

The Farm

The evening sun lay large and bright just above the clear-cut line of the undulating hills, whose captivating forms towered above the tumultuous city in radiant beauty seeming not of the earth with all its hustling, active swarms of humanity but veritable projections reposing on the soft, serene sky. The atmosphere was impregnated with a slumberous, impalpable quality, soothing as the gentle sound of rippling water. Over a village situated near the Hong Kong side of the border that separated the colony from the province of Kwangtung, all this magical influence of time and weather descended in all its glory as an appropriate close to the peasants' daily toil. Spirals of smoke rose from the houses, indicative of the culinary activities of the women as they boiled rice and cooked their scanty dishes. The wet rice fields gleamed in the vicinity, their stalks swaying ever so lightly; stacks of hay rose higher than the huts; and the cows reclined wearily in their sheds, looking as resigned as their masters, the monotony of whose bleak, gray lives, toiling to live from hand to mouth, had rendered them impervious to the subtle beauty of their surroundings. Their days were vacant caverns.

Along the straggling lanes of the village sauntered Ho Fook, the gardener, with his arms locked behind his back and wearing a blue coat that, totally unbuttoned, revealed his broad, sunburned chest. He was no stranger to the place, judging from his unfaltering step and the direction of his eyes, which, riveted to the ground, displayed a lack of interest in his surroundings more than usual even for him. His leaden apathy was most remarkable, but that his mind was at ease was sufficiently indicated by his leisurely motion. Emerging from the village, he saw on a small piece of sandy ground a group of boys playing shuttlecock with their feet, kicking it from one to another and trying to keep it in the air all the time, a feat not easily attainable, judging from its fall every few minutes. Two bigger lads were flying huge kites in competition, which, moving close together, got entangled and had to be pulled down after vain attempts to free them had been made. The owners shouted volubly, blaming one another for the mishap, while other urchins clapped their grimy hands and laughed merrily at their discomfiture. One or two venerable ancients, patriarchs of the community, sat on stools watching the lively scene, feeling very well satisfied with life and almost as happy as the youngsters; theirs was not the excitement of activity but the joy of a placid heart. Ho Fook shook his head gently as a sign of regret that he was too old to permit himself any of the luxury of the feelings of the boys and too young to be able to achieve the calm of hoary decrepitude. His was the toil and care of vigorous manhood.

Entering a narrow, muddy path that traversed a rice field he came to a wooden hut that, though still serviceable, was in need of repair and looked as if it could be easily demolished with one forceful blow of an axe. The two lengthy strips of paper covered with words of beneficent omen that were pasted on the doorposts the previous New Year had largely peeled off, and their color had changed from a bright crimson to a dull pink. A huge pig, sprawling contentedly before the open door, grunted with displeasure as Ho Fook stirred it with his foot in order to get it to make way for him. The interior of the hut possessed hardly any furniture beyond some stools, a crazy table, and a meager array of culinary utensils and crockery. Nevertheless, the owner of this unpretentious abode might well congratulate himself on having more desirable quarters than the occupant of a horrible room in a slum tenement in the city, a room often shared by a score of people!

As Ho Fook entered the hut, he greeted the host by placing his hands together and shaking them up and down while he murmured, "I respectfully wish you happiness." The salutation was returned with the words "I owe you my good luck." There was an unusual gathering, comprising about a dozen people, all looking more or less jubilant and, for the time being at least, free from care, as befitted the occasion.

They were gathered to celebrate the "completion of the moon" of the son of the host; the child was born one lunar month ago, and a feast was being given in his honor. The unfortunate man had so far produced four daughters to his extreme chagrin and had begun to think that there was something wrong with his wife, to whom indeed he attributed the whole of this misfortune, when to his immense joy a son was providentially born to them. Great as his satisfaction was, it was nothing compared to that of his wife, who had never doubted that he was quite right in his views regarding her. If he were rich, she would undoubtedly have suggested to him the logical solution, which was that he should take unto himself a concubine; as they were poor, however, she had been driven almost to distraction in consequence of her own perpetual self-recriminations. But heaven was merciful, and as a fitting reward for blameless conduct in a former existence, she no longer had to bear the stigma of a woman who could not produce a man-child!

Ho Fook was among those invited to the festive board of the lucky man, whom he had known for quite a long time and who, bearing the same surname, was regarded as a kind of relative. The farmer had been instrumental in helping him to get his gardener's post with Mr. Chu Weng, whose land he used to till, though now he possessed his own plot and independence. Unlike Ho Fook, he was of a cheerful disposition and, except for the unfortunate production of four daughters, had met with no evil to sour it. The solitary table was now carried outside the hut and placed near another that had been borrowed from the village. The feast did not last long, and after it was over the guests, instead of dispersing, talked with great energy.

"How is it, though you aren't blessed with a son, you haven't married again?" asked a carpenter of Ho Fook. He was an anemic person with protruding teeth, as discolored as any teeth could possibly be. They eyes of all the men converged on Ho Fook, who did not turn a hair.

"Oh, plenty of time to consider that," responded Ho Fook. "I haven't got the money yet."

"I think you must have saved quite a bit by now," continued the carpenter. "You could get a woman very cheaply."

"Oh yes," chimed in a factory worker. From his tone it was evident that he had made a very good bargain in the matrimonial market. "There are so many of them."

"Still, one has to support her," said Ho Fook with a mien as impassive and stolid as ever. Really, nothing seemed able to rouse him, not even the exciting topic of women. Is it desirable to possess such a queer temperament?

"You don't seem to enjoy life at all," observed a bus conductor, who spent whatever he earned on the members of the lurid profession. "What is the matter with you?"

"I don't suppose there is anything wrong with me," replied Ho Fook, looking at his thick, rough fingers. "I am quite contented with my lot."

"Every man has his own temperament," said the host, who was picking his ear.

"After all," put in a noodle hawker, who had unbuttoned his blue shirt and was fanning himself with a wooden fan, "Ho Fook does not waste his money needlessly on senseless pleasures." He glanced at the bus conductor, who suddenly found a great deal of interest in his hair, which he pulled over his eyes. "What does the proverb say, 'One turnip, one pit'? We should make good use of what we earn. I shall not be surprised if he grows to be a rich man. He is given to thrift and industry."

"Those traits don't make one rich," growled the factory worker. "Only crooked methods make for success."

"What is the use of working yourself to death and having no fun at all in order to save a lot? You can't carry your wealth with you to the grave. Better give yourself some little pleasure while you are young," said the bus conductor with a sniff.

"I agree that it's more sensible to pass the days as happily as one can," intervened the carpenter, who was using a splinter from a log of firewood as a toothpick, "though I wouldn't go in for joys that are immoral."

"What is the use of morality?" protested the factory worker truculently. "Nobody admires you any the more for it. The richer a person is, the more vicious he becomes and the more looked up to. Take, for example, my employer. Do you know how he made his money? They say he used to be a poor official in a small town near Canton. He did not stop at any kind of trick to squeeze as much as he could from the people. He even went so far as to be in league with a brigand, secretly, of course. Later on he and the brigand fell out, and collecting his ill-gotten gains, he came here. They also say that till two or three years ago, while pretending to be engaged in legitimate trade, he was actually a smuggler. Now he has made so much that he can afford to be good in his business methods and even to indulge in occasional philanthropy. He is no longer unscrupulous in the acquisition of wealth, but the way he spends it! Though he is nearly fifty and possesses several wives, he still goes after bad women. But nobody despises him or hates him. You will find his name in the newspapers mentioned with respect. I have heard poor men who have received some little charity out of his superfluous and unholy riches go into raptures over his generosity. Truly it is said, 'Men respect the wealthy: even dogs bite the ragged.' Morality, indeed!"

"Why do you work for such an evil man then?" questioned the noodle hawker, laying down his fan and inspecting his toes, which were almost destitute of nails.

"What can I do?" was the angry response. "I have to live. I only wish I had no need to eat."

"The mere fact that some bad persons have become successful and consequently respected does not prove that virtue should be discarded," put in the host, turning round after casting a joyful look at the sleeping baby, who did not seem to be in the least disturbed by the loud discussion. "We should practice it for our own good. Money is not everything. I don't want to be wealthy. We may have our miseries, but we have our compensations also. The rich have misfortunes of their own too and …"

"What misfortunes?" impatiently argued the factory worker.

"It's queer, but many of them are childless, and those children they have are usually very unfilial," replied the host, casting another glance at the little boy, who, having a rubber teat in his mouth, sometimes sucked it with his eyes closed, drawing in only air.

"They probably prefer to have no children and thus have less worry," retorted the factory worker, slowly lifting up a hand and with a sudden rapid movement seizing and crushing a fly that had been buzzing round his ears for the last five minutes.

"Then again," continued the host, unimpressed by the other's statement, which appeared to him utterly and completely preposterous, "their wealth is not glued to them, and they are forever living in fear of losing it. Their state of mind is not to be envied."

"Whatever they may suffer, they don't have to bear hunger, and I don't know of anything worse," affirmed the factory worker forcefully.

A fat brown hen that had just laid a very fine egg clucked loudly, proclaiming to all and sundry her glorious feat, moving restlessly here and there in her perfervid enthusiasm. The pig, which had resented Ho Fook's interference with its right to stretch itself luxuriously across the doorway, now felt scandalized at the forward behavior of the hen and grunted its anger in surly, unmistakable tones. The hen saw it lumber toward her threateningly and scampered away to waft her tidings elsewhere to more appreciative ears. The pig, after its triumph, which bore a strange resemblance to the deeds of some human dictators, made its way to a tolerably big pool of mud and lay there, blinking blissfully.

"Each one of us does a different kind of work," observed the carpenter in an attempt to dispel the silence that had momentarily descended on the company. "Who has the best job? I don't like mine, though I have gotten used to it. It's pretty awful to be playing with pieces of wood all day long …"

"Your work is inspiring," stated the bus conductor. "You actually make something. To construct a chair or table is to produce what is useful. Now I can't claim to be productive. Standing in a bus and clipping tickets isn't of any real benefit to society; in any case, I don't make anything. Of course, there are many occupations that are even more worthless than mine. However, I am not interested in work. I care only for the money I earn, which will buy me some pleasure."

"The easier a job is, the more money it brings," said the factory worker. "The actor who does nothing needful to life earns a great deal, while those of us who slave all day long get just sufficient to keep ourselves from straightway going to Yin-shih to become devils."

"I like to see people eat," laughed the noodle hawker. "So I have nothing to complain about my work."

"It would be more fun to do your own eating," suggested the bus conductor.

"Perhaps so," conceded the noodle hawker. "I daresay I may be rather queer in this respect. But when I see people heartily enjoying a dish I have cooked I feel keen pleasure. I myself can never enjoy my noodle so much, for, whether it is good or not, I see so much of it I feel no appetite for it. Sometimes I give a free dish to a miserable street-boy for the sake of seeing him swallow the stuff."

"You are certainly very strange," muttered the bus conductor. "Finding pleasure in other people's pleasure is what I don't understand. One may practice kindness as a duty, but that one could really enjoy it is … is positively queer."

"How do you like your job?" questioned the carpenter, turning to Ho Fook, who all this time had maintained a tremendous silence. His talent for holding his tongue was truly colossal. Whether he was interested in the discussion or not it was hard to say, for, with his eyes on the table, he was to all intents and purposes a sympathetic listener, though the muscles of his face were possessed of an almost inexpugnable rigidity.

"I don't mind it," said Ho Fook in a tone into which he did not mean to infuse any special meaning. In spite of that, all inferred that every variety of work would be welcome to him, so long as it was legitimate.

The carpenter gave a smile stamped with approval. Lighting a short pipe that, until one scrutinized it closely, would have been taken for a shapeless rod with irregular twists and notches whose use was doubtful, he commenced to smoke with wonderful gusto. With the thin rings floating deliciously about his face he said, his eyes politely directed toward the host, "After all, every occupation must bow before that of the farmer, the oldest and most beneficial. Others may or may not be of some use, but this one is absolutely essential to our very existence. The overwhelming majority of our people are farmers. Quite right and proper! If the day should come when our country has more people laboring in the shops and factories than in the fields, it will be unfortunate for us. We shall lose a great deal of our virtue, simplicity, and honesty. The peasantry is the real foundation of China. I was born too weak to till the fields. Blessed is the countryside!"

"Don't you like cities?" interrogated the factory worker.

"They are very bad," replied the carpenter. "I see no sense in so many hundreds of thousands of people huddled together in a space of a few square miles. Why are people who live in cities so much more vicious than those in the country?" The bus conductor again discovered that there was something queer and vastly entertaining about his hair, which was loose and flying in all directions. He took from his pocket a small comb and began to touch his head with great care without the aid of a mirror. "Look how friendly the villagers are," continued the carpenter. "Contrast them with the townsfolk, so brutal, selfish, and quarrelsome. It is only in cities that you find thieves and villains of all sorts. You also find another evil, unemployment. Outside their limits such horrors are absent ..."

"I don't agree with you." The factory worker checked the loquacity of the panegyrist of the village, who was waxing more and more eloquent. "The country places can harbor quite awful persons too. Brigands have their dens there, and they are the consequences of unemployment. Doubtless, villagers have a more simple nature; still, that's hardly any compensation for their misery."

"The country air is purer than that of the town," observed the host. The sentiment sounded strange from the lips of one who dwelt comfortably amid surroundings that were none of the cleanest; as for the element he breathed, it smelt of dung and pigsties.

"People who dwell far from the cities are always more robust than those in them," added the emaciated carpenter.

"That's true," agreed Ho Fook, breaking his silence on his own initiative. He had spoken so rarely during the discourse that all now turned their heads toward him as if oracular words had come from his mouth. "The farmers live longer than others. My grandfather was 107 years old before he left us."

An awed silence befell the company. They meditated for thrice sixty ticks of the clock over this wondrous piece of news.

"Was he ... was he able to move about toward the end of his honorable life?" The bus conductor stammered the question. He felt that it was rather embarrassing to imply that the old man by living to such an unusual age was probably a burden to his descendants and a perfect decrepit.

"He was quite healthy," replied Ho Fook. "He never complained of any illness and could walk, see, and hear well. His senses were intact. He ate half a bowl of rice twice a day and at night slept for five hours."

"It's doubtful whether it's worthwhile to be in the world too long," observed the factory worker gloomily.

"Why not?" said the carpenter. "People naturally love life, so much so indeed that formerly vast numbers of magicians tried to find the elixir of immortality. It is said that some emperors even died from drinking the products of quacks."

"Serve them right!" exclaimed the factory worker. "Having no misery they might want to live forever. It's different with us. I personally am not afraid of death."

"One might as well think of death calmly," stated the host in a tone brimming with resignation and fatalism. "One must go away on the day fixed by the decree of Yen-lo (King of the Nether Regions). If people could never die, then the world would be full only of graybeards and there would be no children. Imagine a man ten thousand years of age!"

Loud laughter greeted this facetious remark.

"Then Peng Tsu, who lived to be eight hundred, would lose his glory," added the noodle hawker.

"We must be going, I think," said the carpenter.

They all thanked the host for his hospitality, showered blessings on the baby, and went their separate ways. The sun had slid softly behind the hills, and the evening had changed its color from golden to glamorous rose and was now mantled in darkness. The fowl composed their wings in their coops, and the pigs slumbered soundly. As Ho Fook took his departure, he left the host standing at the door, on his lips a farewell smile that became invisible to him after he had stepped a distance of two yards. When he emerged on to the main road, he turned round for a last look at the hut, whose position was indicated by a feeble kerosene lamp that seemed to be suffering from the palsy as its light trembled restlessly.

As he walked more briskly than usual toward a stand to catch a bus for home, warbling birds and shrill cicadas pealed their luscious notes among the wayside bushes and grass, and glowworms on dewy seats, tiny lambent flames, glimmered in peace. Close-grained as his mind had become to beauty or happiness, not even he could entirely escape the ineffable influence around him, and he felt a strange, though mild, exhilaration.

Chapter 11

The School

On a narrow board running transversely along the front part of a corner building that abutted a quiet road in Kowloon were painted, in square Chinese ideographs, the words "Chung Shan Boys' Chinese School." The house, with its recent coating of green paint, looked clean and pleasing. On pushing open the folding doors, one entered the school, which occupied only the ground floor, divided into a number of apartments. Even without the sign, a casual observer could tell that here was an institution of learning from the way the tables and chairs were ranged. The school, which had been established by public subscription, was conducted on modern lines; that is to say, it was divided into classes with a teacher in charge of each, teaching all his pupils collectively. Blackboards were in evidence, and chalk flourished. The boys gazed dumbly at their masters, listening with pretended attention, not daring to look out of the windows for five minutes on end or to talk among themselves except in guilty, surreptitious whispers, which tended to promote at least one art, very valuable and wholesome—voice control.

How different from the old system! A school consisted of a single teacher with a score of boys, who each studied on his own. Although there were given hours of study, the pupils need not necessarily all be in class at precisely the same minute on the ringing of a bell. They entered singly and in a leisurely, dignified manner round about the usual time, not minding in the least whether they were earlier or later by fifteen minutes or even more. They had no need to look at their watches and, finding that the awful bell was about to ring in another minute or so

117

when they were still a good two hundred yards away, rush with panting bosoms and unsteady steps into class to receive an ominous look from their masters. When they arrived at their desks they took out their ink slabs, ink sticks, small bottles of water, brushes, writing paper, and books. See them pour water on the slabs, gently, not too much, and grind the ink sticks till a black liquid of fair consistency is produced! Now they pick up their brushes, scrutinize them as though are were rare curiosities, remove one or two loose hairs, dip and roll them in the liquid, and commence to write. And what do they so earnestly indite? Why, they are just copying out the words in their textbooks so that they may acquire a beautiful hand; whether they grasp the meaning of the mystic symbols or not doesn't matter so much. Now all have laid down their brushes and there is a pile of writing pads in front of the teacher, who corrects them. The boys are at present immersed in reading, each from their own textbook. They chant the words loudly, the greater the din the merrier, striving to imprint the passages in their minds. The pupil who thinks he has now mastered his stuff goes up to the teacher, to whom he gives his book, turns his back on him, and rattles off the words as rapidly as memory and the tongue permit. In this way he has pursued his learning. Occasionally, after so much shouting, a boy may lose his voice for a day or two and only speak in whispers.

Returning to the particular school under discussion, we find Choi Ching Kee, who was the headmaster, sitting alone in a small room. The day, being Sunday, was a holiday. He was reading aloud with enthusiastic mien the poem called "The Eternal Woe," written by one of the greatest poets of the fertile Tang Dynasty, Po Chü-i. The poem, which is of considerable length, deals with the frantic love of Ming Huang, the sixth emperor of that dynasty, for a concubine, known to history as the beautiful and hapless Yang Kuei-fei.

For many years the emperor had failed to discover a beauty fit to subjugate nations. Finally, his dream was gratified in the person of a maiden of surpassing beauty of the Yang family. He became oblivious to all sense of duty; love and banquets occupied all his time. Three thousand damsels filled his palace, but he had eyes and ears for only one. Her brothers and sisters were raised to positions of honor, and such good fortune caused every parent to long for the birth of a girl and deplore that of a boy! At last war uprose, and the court fled to the southwest. On the way, the troops of the emperor revolted and demanded the death of the lady. He covered his visage, unable to prevent the slaughter. The army then proceeded to traverse sandy plains and cloudy mountains and dark waters, and all the while the emperor was consumed by inconsolable grief. In the course of time, he returned to his capital, and during the journey he lingered at the tragic spot looking vainly for her whom he loved. Home at last, and all the old, familiar things were there, the pool and the hibiscus; all save her. He sat in grief through the long nights, his companions the fireflies and the constellations. Years passed till a Taoist priest, versed in the art of recalling spirits from their abode, was ordered to undertake an intensive search for her. After soaring through the sky and diving under the earth, he eventually located her dwelling place, an island in the middle of the ocean, peopled with immortals! He came to a golden palace and stood at a jade door waiting for the fair one. She went hurriedly to meet the imperial envoy and told him of her unchangeable fidelity. She produced the old tokens of their love, a golden hairpin and an enamel brooch, broke each of them in two, and told the necromancer to take the half pieces back to the emperor and convey to him her advice to be strong in heart like the gold and enamel and they would one day be reunited either in heaven or on earth. She spoke of a secret pledge made by the emperor to her at midnight on the Seventh Day of the Seventh Moon in the Hall of Immortality to the effect that forever and ever they would live like one-winged birds or like the tree with intertwining branches. Although heaven and earth endure for ages and ages, they will one day disappear; this tragedy will, on the contrary, last unto eternity.

Such is the tenor of the narrative poem. The magical words came tumbling out of the mouth of Ching Kee, his sallow face all aglow, the vivid imagery of the verses lending him its life. He was nearing the end of the piece when who should enter but Siu Kam, who had dropped in for a chat.

"Greetings," said Siu Kam pleasantly. "Have you eaten rice?"

"Yes," replied Ching Kee. "I hope you have done the same."

After ascertaining what it was the teacher was reading, Siu Kam, who revered poetry although seldom looked into it, finding it vaguely sublime and boring, remarked (he liked the imperial romance well enough as a story), "Is Po Chü-i your favorite poet?"

"Not exactly," returned Ching Kee, laying aside the book in his politeness. Interesting though it might be, to persist in its perusal would suggest very strongly that his friend was unwelcome, and he would feel very much obliged if he were to remove his intrusive presence. He was a thriving sensitive plant in regard to the delicacies of etiquette. "Of course, I like best our greatest poet, Li Po, the Banished Angel."

"What a remarkable life he passed, to be sure!" commented Siu Kam.

"He was an inspiring wanderer. His life was as romantic as his poetry," proclaimed Ching Kee with a profound sigh, looking as depressed as it was possible to do for one normally so contented with his life and resigned to everything. Nobody loves romance more than one of sedentary, humdrum existence. The unattainable swells into the wonderful.

"Yes and his strange death!" exclaimed Siu Kam. "Leaning over the side of a boat to catch the moon's sweet reflection in the water while drunk and getting drowned! Really incredible!"

"Great he was," proclaimed Ching Kee fervently, "as Tai-shan. It's curious, isn't it, how the shoddy intrigue of a eunuch could make the emperor, who admired him so much, send him away from court."

"Injustice," pronounced Siu Kam portentously, as if he had made an amazing discovery, "has always run rampant in the world."

"True, true," murmured Ching Kee in ready acquiescence.

"I have always been greatly captivated by the story of Ming Huang and Yang Kuei-fei," observed Siu Kam. "Do you think the emperor's infatuation was right?"

"Emphatically not," declared Ching Kee, shaking his head vigorously in confirmation. "Emperors should never fall desperately in love, nor indeed should anybody else."

Siu Kam stirred uncomfortably in his seat. "Of course, he went too far," he observed after a pause.

"It was a most unfortunate business altogether," Ching Kee pronounced. "His character was naturally noble. At first he made such a good ruler, simple in his habits and benevolent. What admirable impulse prompted him shortly after his accession to burn all silks and luxuries! And yet he could ruin an empire for the sake of one person! What a terrible influence a woman can have!"

Siu Kam looked at his chair as if searching for the pins which were pricking him. "Yes indeed," he murmured.

Ching Kee moved over to a shelf and took a water pipe; stuffing it with a pinch of tobacco from a small pouch, he commenced to smoke. Each plug lasted only half-a-dozen puffs, and so his pipe had to be continually refilled, the ashes being blown off every time this was done. To save matches he lighted a long roll of paper that, burning slowly at one end, could by a few breaths burst into flame whenever its services were required.

"Of course, not all emperors were as unlucky as Ming Huang," he stated ruminatively as he enjoyed his pipe. "The empress of Li Shih-min, our greatest ruler, exercised an admirable power over him for the public good. It all depends upon the woman."

Siu Kam found that the pins in his chair had magically vanished. "Naturally, that goes without saying."

"As for Yang Kuei-fei …," began Ching Kee.

"We had better not talk ill of a woman," said Siu Kam gallantly.

"Oh, I wasn't going to say anything against her," said Ching Kee, darting a swift look at his friend and rising up his head toward the ceiling, his forehead wrinkled with thought. "She met a most lamentable end. Whether she deserved it or not—ahem—well, she was not exactly good, still … well, her death was frightful."

Siu Kam searched the room with his eyes, as his custom was, and ultimately came to rest on a portrait of Yo Fei, painted with skill. He mused over it.

Yo Fei, who lived in the Sung Dynasty in the first half of the twelfth century, had come to be immensely admired as the type of the patriot, and his portrait was conspicuous in schools. His parents gave him the name "Fei," meaning "to fly," on account of the unexpected appearance of a big bird on the wing when he was born. He possessed great strength, mentally and physically, and was a brave, skillful military commander. At that time, the empire was in process of disintegration; besides internal rebellions, which he helped to suppress, the Chin or Golden Tartars were in possession of Northern China. He once defeated one hundred thousand of these invaders with a force of only five hundred intrepid riders! He burned with a fiery zeal to recover the lost territories. The hero, on whose back his mother had in his childhood tattooed four inspiring characters, "Chin chung pao kuo" (forever loyally guard the nation), was a thorn to the barbarians. Unable to conquer him by force, the Chin ruler resorted to stratagem. He bribed and won over the Sung emperor's corrupt prime minister, who thereupon falsely charged Yo Fei with treason and cast him into prison; but, as all accusations against him fell to the ground for lack of evidence, he could not be formally executed. He had been in confinement two months when the venal minister had him secretly killed and ordered the jailer to memorialize the throne, saying that Yo Fei had died a natural death. Thus the hero, whose one aim in life was to win back the hills and rivers of his country and who years later was canonized, met a tragic fate, the victim of a purblind emperor, a treacherous minister, and a wily Tartar.

Ching Kee looked in the direction of Siu Kam's eyes. "What a noble character was Yo Fei's!" remarked the teacher.

"Yes," replied Siu Kam, turning his eyes away from the portrait, "it's difficult to find his like."

"Noble persons usually have an unfortunate fate," said Ching Kee, shaking his head.

"Truly, as people say, 'Heaven has no eyes.' He was a patriot, if ever there was one." Siu Kam sighed with profound regret.

"Of course," remarked Ching Kee, "most men love their countries, the number of traitors being seldom considerable, but the degree of patriotism, as of any other virtue, varies from man to man."

"When one comes to reflect on it," said Siu Kam ruminatively, "patriotism, like all those virtues concerned with upholding the interests of the group, is merely extended selfishness. As one's welfare is dependent on that of the group, it would be easier and more sensible to care for one's own group than for other groups. A traitor is not just wicked; he is stupid to boot."

"I quite agree," said Ching Kee. "There is nothing worse than a traitor to one's country."

"The problem is not so simple," mused Siu Kam. "Take the case of a man who is persecuted by the government of his country on ideological grounds. He flees to another country, which he starts aiding against the government hostile to him. Would you call him a traitor on the same plane as he who sells his country for financial rewards?"

"There are redeeming circumstances, to be sure, but I would term him a traitor. I don't consider it right that a man should repudiate his country, however extreme the provocations."

"But if the government of a country is oppressive, would a patriot endeavor to overthrow it?" pursued Siu Kam.

"I suppose he could," reluctantly conceded Ching Kee. "But he should not conspire with a foreign country to do so."

"If the foreign country has a design to conquer his land, then he certainly should not conspire with it. But if there is no such motive, I am doubtful whether he may not be justified, especially if internal resources are inadequate."

Ching Kee was stubborn. "How can one be quite sure that the foreign country is free from evil intent and acts purely for altruistic reasons? Nations are even more selfish and calculating in their actions than individuals. Historically, when a foreign army was invited into a country by some interested party for its aid, the usual outcome was for it to acquire control of that country. Look at the Manchu army, whose assistance was sought by General Wu San-kuei to overthrow the rebel Li. It proceeded to capture the Middle Nation, which thus came to be under alien rule for more than 250 years."

"Quite so," assented Siu Kam.

There was silence for a while as they drank strong tea.

"Talking of history," remarked Siu Kam, "what do you think of the multifarious revolts and civil wars that have beset China from ancient to modern times?"

"Nobody could possibly regard them as anything but deplorable. Sometimes when an emperor was peculiarly vicious and tyrannical it might have been necessary for a rebellion to arise for him to be overthrown, as in the case of Chieh and Chou, but even then it is doubtful whether war was the right solution. It would have engendered less misery if the tyrant had died at the hands of an individual assassin or was allowed to live out his normal span of days!"

"I presume that one contributory factor for the revolt was the Confucian doctrine that an evil ruler forfeited his right to govern," observed Siu Kam. "Every ambitious person could therefore give forth the excuse that the reigning sovereign was a villain and he himself was the rightful supplanter."

"The doctrine was sound, but of course, like all others, it could be distorted by evil people for their own purposes," said Ching Kee in a severe tone.

"Supposing, however, that the right to rule was conferred by birth and the emperor could not be dethroned for any reason whatsoever; there would not have been so many rebellions."

"That is possibly so. Such an ideology would have discouraged revolt in general, but it would not have prevented members of the ruling family from contesting for the throne. However, there could have been fewer upheavals."

"Of course, I don't mean to say that an evil ruler should be allowed to rule until he dies. But replacing him by force with another autocrat is not a proper solution. That is why I think that democracy is superior to monarchy. A ruler whom the people don't like is gotten rid of by a peaceful election."

"Democracy," retorted Ching Kee, "is not necessarily a blessing. Elections can be quite chaotic, and sometimes the differences between parties end in civil war."

"To be sure," sighed Siu Kam, "no system of government is always right in practice. Human beings are born pugnacious and acquisitive, and these traits will sooner or later wreck a system."

"Don't you think that man is born good?" Ching Kee spoke in a tone of curiosity. "Do you remember the first twelve characters of the Trimetrical Classic stating that human beings are by nature originally good and that they are close together as regards their nature but are far apart in their conduct?'

"If their nature is the same what makes them behave differently?" retorted Siu Kam in the form of a counterquestion. "If they are born good, what makes them act evilly? No! I do not subscribe to the theory of the innate goodness of man."

"Do you consider then that he is born evil?" asked Ching Kee with a flabbergasted demeanor.

"Not at all," replied Siu Kam. "What is good and what is evil? Man is born with certain characteristics, of which the chief is the instinct of self-preservation. There is no question of morality involved. But according to our moral code, certain forms of behavior are deemed moral and some immoral, and as most of the commonly displayed human traits fall into the evil category, some say that man is born evil. Others, however, consider man originally good and then try to explain his evil actions away. The truth is, of course, that he is neither good nor evil."

"People must be either one thing or the other," observed Ching Kee stubbornly. "The moral code is not an arbitrary set of rules but is a necessity of life. Conscience distinguishes for us right from wrong."

"If that were the case," retorted Siu Kam, "how did there arise so many moral systems? Even in the olden days there were the competing systems of Confucius and Laotze and Moti and Yangchu. How do we reconcile the preaching of Confucius that one should actively fulfill one's social duties like those of emperor and subject, father and son, brother and friend and the theory of Laotze that one should do nothing and should live in seclusion and retirement? Moti talked of universal love and Yangchu of egoism. I think that moral ideas are human products like chairs and tables."

"The fact that there are different moral codes does not mean that none is right. Confucianism won the day because it was true," said Ching Kee naïvely.

"As it is now losing the day to other theories, it is therefore false," retorted Siu Kam. "It is ridiculous to equate success with truth. There have been all sorts of theories in the world contradictory to one another and commanding wide support. They could not all be true."

Ching Kee wriggled in his chair and felt none too happy.

Siu Kam suddenly looked at his watch and exclaimed, "Oh! I have completely forgotten the time. It's getting late and I must go home."

Ching Kee did not detain him, but he said, "We have had a most interesting discussion. Such discourse is very useful in clarifying one's mind."

"I meant no offense," said Siu Kam, "in my arguments. I was just talking for the sake of talking." He laughed loudly as though he had cracked a good joke.

Ching Kee laughed in unison. Still laughing, Siu Kam took his departure; on emerging into the street, he looked at the sky and increased the rapidity of his gait.

Chapter 12

The Wedding

In spite of the opposition of his parents, Siu Kam persisted in his determination to marry Wai Hing. Partly from the realization that their son's mind was unchangeable and partly due to the gentle persuasion of Silver Moon, who, among other arguments, often repeated to them the theory that what could not be avoided had best be endured with a good grace and the consolatory fact that after all the bride was not a sing-song girl, Mr. and Mrs. Yuen Ko resigned themselves to it. They, that is to say, did not break off relations with him altogether but passively allowed him to do whatever he liked. Mr. Yuen Ko, who was chiefly concerned over his honorable reputation in society, was more easily reconciled than his spouse, whose indignation was based on a more serious grievance: that she was not consulted on the choice of a daughter-in-law of hers. This fact rankled in her mind. She had never set eyes on her husband before she married him; his mother was the person who chose her for him. Therefore, it was manifest injustice that she did not pick out her son's bride. She was prepared to find nothing good in her. As it was not desirable that the family should become notorious and a laughingstock, a contingency that would happen if they were to disown their son forever, she would shut her eyes to the marriage. Both she and her husband came to the conclusion that the most sensible course to pursue was to let the wedding take place with due regard to the customary formalities and hope for the best.

Now there were several types of wedding ceremony in current use. One, rapidly going out of fashion, was the traditional variety, compounded of elaborate rites, kowtowing, noisy drums and cymbals, and the flowery sedan-chair, wherein the invisible bride jolted to her new home. It was undoubtedly picturesque though ruinous to the purses of the harassed parents. Its complicated ritual could only have been formed through the accretions of centuries, for all ritual needs time to grow; Confucius, it will be remembered, did not create but transmitted rites. Republican China initiated a style of marriage based on the Western, its chief difference being that instead of taking place in a church, it could be held anywhere: guild house, club, restaurant, or any convenient spot. Its chief recommendation was its low cost; most ordinary young folk preferred it for the very good and decisive reason that it was not old-fashioned, an epithet that bestrode their minds like a monster of iniquity.

The modern damsel, Wai Hing, positively refused to have anything to do with the old-style marriage, for she wasn't going, she averred, to suffer the indignities and inconveniences associated with it; so Siu Kam suggested that they hold their wedding in a hotel, a simple, brief affair. In the normal course of things, his venerable parents would have strenuously opposed this; but, as the marriage was to them in any case distasteful, they made little objection to this last instance of their son's depravity.

Siu Kam was a good deal troubled by all this strife, which formed an ominous prelude to a peaceful, happy, new stage of life; and on the morning of his wedding day he woke up with gloomy thoughts running round his head. An eavesdropper—luckily there was none present or he would have concluded that he was in the presence of a man whose faculties were in the process of derangement—would have heard him thump his chest and address the wall in a plaintive tone, asking why fate should treat him so unkindly, and, in spite of his best intentions, contention and misery should thus descend on him. He tried to draw comfort by mentally subscribing to the proposition that love should override all other considerations and should be its own justification, but his conviction was by no means completely whole-hearted.

As for Wai Hing, she was in the highest spirits. Siu Kam had not told her anything about his parents' attitude toward her, and in her own eyes, she certainly could not see why anybody should object to her. The idea that she was the cause of a considerable amount of altercation never entered her head. She had visited her fiancé's home only once so far and found that her future parents-in-law were polite and formal as it should be. Of course, it would have made no difference to her what their attitude was in any case as she never consulted others about her inclinations and actions.

They spent their honeymoon in Honolulu, where the sun shone brightly all the year round on a modern city surrounded by enchanting countryside. Siu Kam had known this place before but never found it as interesting as now. He had never experienced such happiness hitherto, and he concluded that the most momentous step in his life was also the most blessed. He lived as in a dream, and it was with a shock that he found himself returning to Hong Kong with Wai Hing by his side to resume the daily round, the common task.

Although his relationship with his parents was none of the pleasantest, Siu Kam brought his wife home to stay with them. To set up a separate establishment not conforming to the usual custom would be tantamount to effecting a serious break with them. The house was quite ample to accommodate them all. He possessed a lingering hope that the breach would eventually be healed, placing reliance on Wai Hing's charm and gentleness, but from the first he found his illusions shattered.

His father indeed was not so unrelenting. On finding that the marriage was by no means as disastrous as he had anticipated and that his "face" was almost as unblemished as ever, he gradually ceased to feel so hurt. Mrs. Yuen Ko, however, was made of sterner stuff. It was not reputation that she cared for so much as parental rights, which had suffered irreparable inroads, and her ingrained antipathy to the type of girl represented by Wai Hing. She could see no good in her, for though she might not be a sing-song girl, she certainly was no model of propriety; she knew no manners, no idea of correct behavior.

A daughter-in-law with a sense of duty would rise early in the morning and bring tea to her mother-in-law. She would wait on her at meals, standing respectfully behind her chair, ready to refill any empty dishes. She should not sit in the presence of her elders and should always speak with a soft, pleasant voice. Late to bed and early to rise is her maxim. Before marriage her devotion is directed toward her parents, but after "leaving the home," she is part and parcel of another family.

Wai Hing lamentably fell far short of these ideals; to record the unvarnished truth, she embodied in her charming person the direct antithesis of all of them. She sat down at table even before her mother-in-law did so; she was out of the house most of the time on her visits to friends; she did whatever pleased her. Of all the traditional rules, she might be said to fulfill only half of one: she went late to bed, after shows, parties, and whatnot. Is it any wonder that Mrs. Yuen Ko's wrath against this precious daughter-in-law of hers had no tendency to abate, rather the reverse, in fact? But she controlled herself and did not display any open animosity.

Wai Hing was decidedly attracted by Silver Moon, just as the north pole of a magnet turns toward the south pole of another. She seemed to her a queer specimen, a type rapidly becoming extinct. She could not for the life of her understand what she lived for, why she didn't find time hang heavy on her hands, how she could be so shy and retiring. Silver Moon presented to her an intriguing problem, and they chatted for long hours to the immense satisfaction of both. Silver Moon also found Wai Hing interesting; not bad, as her mother averred, but high-spirited. Sometimes she envied her freedom and vivacious gaiety, though, it must be confessed, not often, for she felt that, after all, she did not clearly understand why her own serene days promised less strife, to which she evinced a tremendous aversion.

One day, unable to issue from the house due to a drizzling rain that looked as if it would never cease, a meteorological phenomenon not unusual in this part of the world, Wai Hing sat in conversation with Silver Moon, who was knitting with a pleasant expression on her soft face. After watching her intently for fifteen minutes, Wai Hing exclaimed: "You seem never to leave the house. How can you bear it?"

"Easy enough," smiled Silver Moon. "I find it tiresome to go out. I suppose I am very lazy."

"People are lazy in regard to work, but this is the first time I find a person too lazy to move about," laughed Wai Hing. "You are really very curious. I never saw a girl like you before. I think I am given to idleness, and no mistake—I don't like work as you do. But I find it hard to sit still."

"You are not used to it," stated Silver Moon sagely.

"You should go out more often," urged Wai Hing. "Don't you love the sight of the streets and shops?"

"I am afraid of men," said Silver Moon shyly.

"What!" exclaimed Wai Hing contemptuously. "They are not tigers. They can't eat you."

"Maybe not," conceded the other. "But I feel so uncomfortable when I find a man staring at me. Do you notice one thing very curious? When a man looks at a girl, he always grins. Now what's the reason for this?"

"I don't know," said Wai Hing after a pause. "I never thought of it before. All men are fools," she concluded in an authoritative tone.

"Are they?" queried Silver Moon doubtfully. "What about my brother?"

"Most men, that is to say," replied the other, correcting herself. "Of course, there are some exceptions."

"I think men are cleverer than women," remarked Silver Moon judiciously. "They have always done most of the work that keeps civilization going. They were responsible for poetry, music, art, inventions. Women have hardly done anything."

"That is only because men have always tried to prevent women from doing any great work, and they enforced their will by their superior strength," retorted Wai Hing angrily. "All men are villains; most men, that is to say," she added hurriedly.

"So you think, if we had free competition, we could surpass them," said Silver Moon with great interest.

"I am sure we could," was the vigorous reply. "We are now being emancipated. The world does not belong to men alone. They are usurpers."

"I believe the woman's place is in the home."

"I think nothing of the sort" came the severe retort. "Her place is in the world. Both sexes inhabit the same planet, and I don't see why we should be confined within the four walls of a house and live only to look after their comfort."

"They get money so that we can keep the home going."

"We can also earn if we are allowed to do all the work they do."

"Why are men so fond of working anyway? I suppose it isn't very enjoyable," observed Silver Moon innocently.

"It's not that they like toil. But organized as our society is, an occupation means money, and money means pleasure and power. If they can have the money without the work, they'll be only too happy to do so."

"I dare say that's true. The hardest job is usually the worst paid. Nobody wants to be a coolie if he can help it, yet he has more strenuous work than anybody else."

"Exactly so. Men are selfish and cruel. Look how they kill one another in war. Have you ever heard of bands of women indulging in mutual massacre?"

"That is because we are afraid of blood. We are not brave enough."

"When courage leads to such horrors, I don't see what good it holds. It's an evil rather than a virtue."

"If we go out into the world and struggle like men, do you think it would be for our benefit?" questioned Silver Moon after a moment's silence. "Would we be happier?"

"At least we would be free and cease to depend on the whims of men," answered Wai Hing with extreme heat. "I can conceive of nothing that makes for greater happiness than to do as one pleases. Our slavery, which is even now only partly removed, is hideous. It's against nature."

"And yet," smiled Silver Moon, "this unnatural state of affairs has lasted for thousands of years."

"The length of a tradition doesn't in the least prove that it's good or even natural," affirmed Wai Hing. "You don't deny that bound feet are not to be found in nature; the distortion is purely artificial. Still the monstrous custom existed for a thousand years, ever since a foolish Sung emperor took delight in a concubine who possessed very small feet. You will notice that the custom was due to men; the women did it to please them. We always do things only to attract them; men don't do things to humor us. How do you like to have feet with only one toe on each clearly visible?"

"I am glad I don't have them," conceded Silver Moon.

"The misery we suffer due to the different treatment of the sexes is really too much," said Wai Hing with a flush upon her cheeks. "It's very strange how women could have accepted their despised and inferior state for so many ages without the shadow of a protest. Indeed, they seemed to glory in it. Sometimes I despise our sex."

"You seem to be contradicting yourself," put in Silver Moon, winking ever so slightly. "I thought you admired it."

"Of course I do," retorted Wai Hing warmly. "I only despise women for being so submissive; I dislike such an attitude as yours, for example."

Silver Moon blushed in confusion and appeared as ill at ease as it was possible for her to be. Wai Hing regretted her hasty and cutting remark on perceiving its effect and said in a soothing tone, "Well, you are born gentle. I love you enormously."

Her colossal affection was without a doubt very satisfying, for Silver Moon smiled, and her confusion vanished like the gray cloud before the rising sun's golden rays.

"Really," mused Wai Hing with a faraway look in her eyes, "we have still a long way to go before we are fully free. It's so hard to destroy prejudice. We are not economically equal with men. There should be as many women as men in every vocation. It is very absurd that most women are confined to doing unpaid work in the house. I protest against this."

It was not certain to whom she was protesting with such vehemence, and Silver Moon smiled but maintained silence, not wishing to provoke her anger by any inappropriate observations. After reflecting with ungraceful gloom for some time over her grievances, Wai Hing resumed her discourse: "However, we are free now in one respect. We can go out as we like. At least I do. I must take you out. It's not good for you to stay cooped up at home the whole time."

"But I find no fun outside," spoke Silver Moon pathetically.

"That's because you have not known how to move about properly," stated Wai Hing with becoming condescension. "Do you know how to drive a car?"

The other shook her head in horror.

"Of course not!" exclaimed Wai Hing in triumph. "I'll teach you. Have you ever climbed a hill? Next week a party of us is going up Tai-mo-shan. You must certainly come along."

"But hill climbing is so dangerous and tiresome," observed the timid one helplessly.

"Don't be a coward!" exclaimed the strong one impatiently, looking very brave. "I suppose you don't know how to swim either. Oh dear, you have a lot to learn!"

Silver Moon did not look as though she wanted to be instructed in all these wondrous arts, which did not seem to her to promise any fun at all. In spite of this, her self-constituted patroness ran on with ardor: "You'll adore swimming in the sea when you have had some experience. I learned it when I was still a little girl."

"I wonder what Mother will say to all this. She will be angry with me if I do them," observed Silver Moon wistfully.

Starting in unpleasant surprise, Wai Hing found her enthusiasm come to a halt as abruptly as a train that encounters a red signal.

"Why, doesn't she approve of them?" she asked in consternation.

"Of course not," replied Silver Moon slowly. "You don't know how conservative she is. She doesn't like to see girls in the streets at all."

"This is monstrous!" exclaimed Wai Hing, reddening uncomfortably. "I never knew she was so strict. I understand now how your behavior is so old-fashioned. Well, I don't care. I can't bring myself to act in such a way as to suit her prejudices."

"After all," observed the other uneasily, "she is my mother."

"Filial piety can be carried too far," remarked the modern one in a tone noticeably devoid of respect. "Parents must be reasonable. I would never follow the wishes of my seniors if they were not right."

"Or if they don't accord with yours," breathed the other with an odd smile.

"Well, perhaps it is the same thing," conceded Wai Hing. "But it can't be helped. We can't make our minds believe what we think is wrong. And every person should have a right to live her own life. In any case, that's my opinion. And I advise you to be less timid. You would be happier. That, of course, you would say is again my opinion," she laughed merrily. "The rain has stopped. I am going out. Would you like to join me?"

Silver Moon shook her head in gentle decline of the invitation.

Chapter 13

The Theatre

As the days progressed, Siu Kam's commercial prosperity increased, and though he was very much in love, he did not neglect his business. This was as it should be and demonstrated clearly enough that he was a man possessed of great common sense and was not needlessly given to romance. This did not mean, of course, that he neglected Wai Hing; on the contrary, he was too attentive, yielding to her slightest wish. In fact, with his friends, he bore the dishonorable reputation of being uxorious. With the air of the worldly wiseacre, they gave the usual explanation that one who never had any association with the opposite sex before was apt to fall more desperately in love than any other, implying that it was not the rare excellence of the beloved that inspired such devotion but his lack of experience. A person of a contrary view could refute this dictum by pointing out that most of the world's great lovers were not saints who went crazy over one woman but men who indulged in fashionable living, like Mark Antony. Naturally, Siu Kam could not afford to spend as much time with his friends as he did formerly, though whenever he was free and Wai Hing could spare his company, he would gather in the evening with them in a teahouse or their club.

On a certain fine evening he was in a theatre, whither he repaired sometimes for relaxation. The cinema, especially American pictures, claimed his preference; still, as befitted his liberal mind, he was not averse to the Chinese drama, which was one of the last strongholds of conservatism in a culture whose retreat before new influences since the revolution of 1911 was rapid enough. This drama was an unmitigated bore to the majority of the young of both sexes; Wai Hing looked down on it as being associated principally with noise.

"Why do you want to see such stuff?" she murmured to Siu Kam when he announced his forthcoming treat. "I thought you were a modern and progressive person."

By the way, the word "modern" was to her sacred and the justification par excellence of all ideas, manners, tastes, behavior, and deeds. She flatly refused to join him in such a highly unentertaining entertainment, though she graciously granted him permission to go with his friends.

The theatre was clean and elegant, being the best in town; one says clean because not every hall could boast such an epithet. Several green dragons reposed in carved majesty on the ceiling. Only a person well versed in the subject could tell what variety of that mythical species they represented—whether they were dragons who passed their existence beneath the waves in resplendent mansions or those evil nagas who had their abodes in desolate mountains. Was their work to produce wind and rain, or was it to look after the palaces of the gods? Were they connected with any particular legend, or were they ordinary dragons, of which a tremendous number existed?

"The show promises to be good," remarked the merchant, Gaw Lok, shortly after the play began.

"I hope so," said Tak Cheong, the lawyer, solemnly, as if he were speaking to a prisoner in the dock who had the misfortune not to be his client.

"The story of Wang Chao-chun is romantic," chimed in the mild-looking pedagogue, Ching Kee. "Very absorbing."

"The tale may be interesting; the performance may be the opposite," said Tak Cheong without relaxing a muscle of his face.

It is to be feared that his pessimism had its basis in something totally unconnected with the present show, for he had lost one of his most important cases in court that day, though according to him, he had never spoken better in all his life.

"Well, let us wait and see," interposed the agreeable Gaw Lok.

His habitual good humor was vastly enhanced that day, for it was his fiftieth birthday. Of course, he had celebrated it with a fair degree of enthusiasm and a not unfair amount of ceremonies. The contrast between ancient Chinese and modern Western attitudes toward the variegated problems of life is nowhere more striking than in reference to age. Then, age was a venerable institution; now, youth is an idol. Then, the man, and still more the woman, was respected the greater their number of years; now, the man, and still more the woman, assiduously strive to conceal the true digits. Then, in polite conversation with a senior, one lamented one's yet contemptibly short span of life; now, the senior jocularly, if he is jocular enough to do so, points with a wry face to his gray hairs, while the youth strives to prove to him that he is still young. Fair, fat, and forty is a facetious description that did not occur to anyone in the Celestial Empire. As Ching Kee once observed to his friends, "Why there should be such pother over either youth or age is mysterious, considering that everyone is young once and must be old someday, irrespective of his merits. A person can truly boast only of personal achievements and not of something that sooner or later descends on him. And age can be just as pleasant as youth."

The suggestion of a visit to the theatre originated from Gaw Lok and was enthusiastically seconded by his friends; after a sumptuous banquet there could be nothing more agreeable than relaxation in comfortable seats with a show in front.

And here they were, ready to applaud the play, with the exception, perhaps, of the unfortunate lawyer.

"The Chinese theatre compares very unfavorably with the foreign cinema," gloomily remarked Tak Cheong, sweeping the hall with a severe eye. "Very unfavorably indeed," he repeated with a rhetorical roll in his voice.

"Why do you say so?" Ching Kee inquired, in the mildest of mild tones.

"For a variety of reasons," replied Tak Cheong pompously. "First, in our dramatic performances the action is extremely slow. Lengthy dialogues chanted in a falsetto voice ..."

"But the conversations tell the story," interrupted Ching Kee.

"More often they are mere padding, put in so that the play may last the requisite length," said Tak Cheong irritably.

"Doubtless," interposed Siu Kam placatingly, "sometimes they are unnecessary."

"Secondly," continued Tak Cheong, "in the cinema you see before you the scenery, background, and all things as they are in real life. In the drama we have to be conversant with the conventions in order that our imagination may supply what is lacking. Take a man riding a horse. Do we see an actual horse?" he asked so loudly that a goodly proportion of the audience turned round in surprise.

After fully two minutes, when all eyes were again transfixed on the stage, Tak Cheong answered his own question in a lower tone, "No, we don't see anything that bears the faintest resemblance to that quadruped. Instead the rider is supposed to mount a horse when he makes a sweeping curve with one leg and then he waves a whip up and down as he walks round the stage. What could be more ludicrous?"

"Now that I come to think of it, it's certainly curious," murmured Gaw Lok.

"Consider the other queer conventions," pursued the lawyer with a triumphant visage. "A door is opened by making gestures and sliding an imaginary bolt. Four men shouting and waving flags form an army ..."

"You don't expect to behold ten thousand persons on the stage, do you?" asked the teacher in a tone of gentle remonstrance.

The lawyer did not deign to reply. After a pause he continued, "Thirdly, there is a lack of decency in exhibiting certain things. A woman is shown giving birth to a baby right in front of you. The supposed infant is of course only a doll. A man sits lolling in a chair picking his ears. Bad words are often spoken."

"Well," argued Ching Kee, "such things occur in real life, and I thought you loved realistic effects."

"There are certain common events that are not suitable subjects for representation," retorted Tak Cheong in a hurt, dignity-charged tone. "Fourthly, with progress all round us, our drama is almost as conservative as ever."

"No film," Ching Kee stated with conviction, "is as interesting to its audience as our plays are to people like me. And to give pleasure—what more can we ask of anything? These stories have enchanted generations."

"No desire for progress and variety—that's exactly what I deplore," interrupted the other with ungraceful violence.

"What's the use of variety for its own sake? I would much prefer to have one good thing, which has come down through the centuries, than ten indifferent novelties."

"Your course is certainly the easier to pursue," laughed Tak Cheong sarcastically. "All lazy people follow it."

The pale face of Ching Kee assumed a red glow, which rapidly increased to a beautiful crimson and then more gradually retreated, as flows and ebbs the tide.

"I think our romances are charming and instructive," quickly interposed Gaw Lok, casting oil on the troubled waters. "I like them enormously."

"Well," added Siu Kam, as usual trying to sit on two stools, "our theatre is excellent, though it needs reform."

In the meantime, the play had started and was now in full swing. It dealt with the romance of Wang Chao-chun, a dazzling beauty who became the concubine of a Han emperor, Yuan-ti. An official, Mao Yen-shou, who was sent by the emperor to choose damsels for his palace, was an avaricious villain; failing to get a sufficient bribe he disfigured the portrait of Chao-chun so that the emperor, who based his judgment on pictures, did not see her and she was relegated to the cold palace, the place where ladies who had fallen from the imperial favor were confined. Accidentally the emperor encountered her, was thoroughly captivated with her beauty, and on learning from her the true story, ordered the arrest and execution of Mao Yen-shou. He, however, unlike some loyal ministers, had no taste for this treatment but escaped and made his way north to a Tartar country, to whose king he showed a portrait of the lovely Chao-chun. The Tartar khan thereupon became violently enamored with the original. He demanded the hand of Chao-chun from the emperor, who had no general capable of defending the country against the powerful barbarian and was forced to accede to his request. Chao-chun, who was very much in love with the emperor in spite of having been in the cold palace, set out on her journey in tears. The khan received her with the greatest honor. But at the Amur River, which separated the Middle Nation from Tartary, Chao-chun ended her life by jumping into the cold waters. The khan was terribly upset and laid the calamity at the door of Mao Yen-shou. He made peace with the Han emperor, and Mao Yen-shou was executed.

Whenever any point of particular interest occurred in the course of the play, the audience cried, "Good!" At the conclusion of a lament played by Wang Chao-chun on her lute bewailing her fate in the cold palace the ovation was thunderous.

"Such enthusiasm," observed Ching Kee, who himself had shouted "Good" with ardor, "is in itself a delight to behold."

Tak Cheong maintained a dignified silence but curled his lips ever so slightly: he was to all intents and purposes weighed down with weariness at the irrational behavior of people.

Just then a child ran from the wings almost to the center of the stage but was quickly retrieved by its mother. This incident showed one of the curiosities of the Chinese stage in that no effort was made to create the illusion of reality. Everybody was fully aware that what he was seeing in front of him was just a piece of acting; therefore, incongruous effects were not rigorously excluded. While the play was in progress, those actors and actresses who were not actually engaged in speaking at the time refreshed themselves with a cup of tea or conducted conversations with one another; those who fell down dead rose immediately and retired; the property men moved about arranging chairs and tables; members of the troupe stood in the wings in full view of the audience to watch both the play and the spectators.

"Very realistic effect," exclaimed Tak Cheong sarcastically, pointing to the child.

"I agree with you," said Siu Kam, "that such incidents should not be allowed to happen."

The music from the pipes, fiddles, cymbals, gongs, and drums became rather clamorous, and our friends were silent for some time.

"The story of Wang Chao-chun," said Tak Cheong "is a typical example of the decadence of ancient China."

"Why do you say that?" queried Gaw Lok, his eyes round with surprise.

"An official was sent round to pick girls for the imperial harem, to which they were forcibly transported whether they wanted to go or not. This particular official was a corrupt specimen and was quite typical of his class. Without any further inquiry and for no crime whatsoever, the girl was condemned to dwell for the rest of her life in a prison. The country was weak, and the emperor sent her, although reluctantly, to an inhospitable clime to wed a person who got her by force. If the emperor had devoted his energies to making the country strong instead of looking for beautiful girls, he would not have been in the ludicrous position of having to surrender his wife, although only a secondary one, to a foe. The record of autocracy in China is unedifying." Tak Cheong wiped his brow after this peroration—the night was hot.

"It is not fair to condemn all emperors because one was weak," argued Ching Kee.

"One!" sneered Tak Cheong. "Almost every emperor in China was an amorous good-for-nothing. How did the dynasties come to an end? Consider the number who perished as a result of the crimes or follies of the rulers."

"Love and war," stated Siu Kam sententiously, "are common to all races."

"But it is only in absolutisms that the lives of millions of people are made to hang on the caprices of a single man," contended Tak Cheong. "What a shocking, unnatural state of affairs!"

"So you oppose Confucianism?" questioned Ching Kee with unwonted vigor.

"I have no use for it," retorted the other just as forcefully.

"Then how do you account for the fact that it was firmly established and venerated for so many centuries?"

"Its success is no proof of its value. Why was the crippled foot the fashion for a thousand years? Wrong judgments, confirmed by habit, explain both."

"Are you a Chinese?"

"I certainly am."

"I am surprised. You seem to approve of nothing that originated in the Central Nation."

"It does not mean that to be a good Chinese one must believe that the cause of an eclipse lies in the fantastic attempt of a voracious dragon to swallow the sun or digest the moon. You are arguing like an ignorant peasant instead of an intelligent scholar."

"It is very warm tonight," said Gaw Lok hurriedly and apprehensively, fearing an explosion. "Shall we order some drinks?" Without waiting for a reply, he gave the necessary instructions to an attendant who happened to be standing close at hand.

After a long silence, wherein everybody's eyes were riveted on the stage, Siu Kam said, "The Chinese cinema is increasing in popularity. It has a more modern appeal, though many of its stories still deal with the life of past times."

"I don't particularly like the cinema," said Gaw Lok, "as I am not fond of sitting in darkness."

"You'll get used to it if you go more often," said Siu Kam.

"The cinema is really a strange form of entertainment," observed Gaw Lok. "Next to the radio, I consider it the subtlest of all inventions. Familiarity has made us cease to regard it with wonder. I once came across an instance of its effect on a person seeing it for the first time. The man was a peasant. He was exceedingly astonished and muttered in a trembling, fearful tone, 'This is undoubtedly a play enacted by ghosts. I see shadows but no living beings. I hear voices which seem to come from the moving shadows. This is frightful.' Thereupon he rose with a wild look of horror on his pale face and precipitately rushed out of the hall."

"That's very curious," commented Siu Kam with a smile.

Chapter 14

Conflict

Relations between Wai Hing and her mother-in-law, Mrs. Yuen Ko, deteriorated day by day. Once or twice they went to the extent of exchanging words that were by no means of the pleasantest. Their points of disagreement, as mentioned before, were numerous and varied: they looked at life through diametrically opposite windows. There was no plane on which they could meet. Mrs. Yuen Ko was resentful of the fact that her son no longer looked up to her as the guide of his life; Wai Hing, on the other hand, wanted to monopolize all his love and in every single thing, great or small, wished him to submit to her decisions. Another potent source of friction came from the gentle Silver Moon, who under the influence of Wai Hing began to take an interest in the great world outside. In her, Mrs. Yuen Ko fancied that she discerned faint gleams of incipient revolt against parental authority and the conventional virtues and verities. Persistently egged on by the tireless Wai Hing to do things for which she felt no real inclination and scolded by Mrs. Yuen Ko for acts she never committed, the modest Silver Moon led a life that would excite envy in few. She sometimes sighed and wondered why people were so devoid of reason.

According to a noted philosophic theory, the universe is subject to necessity: every event comes to pass predetermined from the beginning of time. This profound view looks suspiciously like a variation of the simple Oriental peasant's belief in fate. Any person who wanted to know what an efficient drug fatalism is should have stood in Hong Kong on an evening watching the boatmen reclining in their vessels. How stoical they looked! The wisdom of the East, which sounded so romantic in the West, seemed to shine through their weather-beaten faces. They serenely took whatever came along, without complaint, without murmur.

The above digression is made in order that an excuse may be furnished for the luckless Siu Kam, who at first sight appeared to be the actual cause of the doleful atmosphere in his home, for if he had not given his heart away so injudiciously, supreme peace would without a doubt have reigned in triumph. He was really guiltless as the conflict was foreordained from eternity and he was only a hapless, involuntary instrument in the hands of destiny. Although we presume to possess quite a good knowledge of his life and although we are not supinely ignorant of the salutary truths of science and philosophy, we confess with shame that we are wholly unable to trace the stupendous chain of events that, starting millions of years ago, led inevitably and inexorably to his domestic troubles. We have to take for granted that he was not responsible for them. We feel convinced that our conclusion is right, the more so as he earnestly deplored the discord and was the chief person on whom it bestowed its hard kicks. His mother reproached him; his wife showed her vexation with the imperfect extent of his love; his sister looked at him with wistful eyes on whose shining surface trembled soft tears; his father deemed him uxorious, feeble, and good-for-nothing and never met him without a frown. In a word, as he told himself, he was not happy, not happy at all.

But he could do nothing to put right this lamentable state of affairs; torn between filial piety and conjugal love, he found himself helpless. He dared not say even a word to his parents to justify his wife's conduct or his own, for it would have been the height of presumption. He gently admonished Wai Hing, begging her to subdue her behavior and endeavor to please the old folks as much as was needful; but the recompense for his well-meant advice was a fine display of rage and scorn, of which he had never dreamed her capable. Among other things, she averred that she was born in the twentieth century; that she was not going to kowtow like the wretched daughter-in-law of former ages; that if he didn't like her behavior he should never have married her but should have trusted for his happiness to his parents, who would, she supposed, have chosen an unexceptionable bride for him;

that she had never obeyed even her own father and mother; and that she was ashamed of his weakness in submitting to atrocious injustice and monstrous tyranny. She then evinced her strength by bursting into a flood of tears. Siu Kam retired with unseemly haste and, an hour afterward, was found by Tak Cheong in their club, gazing gloomily and steadfastly into the depths of a turbid glass of wine with the forlorn look of a would-be suicide.

This wretched muddle wriggled along for nigh upon a year before it terminated in a clamorous crash, which was to be expected. One day, in the absence of her mother, Silver Moon was enticed by Wai Hing to follow her to a party whose major interest was dancing. Silver Moon did not know how to dance, and she was just an uneasy spectator. They arrived home late at night. The next day Mrs. Yuen Ko obtained from her an account of her activities of the previous evening, the upshot of which was a sustained piece of invective of remarkable length. She was dubbed a bad girl and a corrupt hussy and given other ungraceful titles and finally was forced to resort to the wet language of the eyes to express her contrition. Wai Hing, feeling that she was to blame for this sad result, valorously came forward in her defense. She started off by stating that she was responsible for the visit to her friend's house and that Silver Moon did not dance. Not content with this, however, she went on to affirm with a needless display of profound conviction that dancing was a meritorious and wholesome pastime and she could discern not the slightest bit of harm in it. Mrs. Yuen Ko now directed all her wrath against this stout champion. The range of her voice was a revelation and its power awful, as, commencing with a hoarse mutter, it rose to a shrill screech. She accused Wai Hing of all the crimes that modern girls were capable of committing, reviled her up hill and down dale, called her names that would generate a blush on the most hard-boiled libertine, cursed her family and all her ancestors to the remotest generation, summoned heaven to witness all her iniquities, was sure that she would live a short life, die a violent death, and wander a hungry ghost, and finally ended by ordering her to leave the house and remove the contagion of her presence. Wai Hing, who was never at a loss for a word and boasted her power to floor everybody, was, for the first time in her active life, completely flabbergasted. She stood transfixed to the spot as if she were enjoying the rare privilege of listening to some celestial melody; a stony silence sealed her lips. When she awoke from her blissful trance and all of a sudden remembered that she was not a statue but was gifted with the faculty of motion, she—it would be better not to insult her by saying that she ran—walked off at an unusual pace. Then, in her room, she vented her tears and wrath on Siu Kam.

That ill-fated gentleman, unconscious of the treat in store for him, had returned home a few moments earlier in time to hear the latter portion of his mother's breathless peroration. Hardly knowing what the trouble was, he discreetly withdrew and now found himself in a lamentable situation. He silently cursed his life and—though it is singular in one of such mild character—the female part of humankind. "Oh, these infernal women!" It is painful to have to record that he actually breathed these words, though in such a low voice that only one gifted with the powers of Sun Hou-tzu, who could assume a variety of transformations, could possibly make out what he was saying by becoming a mosquito and settling on the tip of his nose.

"You and your family!" stormed the lovely Wai Hing. According to personal taste, an angry beauty may seem more enchanting or quite repulsive. Siu Kam wished heartily that such a vision was not vouchsafed him; he had no mind for this kind of charm. He looked out of the window with the sorrowful eyes of a martyr and remained dumb.

"You should have told me long ago what kind of people they were," continued Wai Hing. "Oh, how I wish I had never entered this house!"

"I wish it just as heartily," he muttered in a misery-ridden voice, almost sepulchral in its effect.

"You are telling me that you regret your marriage?" Her eyes flashed with the brilliance of lightning.

"I only meant that it would have been better if you had not come to live here." He possessed the endurance of the hill.

"So you have awakened to your senses at last," exclaimed Wai Hing, calming down a bit. "When do we move?"

He was taken aback. "Well—I don't know."

"At once," she asserted with ungraceful peremptoriness.

And thus it came about that Siu Kam had now perforce to set up a separate home. They lost no time in hunting for suitable apartments and were soon in possession of the second floor of a large and elegant building in Pokfulam, a suburb to the west of Victoria.

For a young couple to start a home of their own is usually something of an adventure, the more so if neither has ever lived alone before. There is a soothing feeling of domesticity about it all, and yet romance heavily paints her rosy hues. The purchase of the requisite furnishings is fun. There are so many articles to buy, so many shops to visit. And the most satisfactory part of the experience is the sensation of novelty—a new life starts its journey accompanied by new furniture!

Though Siu Kam and Wai Hing entered their home in such inauspicious circumstances, still they were not altogether deprived of the exquisite feelings of gratification, especially the latter. The man indeed was not so cheerful as he might be; still he revealed—whether it was genuine or simulated is not to the point—a fair degree of enthusiasm and cooperated willingly enough with his partner in the setting up of their joint abode. The lady, however, was blessed with more energy and enterprise and bubbled with suggestions; there was no question of her hearty enjoyment of the venture. It was delightful, a cure for sore eyes to watch her lively movements, arranging a table here, hanging a curtain there, buying crockery and kitchen utensils, some of which she never knew existed in the world before.

Their flat comprised two bedrooms, a sitting room, a bathroom, a kitchen, and a veranda. Among other things they bought two different sets of chairs, a carpet with blue flowers, porcelain vases, a bookcase, and a refrigerator. They also got hold of a small glass aquarium destined to be the prison of goldfish, the said luckless vertebrates being probably not yet born. With empty rooms to begin with there was verily a lot to buy, as Siu Kam reflected gloomily and as Wai Hing proclaimed happily.

Siu Kam tried to live as peaceful a life as possible. So far as reconciliation with his parents over the breach caused by his marriage was concerned, it was now out of the question; his efforts at a due mixture of conjugal love and filial piety had proved a definite failure. If he were gifted with the talents of character reading and logical ratiocination from given premises, he thought bitterly, he could infallibly have known from the beginning what would be the outcome of his romance. It required no inspired prophet or fortune-teller to reveal it. His attempt to harmonize East and West in family affairs had ended in disaster; social forces and human passions were too strong for him. He himself was only a weakling who could not make up his mind firmly and clearly on any point, momentous or otherwise. He wanted to be a living compromise, to make the best of both worlds, the world of mediaevalism and the world of modernity, but he did not know how, and the inglorious upshot was ruin.

Siu Kam sought consolation in his work and the society of his friends. As his business took him away from home nearly the whole day, Wai Hing found herself alone more than she liked, for she was not one who could extract pleasure from the charms of solitude. Formerly she could divert herself in sweet converse with Silver Moon, whose company she now missed acutely. She took to going out more often than ever since her marriage and frequently returned hours after Siu Kam was already in his armchair shaking his legs in languid ease. Tired of waiting for her, he would sally out to find some amusement and, in his turn, came home when she was preparing to climb into bed feeling vexed and hurt. This kind of situation was not calculated to engender marital concord; still, they loved and admired each other well enough not to indulge in mutual reproach. But a series of petty annoyances, familiarity, which blunted the appreciation of excellencies and heightened the awareness of defects, and a sense of remorse on the part of the man and quick resentment on the part of the other at any fancied sign of this quality, which seemed to accuse her as the cause of his family troubles, insensibly cooled the warmth of their mutual affection and esteem.

Chapter 15

The Dragon-Boat Festival

The fifth day of the fifth lunar month, one of the major festivals of the year, rose auspiciously, with a fat, good-natured sun. There was no likelihood of rain, and the thought gladdened the innocent heart of Silver Moon. Her radiant face broke into a gentle smile, and intoxicated with it, a man might walk miles and miles, not on a lonely country road, but within the confines of a populous city, in search of such another soul-stirring specimen, and he would be sure to fail in his rash quest. There was no doubt of it: he could more easily have won a sweepstake.

As for the festivals, which were separated from one another at convenient though not at exactly regular intervals, they were rapidly losing their importance. This is rather a pity, as they served as highlights in the lives of the peasants, who, having hardly any enjoyments all the year round, may be said to have lived only for them. They looked forward to one that was approaching; they looked backward at another that had just receded. Though the lunar calendar was officially at an end, the populace continued to celebrate these festivals.

Due to some strange freak of the human mind, many festivals all over the world take their origin from deaths and other gloomy events, though they are seasons of rollicking fun. The Dragon-Boat Festival commemorates the tragic end of a national hero. Chiü Yüan lived toward the close of the Chou Dynasty about twenty-three hundred years ago. Loyalty was his creed, and a more faithful minister never breathed. But his obtuse prince, like so many others of his ilk, suspected him of treachery, and he was disgraced and deprived of his rank. Disconsolate, lamenting the woes of his country, he wandered by the banks of the River Mi-lo. Like the Romans, the Chinese regarded suicide as noble under certain circumstances, and Chiü Yüan preferred the more congenial embrace of the lambent waves to an inhospitable clime. The boat races, held on the anniversary of the day of his death, signify a ceremonial search for his body.

Silver Moon got up early to prepare the dishes and other mysteries of worship; she was very much in her element as she reveled in such things. Candles, incense sticks, paper to serve as currency in the invisible world, and viands seldom prepared on ordinary days were very much in evidence. The altar almost creaked beneath the mass of sacrificial offerings. She held incense sticks in her symmetrical hands, which were tightly clasped together, and shook them up and down in prayer. She wore a solemn face, quite entrancing to behold.

Some special kind of food or cake is prepared, offered in prayer and eaten afterward in connection with a particular festival. "Tsung" is associated with the one under consideration; it is a dumpling made of rice wrapped in bamboo leaves. There are many varieties according to the ingredients composing the package, which is usually made in the form of a four-sided figure with sharp corners and is cooked by steaming. The rice turns into a glutinous mass. It is made for the benefit of the spirit of Chiü Yüan; the pious people who attempted to rescue the hero threw their offerings of food to him into the river, by whose side grew the plant whose leaves provided a convenient covering for them.

Boat races were organized by different societies to celebrate the event. The boats, which were decorated to represent dragons, were supposed to be engaged in the holy task of searching for the body of the tragic minister. A visit to a beach where such a competition was held in the service of religion was one of the few occasions when Silver Moon was graciously permitted and encouraged by her parents to step out of the house. Hence her concern over the weather was enormous, and no person, unless he was possessed of a heart of stone, could possibly refuse to vibrate in unison with the trepidations of her anxious heart.

But, as stated before, her worry was but transient, for the day showed every promise of being exceptionally fine, and her sympathizer would do well to smile with her.

Silver Moon and her younger brother, Siu Yip, accompanied Mr. and Mrs. Yuen Ko to a village possessed of a fine swimming beach, where the Mutual Aid Society had established a bathing pavilion. The concourse of spectators was tremendous, and all the buses that ran in that direction were packed to capacity. The pavilion was enclosed by a wooden fence, and the only entrance was a small gate three feet wide. Crowds lined the road, peered through the planks, and stood on the roofs of neighboring houses; the more adventurous even climbed a hillock and sat in comfort on craggy seats that commanded a full view of the gleaming sea a quarter of a mile away. Like other benevolent organizations, which eagerly pounced upon every opportune occasion to collect subscriptions from the greathearted public, the sponsors of the race, the Mutual Aid Society, admitted onlookers within the precincts of their shed only on the payment of a small fee, which fluctuated in amount according to the quality of the purse or heart of the donors. As the entrance was none of the biggest, it was not an easy task to secure admittance in the rush. In front of Silver Moon, two corpulent men pushed forward at the same time and inadvertently found themselves jammed together. After a tremendous struggle, which afforded a good deal of amusement to the bystanders, one of them managed to shoot himself in; they were both red in the face with embarrassment, muttered some incoherent words, and bowed to each other. Silver Moon followed in their wake.

A small part of the sea was flanked by two creaky wooden piers; this was to serve as the finishing point of the races. Though it was only three o'clock, a good hour before the competitions were scheduled to commence, one could hardly walk a step without jostling somebody. Luckily Mr. Yuen Ko knew the secretary of the society, and he and his party secured comfortable seats in the main shed, right in front of whose base washed the water, which was to halt the boats in their arduous career.

Swimmers, boys and girls, splashed in the sea. Further away sampans rocked gently to and fro, crowded with spectators, who seemed to think it much more convenient and interesting to watch the races thus than from the shore. On all sides small craft could be seen plying amid the gleaming waves.

"How enchanting!" murmured Silver Moon to Siu Yip in a rapturous voice.

"Very!" agreed the boy laconically. He would have found it more enchanting if he were allowed to go down among the swimmers and enjoy a dive, as another boy about his own age was doing at the moment. Wistfully he gazed into the depths.

"What's the matter?" asked Silver Moon. "You don't look too happy."

"I have a headache," replied the boy pettishly.

"Siu Yip has a headache," Silver Moon informed Mrs. Yuen Ko.

"Really! When did it begin?" Mrs. Yuen Ko turned to him fatuously.

"What's the trouble?" Mr. Yuen Ko wanted to know, becoming aware of the slight commotion about him.

"He has a headache," replied Mrs. Yuen Ko anxiously.

"Who?"

"Siu Yip."

"Oh, it will soon pass off," commented Mr. Yuen Ko irritably. "It's due to the heat, that's all."

Mrs. Yuen Ko, however, was not satisfied with any such treatment. She immediately fished out from her bag a bottle of a popular medicinal balm, which, besides curing headaches, was reputed to banish effectually almost every ill that flesh is heir to.

"I feel quite well now," muttered the boy hastily at sight of the panacea.

"Are you sure?" asked Mrs. Yuen Ko, unconvinced. "Let me apply some of this to your temples."

"I am perfectly all right," replied the boy, backing away a little, and from that moment there was a look of superb happiness in his eyes so that no one could possibly doubt that his recovery was complete.

Shortly afterward, when Silver Moon was, for the first time in her uneventful life, attempting vaguely to compute the population of Hong Kong as she gazed in stupefaction at the immense multitude of people all round her on land and sea, the thundering sound of drums smote on her ears. The races, whose magnetic power drew this immense congregation, had commenced. The dragon-boats approached with surprising rapidity. The rowers cut the water with their oars in spasmodic, uniform strokes, lifting and lowering them in and out of the waves with force and speed. The blades, which were thin and broad and were coated a bright gold or silver, flashed in the sun. In the middle of each boat was placed a big wooden drum, on which a drummer, standing on his feet, rattled away with all his might, thus rousing the energy of the rowers, whose paddles all dipped in time to the beats of their drum. Four boats participated in this first race, and as they neared the goal, the eager crowds, who, like all spectators of all kinds of games, were more enthusiastic than the actual performers themselves, strained their necks and shouted vociferously in the fond belief that their voices, which blended into one huge, indistinguishable roar, would encourage the rowers of the boats they favored. The race was very close, the vessels being just behind one another. The winner was ahead of the second by a quarter of its length.

When the vigorous oars were all at rest and the water was temporarily relieved from their insulting slashes, Silver Moon took a good look at the dragon-boats, inspecting them as carefully as if she were concerned over their personal welfare. The dragon-boat, which was extremely slender in proportion to its length of forty feet, was constructed of ordinary timber and did not bear the appearance of being particularly strong. At one end it was adorned with a dragon's head, which displayed a collection of whiskers of unearthly length, and at the other waved a tail. The mythical creature did not assume a pleasant, happy expression; the lord of the sea was probably angry at its unseemly exposure to the eyes of the vulgar mob. The music, which was so necessary to stimulate action, was provided by a drum and a gong as well. Banners were essential to add gaiety to the scene, and there were several in addition to one of special size that rustled at the bow and was inscribed with the honorable appellation of the owners.

Each boat was manned by sixty rowers who sat in two ranks, each person manipulating an oar. They wore their everyday shirts and trousers, none too clean; but on their heads were tied big hats that possessed a ceremonial appearance. Their tanned faces were tremendously serious; apparently, they were engaged in a matter of life and death. The stern was occupied by the coxswain, who, comparatively at ease and seemingly with less expenditure of energy, steered the course. The banners were crimson; the dragons were green; the oars were yellow; and the hats were purple—truly a riot of color blazed.

The tracks covered by the diverse races varied in distance from 250 to 1,000 yards, running straight from the goal toward the opposite shore. They were lined on either side by the junks of the folk who lived on the water all their lives, hardly ever stepping ashore. Of all the spectators they were the most deeply interested, and poor as they were, they did not grudge the expense of purchasing and firing crackers that resounded as the dragon-boats skimmed along. They were extremely anxious to be wetted by the flying spray thrown up by the competing vessels; they would thereby be blessed by fortune for the ensuing year.

The crowd passed loud comments on the race that had just ended; after a time, a hushed silence descended on them as the sound of distant crackers announced that the second race had started. In their anxiety to view the boats, numbers of people pressed against the railings that surrounded the piers or sat on the steps that led down to the water.

Suddenly part of the railings of one pier on the side facing the goal of the boats gave way, and more than a hundred people were catapulted into the sea. There were two sampans nearby, and as the water here was not deep, the rescue work presented no difficulties. Besides, those who could swim made for the steps, which were only a few yards away. But almost immediately after this mishap the dragon-boats came racing in at full speed. One, in order to avoid running into some of the people who were struggling in the water, suddenly swerved to one side and came into violent collision with another dragon-boat that was coursing side by side with it. There was a sickening crash as both boats overturned, throwing their occupants into the water. The spectators shot forth a yell of horror, mingled probably with a thrill of pleasurable excitement, and tensely waited to see what would happen. The two boats were masses of floating wreckage, and the banners, drums, and oars mingled together in their ruined condition. A multitude of purple hats danced on the water. The rowers encountered different kinds of fate. Some had jumped into the water and looked as if they were there for a swim; others appeared from under the heap of rubbish; several were thrown a distance away and landed with a thump on the steps. Those who were safe and sound immediately swam to the rescue of their less-fortunate comrades. About half the occupants of the two vessels sustained injuries ranging from scratches and bruises to dislocations and broken heads and limbs. When the injured were taken on shore, ten of them were in a rather serious condition and were rushed to hospital. Subsequently, one died on the very night following the accident.

Some time was consumed in clearing away the wreckage and in the rescue work. The crowd chattered volubly. On the spur of the moment, numerous parties arose to contend with one another over the cause and the nature of the catastrophe and how it could have been averted. Their fluent oratory made splendid use of the precise, empirical knowledge of scientists, the close chain of deduction of philosophers, and the luxuriant fancy of poets.

Silver Moon let forth a tiny shriek when the railings collapsed and a full cry when the boats clashed; and she nearly fainted outright at sight of the injured bodies pulled out of the water. She began to regret that she ever came to see such shocking events; she wished she had stayed inside her beloved home, peacefully engaged in needlework or admiring flowers.

"Instead of rescuing the hero, his worshippers have to be rescued themselves," remarked a solemn voice coming from somewhere behind her back.

She turned round at the same time as Mr. Yuen Ko.

"You are here also, Mr. Wong?" said Mr. Yuen Ko in polite tones. "How do you do?"

"Very well, thank you," replied Wong Tak Cheong with the ghost of a smile. "I hope you are the same."

"I am surprised that you find time to attend an occasion like this," pursued Mr. Yuen Ko, not evincing any trace of surprise.

"Oh, I like to see how people enjoy themselves," said the lawyer with a dignified air of condescension. "Races on the sea are evidently as exciting as those on the turf. It's a pity they don't hold lotteries here."

This was probably intended to be a witty joke, for Mr. Yuen Ko chuckled in acknowledgment.

After a short pause, in which he was to all intents and purposes steeped in profound reflection, the lawyer pronounced in an oracular tone that reeked of assurance, "I think it's very strange that year after year for centuries we should be still devoting a day to celebrating the death of a man who, however good he was, could not exactly be regarded as outdistancing all the heroes and sages who have appeared. Don't you think that all this worship of him as a god is absurd superstition?"

Mr. Yuen Ko opened his mouth and closed it again, this time in real and not pretended astonishment. He scratched his right ear, turned round, and looked at Mrs. Yuen Ko and Silver Moon and then directed his gaze at the sky and finally stammered, "Well … I never thought of this before. I just accepted it as a matter of course—as a traditional practice."

"Tradition," observed the lawyer portentously, "is often wrong. I hold no brief for tradition."

Silver Moon listened with both her ears but maintained strict silence in maidenly modesty.

"We should follow the rules of sense and reason," continued Tak Cheong, throwing one leg over the other in dignified ease. "About this absurd festival. What meaning has it got? The hero met an undeserved death. Well, what of it? From my own experience, I find that plenty of innocent folk perish as a result of the violence of rascals. Those who served despotic princes usually suffered from their injustice. Our history is full of such cases. Writers praise them; their memory is therefore assured to posterity. There is no need for us to perform all this mummery." He waved a hand in a magnificent gesture, intended to cover the sea.

"Your ideas seem rational enough," uttered Mr. Yuen Ko in a dubious tone.

"They are just common sense. One of the queerest facts about men is that while they think and act sufficiently well in ordinary affairs, they lose all their sense where religion is concerned."

"But religion," observed Mr. Yuen Ko, "deals with mysterious things, and we therefore can't think of it in the same way as we think of trade, for example."

"Still, we can distinguish between true and false and should not easily believe every superstition, as we undoubtedly do. The masses are ready to swallow every ridiculous and fanciful notion. Some religious practices are monstrous. Mediums, who are supposed to be possessed by spirits, slash their backs with axes or pierce sharp tools through their cheeks. I have seen frenzied fanatics walk over beds of red-hot coals. What is the meaning of all this?"

"There must be something to it, as they don't feel any pain."

"My opinion is that they are lunatics. I don't admire them, nor do I even sympathize with them," said Tak Cheong forcefully.

"Other people hold different opinions," deprecated Mr. Yuen Ko.

"That's the trouble," remarked Tak Cheong with a solemn sneer that became him singularly well. "I despair of the future of humanity."

Clamorous drums again announced the approach of another race, and there was a lull in the conversation between Tak Cheong and Mr. Yuen Ko, or rather in the monologue of the former. The lawyer displayed an interest in the race rather stronger than his strong condemnation would seem to indicate; his behavior reminds one of the society man who avers that he is thoroughly indifferent to pleasure and suffers from such intolerable boredom and still runs after it all the same. This race was quite uneventful and unexciting, and only three boats participated.

When the hubbub had subsided again, Silver Moon turned round and caught sight of Siu Kam and Wai Hing, who had just come in and were standing some distance away. They beckoned to her. Noticing that her mother had moved her seat a few yards away from her in order to talk with a friend and that her father was again absorbed in conversation with the lawyer, she quickly slipped over to their side. She was very glad to be with them, for she had not seen them in more than two months now, ever since their removal to their new home.

Their affectionate intercourse was, however, not so edifying as the discourse of Tak Cheong, who had already cleared his throat and was now saying, "The Chinese are said to have three religions handed down from of old: Confucianism, Buddhism, and Taoism. The first is not strictly a religion as it is wholly concerned with this world: it is a moral system with a political objective. The last two are corrupt versions of what were once abstract ideas, and their real appeal lies in the realm of magic. Although the teachings are unlike, the common people believe all three impartially and mix them up in a hopeless mess. But I would say rather that the real religion of the masses is the worship of spirits, spirits of ancestors, sages, heroes, land, and whatnot. And their one real aim is to secure the protection and blessing of these powers as they feel themselves so helpless."

"Naturally," said Mr. Yuen Ko stoutly. "I don't see what's wrong with that. Men don't do everything themselves."

"And spirits can do very little for them," retorted Tak Cheong. "One of the most curious and obstinate beliefs is that, though their worship brings no results except waste of time and money and their prayers are never answered, otherwise most men wouldn't be leading such frightfully wretched lives as they do, they continue to worship and pray all the same. This kind of stubbornness, in the teeth of their daily experience, is positively mulish."

Mr. Yuen Ko shifted his legs uneasily. He felt some slight anger, though out of courtesy he showed no signs of it.

"Their prayers are sometimes answered, and in any case, they fortify their souls with them," he said after a pause. "There must be some truth in beliefs and practices of such universal character and such old standing."

Just then Mrs. Yuen Ko finished her conversation with her friend and moved her seat back to its former place. She was surprised to notice the absence of Silver Moon. She was alarmed and cast her eyes around in search of her. Eventually she caught sight of her talking with Wai Hing, and her alarm instantly changed to anger. Silver Moon frequently looked to see whether her mother was searching for her; now she found her eyes glaring at her. Wai Hing also followed the direction of her gaze. Mrs. Yuen Ko's countenance thereupon registered haughtiness and distaste, and she turned round to stare at the sea. Mr. Yuen Ko, who had been disturbed by her exclamations about the whereabouts of Silver Moon, found himself the target of Siu Kam's piteous gaze; but he immediately assumed a visage of transcendent immobility, showing no trace of recognition. The lawyer, who had originally come to know Mr. Yuen Ko by virtue of occasional visits to his house in search of Siu Kam and who was not aware of the discord that had arisen between father and son, was surprised at this pantomime but was too discreet to ask any questions. He arose, however, and joined Siu Kam.

Altogether five races were run. When they came to an end, a prize-giving ceremony was held. The winners received banners that were inscribed with words of praise and had, tied to the top, sheaves of dollar notes, doubtless more satisfying than words. The joy of the winners was measureless; the crowd cheered heartily and was as glad as if they were the actual recipients. Their altruistic goodwill was really a subject to excite no small measure of praise. The losing boats had departed some time previously, while the winning ones now sailed away to their homes with all their flags flying gallantly in the breeze and their drums and gongs singing paeans of glory to the heavens. The dragons seemed to look benign, though some of them in the heat of contest had lost many a goodly whisker. But dragons, after all, have hearts and are not immune to praise and flattery.

Owing to the unforeseen catastrophe of the collision of the boats, it was almost dark when the concourse of spectators dispersed. Silver Moon, as she was issuing from the pavilion, hurriedly looked back and waved her handkerchief as a sign of farewell to Siu Kam and Wai Hing, who were still standing in the same place, evidently not liking to come into contact with her parents. She cast a glance at the distant hills, where the clouds of darkness were gathering fast, and she smiled as she thought of the fine day, not spoiled by rain.

Chapter 16

In a Ship

Siu Kam had failed to find any special happiness in his new life with Wai Hing, and his home was not a comfort. He was bitten by the bug of moroseness, and the disease developed apace. Though he had never been a man who always wore a smile on his face, he had, at any rate, usually one at his ready command, but now melancholy seemed to have marked him for her own.

He had become estranged from Wai Hing. Her assurance that her ways were all excellent, her domineering will, her fondness for pleasure, and her constant absence from home in order to attend parties were quite distasteful to him. At the first sign that he was not wholly satisfied with her, she went out more often and began to neglect him. His resentment increased, and he showed it more plainly. She grew angrier still and was not above uttering some stinging remark to him. Thus was established a vicious cycle of mutual aggravation and increasing hostility. She took to going and staying with her parents pretty often, for days at a time, leaving him alone in their flat. She was equally disappointed with him and was at no pains to conceal her anger with his wavering character and his inability to arrive at a fixed, uncompromising attitude toward the problems of life and conduct. She disliked his dislike of her apparent inclination for the society of other men; to her, his remonstrances on the subject were due solely to jealousy and old-fashioned narrow-mindedness. She wasn't the private property of any man. His preference for a quiet family life with a mild recreation now and then, like a visit to the theatre, made her curl her lips in superior disdain. On such terms, existence would be a perfect bore; a day would be a year and a year would be a century, and one might as well be old as young.

He regretted his marriage. Why did he ever enter upon such a venture? His eyes followed the antics of a brown cicada that was flying round and round the room and screaming shrill songs as he asked himself this question. Of all the curious impulses that ever swayed him to a hasty act, his former passion was the most curious. Like a disinterested spectator at a play, he brought himself to review his life for the past year with curiosity. He forgot his present sufferings. While it lasted his romance was pleasant enough; though, considering all its associated miseries and troubles, it should not have been pleasant at all. Why do people call the first meeting and early companionship of two persons of opposite sexes a romance, a commonplace, everyday event though it is, he asked himself. Because it is founded on illusions and the victims will surely awake to reality, he supposed. Just then the big cicada, after alighting for a second on the ceiling, the wall, and the floor and each time commencing its flight again, came to rest on his head. He shot up his right hand, caught hold of it and freed it from his hair, to which it clung with desperation. He gazed at it listlessly for a while, smoothed its transparent, spotted wings, and in trying to avoid its prickly legs, inadvertently pressed its soft abdomen. It emitted a prolonged scream. He stared at it; with its protruding eyes it seemed to stare back at him in wonder. He held it gingerly between his fingers, walked to the window, and with a jerk sent it forth to enjoy the cool night.

He sat on the windowsill and gazed alternately at the numerous stars above and the lights that gleamed from ships on the sea below. He was dissatisfied with many things besides his marriage. He had lost interest in his business, which formerly was so engrossing; such work could not be the aim of life. What solution is there to the riddle of things?

None, so far as he could see.

"Life is a great mistake," he said to himself. "It has no meaning, no sense. We live because we are already born. We are no better than cicadas, and we are less free from pain."

His mental torture was acute. The problem of life was insoluble. He descended from the windowsill and flung himself into a chair and dozed off. He dreamed a dream. He saw the earth crash into fragments, which started to wander aimlessly in space. With convulsive hands, he grasped a rock and floated among the stars, questioning the gods and goddesses who inhabited them—what is the meaning of life? But they only shook their heads and grinned. He then came to a world where a chorus of devils shrieked, "Suffer!" They knocked his head violently. He awoke and found himself on the floor with a bump on his head. He shivered.

All of a sudden, he came to the conclusion that he could not stay at home any longer. He felt stifled. He wanted to escape from perpetual routine, to scramble out of the rut in which he was lying. He must be relieved of business; he wanted to be free to think. He wanted to live a more intense life. But where could he retreat? He pondered the problem and came to the conclusion that he could depart for Singapore. He had visited it before, and it would not be too unfamiliar to him. He was anxious to go away quickly, and he might as well tread its streets as those of any other city.

He woke up early the next morning and went to a travel agency to secure a ticket on a ship sailing for Singapore the next day. He then proceeded to his office and told the manager of his company to look after the business in his absence. On receipt of the information, that worthy character was confounded and stared at him with open mouth, displaying a set of golden incisors. He waited for an explanation, but his employer vouchsafed him nothing more than saying vaguely that he had some business in the South Seas. He settled whatever affairs he might have to settle and went home to pack.

He wrote a letter to Wai Hing saying that he was going to Singapore on business and would be away for some time. The following day on his way to the pier where he was to board his steamer, he dropped the letter into a post-office box, for Wai Hing was with her parents in Kowloon, having gone in dudgeon three days ago after a tiff.

The steamer sailed at nine o'clock in the morning and was soon speeding away from Hong Kong. After lunch Siu Kam was on deck leaning against the railing of the vessel and gazing into the distance, his face grave and tinged with sadness. He noted the white, amorphous masses of clouds that veiled half the sky and scanned the scudding foam tossed up by the passage of the boat. Not being a good sailor, he felt an uncomfortable sensation in the pit of his stomach as the vessel heaved along.

He lay down on a deck chair and on looking round saw on his right side a thin man of uncertain age. The stranger was weak-looking and wore a mournful expression; from his deck chair, he gazed out at the horizon, oblivious to his surroundings. Partly to make conversation and partly from sympathy for his tragic aspect, Siu Kam turned to him and remarked, "It's a fine day, teacher."

"Yes," the stranger replied without enthusiasm.

"I presume you are going to Singapore."

"Yes." The stranger hesitated before signifying his agreement.

"Have you been to Singapore before?"

"No."

"Oh," said Siu Kam, "doubtless you will enjoy it. The place is hot though. Going on business?"

"Not exactly. I am visiting a relative. I have been ill and have been advised that a change of climate and scenery would do me good. I doubt it very much."

Siu Kam was shocked at his hopeless tone.

"I am sure that the change would be beneficial to you," he said consolingly.

The stranger shook his head. After a pause Siu Kam remarked, "Life is sad, isn't it? I feel unhappy myself, and you seem to be the same. I hope your affliction is not of a serious nature."

The stranger sighed and after a while remarked, "Life is indeed a tragedy. I wish I were never born. From birth to death, we experience misery, and after all the fuss we die in pain."

"Truly we have our sorrows, but we also have our joys, which compensate for them," said Siu Kam without much conviction in his voice.

"What joys? If there are any, they only serve to make us feel the miseries more keenly. No joy is unadulterated; it is sure to contain some pain, some annoyance, some fatigue," was the mournful rejoinder.

Siu Kam wondered whether by temperament the stranger was a morose person or whether he had suffered some tragedy. The question was too delicate to broach, and the stranger did not vouchsafe any information of his own accord. Siu Kam himself did not feel like making a revelation of his own problems, although it would seem that they were not so tragic by comparison. This judgment he arrived at from the profound despair and gloom displayed by the stranger in his visage and tone of voice.

Siu Kam fell silent but started speculating on the cause of the other man's sorrow. Could it be a love affair?

Could he have lost some loved one? Could he have been involved in a financial disaster? Was he suffering from some incurable disease? Had he been accused of a crime and been sentenced to a long term of rigorous imprisonment? Had he been leading a life of dissipation and was now a disillusioned wreck? It is said that misfortunes never come singly; possibly he had undergone a variety of sufferings.

Siu Kam looked at him more attentively, trying to divine the mystery. The stranger did not seem to be aware of his gaze but after some time mumbled a few words about going to rest and ambled away.

When he was left alone, Siu Kam fell to pondering more than ever the sorrows of life. There would appear to be an excessive assortment of them. All people are afflicted in varying degrees. The lucky ones are those who are of sanguine temperament or who have experienced a relatively lesser quantity of suffering and who then consider that they have lived a happy life.

What is happiness anyway, he ruminated. Is it serenity of mind, absence of pain? This can be very dull. Can the monks who while away their lives in monasteries be said to exist in happiness? Siu Kam wondered whether he would like this and came to the conclusion that the prospect was not enticing. Does happiness consist in dissipation and having a succession of what are commonly deemed pleasures—drinking, gambling, love making? Such pleasures can prove exhausting, enervating, and wearisome. He considered that such a life could not be genuinely happy. Or does happiness mean moderate enjoyment and useful activities? That was what he had been pursuing, but he had come to be dissatisfied with it all.

After staying on deck for several hours, he went to his cabin and reclined on his bed. He closed his eyes, and his mind wandered vaguely from one subject to another. An eerie feeling came over him, weird as Poe's raven croaking "Nevermore." Once or twice he would seem to have dozed off, but there remained a lingering trace of consciousness. He was not aware of the passage of time.

Meanwhile the day deepened into evening, and the sky had changed. Dark masses of clouds filled the heavens, and a gale blew strongly. Rain fell, and the waves answered with a mournful song. Siu Kam, whose mind was vaguely conscious though he was to all appearance asleep, became aware of the scurrying of feet on deck and voices shouting in agitation. He looked at his watch; it was nearly seven o'clock. In his state of mental confusion and bodily depression, he wasn't at all anxious to leave his bunk; urged on by curiosity, however, he emerged from his cabin. People were rushing toward the stern of the steamer, where was already congregated a goodly throng. He asked a person whose face was decorated with only the faintest vestige of a nose what the commotion might mean.

"Why, a man has just gone overboard" was the reply.

"Who is it?"

"I don't know."

Siu Kam thereupon hurried toward the stern, which was littered with a mass of unsightly baggage and overhung with a singularly dirty piece of canvas. He wedged his way in among the excited passengers, who were gesticulating and talking with discordant clamor.

"The gale was strong and he looked like a consumptive, so he must have been blown overboard as easily as a feather," stated a portly man.

"No, I think he deliberately jumped off the boat," put in another, whose unprepossessing face was badly pitted with the marks of the smallpox.

"He stood near the end of the railing and undoubtedly slipped his foot on the wet floor," averred a youth with hair nicely parted in the middle.

"He was gazing at the dark billows and must have been pulled in by a water devil," stoutly affirmed a gentleman wearing a cap of black cloth closely pulled over his head.

"He was so thin and weak, poor fellow," said the portly man. "And the wind was so furious. I was nearly blown off myself." He evidently still stuck to his theory.

"Who is it?" asked Siu Kam anxiously, a sudden premonition dancing in his brain.

"I don't know his name," said the well-combed youth, unexpectedly lurching forward as the ship dipped and steadying himself on Siu Kam's shoulders. "He had a very sad face. Why, I saw him talking with you."

"He certainly committed suicide," almost shouted the pockmarked man. "I saw him leap into the sea with my own eyes."

Siu Kam was profoundly shocked by the catastrophe. He had a suspicion that the unhappy stranger, shattered in mind and body, had chosen to terminate his life; he recalled his desperate looks and cheerless words. He little imagined at the time, though, when he was conversing with him that he might be planning to leave the world in a few hours' time in this abrupt manner.

The ship had stopped, and its engines throbbed painfully. A lifebuoy that had been thrown into the sea floated and tossed amid the waves in a pathetic manner; a boat, lowered from the ship, cruised about in a futile search for the drowned man. Eventually the task was given up and the ship continued its journey, the storm still blowing.

As the passengers moved away from the stern toward their proper places, still chattering volubly, the gentleman in the black cap said for the general edification of the company, though his eyes were fixed on Siu Kam, "Water devils are really very dangerous. How many cases have I known of people standing near ponds, rivers, and seas who were simply compelled to follow them into the water! That's why I always put myself as far away from such spots as possible. When I am in a ship, I try to avoid standing at the side, and moreover, I seldom travel on the sea."

On finishing his speech, he precipitately rushed away and shut himself up in his cabin.

"Life is really curious," muttered the well-combed youth. "One moment a man can move and speak, and the next he is under the waves, food for fishes. Were you well acquainted with him?"

"No," replied Siu Kam as he sadly went back to his cabin.

He felt dejected beyond measure. He was oppressed as never before by a sense of the stark tragedy of life. Here was a man who, presumably, once passed his days in happiness and honor; then came a calamity not of his own seeking, and finally his tormented spirit found a watery haven, far away from his former home. Was it fate or chance that was thus responsible for his end?

Siu Kam found it difficult to sleep that night. He lay on his bunk thinking and listening to the sound of the waves. On looking through the porthole, he saw nothing but darkness.

"Yes," he reflected, "the darkness of the earth is symbolic of the darkness of life. The world is not a benign place, a pleasant home, but a cruel arena full of sorrow. In primitive times, the life of savages in the jungles was an unmitigated horror. I don't understand how some people could eulogize the noble savage and harbor the ideal of a return to nature if that denotes turning the clock back to prehistoric days. With the advent of civilization, there was more happiness, but this was overwhelmed by the mass of misery still prevalent. Nowadays, material advances have been made in many directions and we might not suffer as much from disease and hunger and toil as before and we might have more conveniences and pleasures, but life is still far from being really happy."

Siu Kam pursued this train of thought until he fell asleep from fatigue deep in the night.

No other unusual event marked the voyage of the ship for the next few days, and eventually Siu Kam found himself with his luggage by his side standing on deck ready to disembark and gazing at Singapore, which originally bore the name of Tumasik or "Sea Town," but which later acquired its present name of "Lion City." Modern Singapore was founded in 1819, earlier than Hong Kong and, like the latter, grew to be one of the greatest ports in the world, a thriving metropolis with an industrious population. In a short time, Siu Kam descended from the ship and entered a taxi that whisked him off to a hotel.

Chapter 17

Singapore

Siu Kam did not stay in the hotel long, for he soon found lodgings on a quiet street in the northern part of the city. He was well acquainted with a few people, merchants and others, resident in this commercial metropolis of Southeast Asia, and he looked them up and visited them pretty often. He was most intimate with a journalist who was formerly on the staff of a newspaper in Hong Kong. The journalist—his name was Pang Yao Wan—was endowed with an ardent temperament and talked with his hands in perpetual motion and wrote articles that read as if his pen always flourished in the air several times before it condescended to alight on the paper and trace out a sentence. He was short, had a slight limp, and did not look at all impressive; but his curiosity was colossal and he was continually running around the city, avid for information. He was equally ready to air his views in conversation, and Siu Kam learned from him many a thing that he would otherwise not have known.

About seven hundred years ago, when the first settlement was made near the mouth of the Singapore River, the diamond-shaped island consisted of forests and swamps and the population was very scanty. When a trading post was established by the British, modern Singapore came into being and grew up to be a humming port. The city is located on the south side of the island, which is linked on its northern side to the adjacent Malay Peninsula by a three-quarter-mile long causeway bearing a road and a railway. Less than eighty miles north of the equator, Singapore has a sunny sky with a temperature of about eighty degrees Fahrenheit the whole year round. It rains every month, the annual rainfall being in the region of ninety-six inches.

Like Hong Kong, Singapore was built from scratch; it was different from, say, Canton, an ancient city deliberately transformed into a modern one. From its setting in the Victorian Age, it absorbed the modern inventions and new ways of the West. The telephone, the radio, and the electric bulb made their appearance. When Alexander Graham Bell found that sound produced at one end could be heard at the other end of a wire, when Marconi developed wireless communication, when Edison made an invisible agent turn night into day, they probably little thought that the City of Rams and the City of Lions would alike bear witness to their triumphs.

Siu Kam spent his time wandering all about the town and from one end of the island to the other, lingering amid spots of interest. However, generally speaking, his attention was somewhat desultory as his mind was tormented by his own thoughts. He was endeavoring, like other philosophers, whether in ivory towers or not, to find a solution to the riddle of life.

He liked to linger in the shade of temples, imbibing the mellow serenity bequeathed by Buddha to suffering humanity. The smell of incense was pleasing to him, the lotus flower, a symbol of virtue arising from evil, refreshed his eyes, and the pagoda, enshrining the idea of man's gradual ascent through successive stages to nirvana, did not fail to elicit his interest. Though he was never really attached to any religion, he was from childhood accustomed to the popular Buddhist worship as known among the masses, and it retained a vague influence over him. Whatever religion most people might profess, they never actually practice its precepts, and Siu Kam was no exception; nor did he ever display any undue interest over such problems. He could not tell precisely in what respects Mahayana Buddhism, the variety adopted in China, differed from Hinayana Buddhism, which was the pristine form, simpler and purer in its doctrines. He would have regarded the question as irrelevant should he be called upon to say what gods and spirits were worshipped by Buddhists and what by Taoists.

He loitered in the parks where he stretched himself beneath the spreading trees or scrutinized the manifold varieties of flowers in gorgeous bloom. He watched the fountains shoot their jets of water or the children run and play. He wandered along the winding paths and cynical smiles of superior wisdom, and drained-to-the-dregs experience flitted about the corners of his mouth as he noticed youthful lovers who were apparently very devoted to one another. "Poor fools!" Thus ran his thoughts. "How little do they know of life! What delusions they cherish concerning those whom they think they love! How misery awaits them!" He spent hours gazing at the birds and butterflies. What do they live for? As the curiousness of the question struck him, he involuntarily emitted a bitter, discordant laugh to the enormous scandal of the bystanders, some of whom were persuaded that he was escaped from a lunatic asylum and rapidly edged away from him. Assuming a haughty, unconcerned mien he sauntered away.

A favorite haunt of his was the botanic gardens, which were cultivated from the natural landscape and included an expanse of virgin jungle. The rubber tree was first introduced into the Malay Peninsula by transplanting a Brazilian sapling from the Kew Gardens in London to this particular garden, whence originated the commercial production of rubber on a gigantic scale. Siu Kam loved to wander round the place scrutinizing the local flora and enjoying the vista of gorgeous orchids or watching the restless monkeys eating the peanuts fed to them by sightseers. Tired of walking, he would sit on a bench and his sadness would overcome him, making him wearily wonder how long he still had to live. After loitering for hours, he would think of time and how ruthlessly it marches on, creating and destroying. As he trod the spacious grounds and strolled from tree to tree away from the urban atmosphere, his hair freely dancing in the breeze, his brain grew cooler along with his body.

He paid frequent visits to Pang Yao Wan's home, which was on the ground floor of a three-story house on a fairly quiet street where women chatted and children played on the five-foot way. The house was in tolerably good condition and the rent was not high. Yao Wan was the original tenant; he rented the whole house but sublet the two upper floors to other families. He was married and had five children, including three boys and two girls. He was quite happy in the midst of his family.

One day when Siu Kam was with him, the conversation switched to the subject of Oriental versus Occidental culture. A friend of Yao Wan's, a calligraphist by profession, was present.

"Eastern culture is much older than the Western," the calligraphist was saying, "and it is mellower, more urbane and more serene. Our ancestors knew how to enjoy themselves; they lived leisurely lives and appreciated the fine arts. They took pleasure in the moonlight and snow, in rivers and sprigs of flowers. By way of contrast, look at the West. There, the pleasures are coarse and noisy, noisy music and noisier sex. The turbulence of modern life is fatiguing and unaesthetic, truly deplorable."

"I suppose," said Yao Wan, "you admire the former Chinese gentleman-scholar. But his knowledge was extremely restricted, and he was more interested in literary culture than in natural truth. He was smugly complacent with his code of morality and thought that he had achieved the acme of perfection. In fact, I consider him an insufferable, absurd character."

"Well," said the calligraphist, "I suppose from our modern standpoint the Confucian superior man may not be all that superior, but I should consider him preferable to the present-day, money-crazy, middle-class fellow with his sports and dancing."

"Times change, and so do manners, customs, and interests," said Siu Kam. "I do not think the past is perfect; neither do I condemn it altogether. It had its good and its bad points. On the whole, however, I think our former society undesirable."

"Why do you say that?" asked the calligraphist.

"For one thing," replied Siu Kam, "there was the imperial system. It was preposterous to let one man, misnamed Son of Heaven, rule the country according to his arbitrary will. Most emperors were effete, some were cruel, few were useful, and all because of the exercise of absolute power committed misdeeds."

"I have no particular predilection for emperors, but they were no worse than our modern dictators," said the calligraphist.

"Then there were the three religions with their mutually contradictory ideas and their superstitions," continued Siu Kam. "I do not find that I can believe in them, though they may contain a truth here and there."

"The real philosophy of the educated classes was Confucianism," said the calligraphist. "It wasn't really a religion and was free from superstition. Without this teaching, the Chinese would have been utterly different from what they were through the ages, and China might not even have endured as a single huge country for so long. It was a blessing and no mistake. It is a pity that it has lost its hold on us."

"There were a lot of absurd customs and practices too," chimed in Yao Wan. "How ridiculous was the pigtail! How monstrous foot-binding is!"

"The pigtail was forcibly imposed on the Han people by the Manchu," replied the calligraphist in a somewhat wrathful tone. "And the bound foot arose during the Sung Dynasty. Aberrations of this sort are not intrinsic to Chinese culture, were not originally part of it, and should not be taken as Chinese characteristics."

"Of course," said Siu Kam, "there were good points. There were the glorious inventions of such things as the compass, paper, and printing. The fine arts like painting were well developed."

The calligraphist smiled. "Calligraphy was a fine art and was an ardent pursuit."

"Banditry was very much in evidence too," said Yao Wan sarcastically. "One could not travel for any distance without encountering brigands whose cruelty was matched by that of the law with its inhuman tortures. People appeared to be very cruel in those days, and frightful revenge was a solemn duty."

"Bandits are by no means absent from the world nowadays," said the calligraphist. "They are as ruthless as those of olden times, although they may live in society instead of occupying desolate hills. I am not so sure that modern people are less cruel whether in war or peace. The weapons of the past were not so ready and destructive as our pistols and bombs."

"I suppose bad people have always existed and will never vanish," said Siu Kam. "They may just change their modes of operation depending on circumstances."

"Look at our present-day Singapore," said Yao Wan proudly. "We have all the modern conveniences and do not have to suffer the hardships of the so-called good old days. Our toil is much lightened by machinery. People do not have to be conscripted and get killed building an edifice as was the case when a prodigal emperor wanted to construct a palace. I do not know why anybody in those days except sovereigns and mandarins wanted to live."

"You seem to equate civilization with material progress," said the calligraphist in a piqued tone.

"And why not?" retorted Yao Wan. "What is it that distinguishes a civilized country from a barbarian community? Principally the quantity and quality of the material productions—the towns, houses, furniture, implements, clothing, food and drink, paintings and sculptures."

"So, according to you, a people with automobiles, airplanes, television, bombs, electric lights, and refrigerators is more civilized than a people without them," said the calligraphist.

"I should think so," said Yao Wan.

"Don't you value religion, culture, literature, music, social organization, morality, and other nonmaterial achievements?" questioned the calligraphist.

"I appreciate certain types. But these can coexist with a high degree of material attainments," said Yao Wan. "The person who travels in an automobile can be just as moral or given to meditation as he who plods on foot."

"What we are concerned about," interposed Siu Kam, "is whether traditional Chinese civilization is superior or inferior to modern Western civilization. Yao Wan's criterion is material progress, whereas this teacher's is intellectual and moral superiority. Are my words correct?" He put on an impressive judicial air.

"Right," exclaimed Yao Wan and the calligraphist together.

"Material achievement requires intelligence, and it was only in the course of long ages that inventions were slowly made," said Siu Kam. "Nowadays, however, there have been a great many marvelous inventions, so much so that we tend to forget the achievements of past ages. In ancient times, we had great philosophers whom modern thinkers cannot rival. Neither do we produce such great works of art. I think that we are also morally on a lower plane than before. But it's difficult to say which civilization is greater. One's preference is a matter of personal taste."

With that, the subject closed, it is to be hoped to the satisfaction of all parties. Yao Wan invited his friends to partake of some snacks; their discussion had made them hungry.

"How do you like Singapore?" asked the calligraphist of Siu Kam.

"Very much," replied Siu Kam.

"The heat," said the calligraphist "makes it not so pleasant a place to stay in as Hong Kong."

"It can be very hot in Hong Kong, too," murmured Siu Kam politely.

"I presume you have been round the island and seen the sights," continued the calligraphist.

"Yes," said Siu Kam.

"And heard the specific sounds and experienced the distinctive smells too," chimed in Yao Wan.

They laughed heartily as at a tremendous joke. "Other than the heat," asked the calligraphist, "what differences between Hong Kong and Singapore seem to you significant?"

"Well," replied Siu Kam, "concerning natural scenery, you have the angsana instead of the pine. As for human beings, you have a variety of races: Chinese, Malays, Indians, and Europeans, all with their different appearance, customs, and languages. Even among the Chinese you have people speaking different dialects: Amoy, Cantonese, Hakka, Teochew, and Hainanese. In Hong Kong, as you know, though there is a scattering of other races, the preponderant majority of the inhabitants are Chinese, and Cantonese at that. This city is thus far more cosmopolitan than Hong Kong. The variety of dress that one sees in the streets is amazing. Different ways of life can be viewed and studied, and it is truly exhilarating to do so."

"Here we have no typhoons, for example" chimed in Yao Wan.

"You have lost nothing," said Siu Kam smilingly.

"Each city has its peculiarities," remarked the calligraphist, "but the similarities are also there, I presume."

"True," said Siu Kam. "I don't find this place unduly strange. As in Hong Kong, there are beautiful beaches here and the harbor teems with similar vessels. The social scene is largely a blend of the Chinese and the Western, not excessively different from that of Hong Kong."

"Have you seen a kelong?" asked the calligraphist after a while.

"Not yet," replied Siu Kam.

"It is an interesting sight," said Yao Wan. "One day I'll go with you to the southeast coast where in the Singapore Strait many of these traps are set up to catch fish. These kelongs are intended for shallow waters and are erected at right angles to the shore. The vertical stakes lead in lines to a small wooden hut perched out at sea. The fisherman sits in his hut patiently hour after hour before hauling up his net into which the fish are attracted by placing bright lights near the water at night."

"Most interesting," murmured Siu Kam.

"I presume you have not visited a rubber estate yet," said the calligraphist.

Siu Kam had to admit ruefully to the omission. "Straight rows in chessboard pattern of tall trees with slender trunks are what you see," said the calligraphist. "The tapper makes a V-shaped incision in the bark of a tree, and from this the milk-white latex flows into a cup. The tapping is done in the early morning and the collection of the latex in a pail later in the day. The latex is taken to a factory where it is coagulated by means of acid. The sheet rubber is then rolled and smoked."

"I should like to visit an estate as soon as possible," said Siu Kam. "Are the trees tapped every day?"

"Nearly every day," replied the calligraphist. "It takes seven years for a tree to grow up and be ready for tapping."

After a short pause, Yao Wan said, "You should pay a visit to a kampong and contrast it with a village in your New Territories. See the attap huts, which seem precariously perched on stilts as though any ordinary storm would blow them down! How leisurely and carefree life seems! In the vicinity, look at the coconut palms raising their slender trunks high above and crowned by feathery fronds and green and yellow coconuts. Sometimes the trunk lies in a leaning position and does not seem safe. It is quite interesting to watch a man climb up a tree with amazing swiftness and pluck off and throw down the nuts."

"The juice is delicious," said Siu Kam looking as though he longed for it at the moment.

The day in question was a festival day, the Chinese Mid-Autumn Festival, on which occasion flat, round cakes called moon-cakes were offered in worship to the moon. They were baked in an oven and consisted of flour enclosing some sweet stuffing, a popular kind being bean paste. During this season, for several evenings in succession, the children would emerge into the streets carrying picturesque paper lanterns of all descriptions, shapes, sizes, and colors, designed to resemble phenomena like the carp, dragon, lion, bird, cockerel, and rabbit.

Yao Wan brought out moon-cakes and invited his friends to feast on them.

"In Singapore," said Yao Wan while slicing a cake, "there is an abundance of festivals. A tourist may come to the conclusion that we have nothing to do here other than to celebrate them. The Chinese heartily enjoy their festivals. Let me see—what are the ones popular with us? There is the Lunar New Year, whose celebration is not confined to one day but lasts half a month ending on the fifteenth day of the first moon, the day known by its Fukien name of Chap Goh Mei. I don't think any other people celebrate their New Year with such exuberance. We eat and drink and gamble and give red packets and firecrackers as though we have no care in the world. Then there is the Monkey God's Birthday with its processions and puppet shows. We worship our dead at the tombs during the Ching Ming season and make offerings to the hungry ghosts in the Seventh Moon. We eat tsung on the occasion of the Dragon-Boat Festival and become temporary vegetarians during the Festival of the Nine Emperor Gods."

"Besides eating vegetables what do the people do at this festival?" asked Siu Kam.

"They pray at the temples," replied Yao Wan, "and operas are staged there. They hold processions of flags and decorated floats and follow the images of the gods."

"You forgot to mention the Festival of the Seven Sisters when girls pray for good husbands," said the calligraphist.

They all laughed, and Siu Kam began to wonder whether he had been a good husband. But before the dim idea could gather shape, he heard the voice of Yao Wan continuing with his narrative.

"Then there are the Malay festivals. The Hari Raya Haji is an occasion for giving alms. The Hari Raya Puasa, which marks the end of the fasting month of Ramadan, is the principal Muslim festival and is celebrated with great gaiety. The New Year is called Muharram. In Singapore we have four New Years: the Chinese New Year, the Muslim New Year, the Hindu New Year, and the Western New Year."

"This must make the foreigner think that life is one long holiday," commented Siu Kam.

"The Muslims celebrate the birthday of their prophet, Mohammed, and the Buddhists honor Buddha on Wesak Day," continued Yao Wan.

At this point the narrative was interrupted by the entry of a neighbor who was also entertaining some friends with moon-cakes and, falling short, came in to borrow some. It was quite a habit for the households of Yao Wan and his neighbors to borrow things from one another.

"We now come to the Indian festivals," resumed Yao Wan on the departure of the neighbor. He seemed to be enjoying the recital. "During Thaipusam devotees carry frames called kavadis and walk in procession with steel rods stuck through their bodies. On the night of Deepavali, candles and oil lamps are lighted and make a merry display."

"What is this Deepavali intended to celebrate?" asked Siu Kam.

Yao Wan could furnish the information. "It commemorates the killing of an evil oppressor by the deity Krishna," he said.

The calligraphist was getting a bit restless and looked at his watch.

"Finally we have the Western or Christian festivals," continued Yao Wan. "You have them in Hong Kong too." He turned to Siu Kam. "You know, Easter and Christmas. Everybody sends greeting cards wishing one another a Merry Christmas and a Happy New Year whether they are Christians or not."

"Your account of the festivals on this island is most instructive and interesting," commented Siu Kam to the great gratification of Yao Wan.

"I have to write about such things in the newspapers in the course of my work," said Yao Wan.

"Yours must be an exciting occupation," observed the calligraphist. "You go round gathering news and interviewing all sorts of people and picking up all kinds of knowledge."

"Oh, it's nothing," said Yao Wan modestly.

The moon-cakes on the table were all eaten. The sun had gone to sleep and night was come. Siu Kam as well as the calligraphist took their leave and went their separate ways.

As Siu Kam trod the streets, he was delighted with the numerous colorful lanterns held by the children; lighted by flickering candles, they swayed delightfully as the merry boys and girls walked about, now proudly showing them off to one another, now peering into their interiors to see how far the lights had run down. Here a child stood still while an older relative relit the candle; there several children were gathered together chattering away for all they were worth. However, the display was not all gaiety, for there would be an occasional toddler howling because a naughty, bigger child had deliberately blown out his candle. "Our sincerest laughter with some pain is fraught!" Alas, that it should be so and no perfect happiness is attainable, whether among mice or men, children or adults! The parents and grandparents sat on chairs on the five-foot ways and discussed whatever parents and grandparents discussed, all the while looking at their progeny.

After taking his dinner in a restaurant, Siu Kam went for a stroll along the Esplanade. The moon on this fifteenth day of the eighth month of the Chinese lunar calendar was round and full and shone brilliantly in the cloudless firmament. According to the legend, on the fifteenth day of every lunar month the beautiful Chang-O, who has her abode on this celestial globe, is visited by her husband, Shen-I, who has his on the sun, and this is the cause of the moon's brightness on that night. Whatever the cause might be, Siu Kam enjoyed the luminous sphere as his uplifted gaze was transfixed on it so much so that he collided with another moon-gazer. Muttering an apology, he proceeded along the picturesque promenade with its trees and plants.

His stroll took him to Clifford Pier, where he stood looking out to sea and gazing at the lights of the ships, tongkangs, and sampans in the harbor. A soft breeze made him feel cool and pleasant. After loitering for a long time, he hailed a taxi and went back to his lodgings. He slept soundly that night.

Chapter 18

Deserted

When Wai Hing received Siu Kam's letter and knew that he had left for Singapore her anger was truly beautiful to behold. She understood at once his real motive in committing this atrocious action: his desire to get rid of her presence, which evidently he could not endure. What a humiliating insult! She never even remotely conceived in her dreams that she would live to suffer such a monstrosity! She had despised him for being an incorrigible weakling, but this sudden act of his savored of strength, which had taken a most untoward turn, worse than weakness. Often when one's wish materializes, it assumes a form most revolting, most revolting! A fine thing to be a married woman without a husband! What a villain she had inadvertently espoused! After indulging in a spate of angry emotion, she gave way to mild weeping; this second act of the drama being over, she grew stern and thoughtful.

It was clearly no use trying to find him as he had left no address behind; besides, as he had run away of his own accord, what good would it do to come into contact with him? In spite of her anger, she felt worried over what might possibly happen to him; she wondered whether he had really gone to Singapore or to some other place. She thought of divorce, but besides being such a scandal, for it was rare in the society in which she moved, she did not want it. To her surprise, she found that she still loved him; however, after such incredible behavior on his part, she was prepared to cherish undying hatred for him. She gritted her teeth and clenched her tiny fists.

She thought of marriage, her own in particular. Why did she ever marry? Because she fell in love! That was responsible for her choice of a man, but it was doubtful whether she would ever have entered into matrimony at all if it were not an institution, a necessity, for girls. She could not very well live with her parents forever; she hated to admit it, but she was reluctantly conscious that her compliance with the custom was what was expected of her by all her relatives and friends. At the same time she could not think of any right alternative to marriage, which seemed so obviously necessary and good that it was ridiculous even to question it. Well, she could not solve the problem.

How had it turned out that their married life was not a glorious success? Not her fault surely! She had done all she could to make a good wife; she could not help his inability to accommodate himself to sensible ways, modern, progressive. Incompatibility of temperament—that was the grand explanation! She should have been more cautious in taking the fatal step, instead of plunging heedlessly and lightheartedly into union with a man whose tastes were diametrically opposite to hers and about whom she knew so little! She was undoubtedly a martyr, the most unfortunate person on earth!

What was she to do now? Obviously the only possible course was to wait till he condescended to come back, if he ever did. That was her humiliating position. If he did not return … What was the use of pondering over the future? She had always prided herself on being realistic and practical, and she never found that it paid to worry over possible contingencies when there were so many problems and troubles present at hand already.

As she sat in the parlor mulling all this over, her parents sauntered in and were struck by her unusually sad face.

"What's the matter?" asked Mr. Chu Weng.

"Nothing" was the laconic rejoinder.

"Why do you look as if you have a toothache?" intervened Mrs. Chu Weng, sitting down right opposite her and gazing at her as intently as if she were a specimen in the zoo.

"Do I look so unusual?" Wai Hing produced an unconvincing laugh, evidently anxious to hide some secret.

Mr. Chu Weng was alarmed. "Come, come! Tell us what it is."

Finding that there was no alternative but to comply with their request, she told them about Siu Kam's sudden departure for Singapore without informing her beforehand.

"Now, what did he go there for?" Mr. Chu Weng stroked his pipe, which, as usual, he was carrying about with him. He was relieved to find that there was nothing more serious than this, and he began to smoke placidly.

"My belief is that he has deserted me," announced Wai Hing suddenly after a short pause.

"What!" exclaimed Mr. and Mrs. Chu Weng simultaneously. Their voices could not have synchronized more perfectly if they had been mechanically produced. The former dropped his pipe in his astonishment and, when he picked it up, found that a slight crack was visible on its stem; as was rarely the case with him, sulfurous anger lit its flame in his heart.

"What is the meaning of this nonsense?" he almost shouted.

"Have you two been quarrelling, or what?" put in Mrs. Chu Weng.

"No, well—slightly," confessed Wai Hing.

"He couldn't have done such a monstrous thing if there hadn't been some very serious cause," said Mr. Chu Weng.

"I never imagined that he would be such a villain," added Mrs. Chu Weng, getting excited.

"You don't know him," said Wai Hing with a bitter smile.

"What a rotten family his is!" proclaimed Mr. Chu Weng with conviction. "I don't know why we ever allied ourselves with them."

"That's not our fault," said Mrs. Chu Weng, turning on her daughter a half-angry, half-sad glance. "We didn't choose him."

"This comes of allowing girls to choose their own husbands," announced Mr. Chu Weng bitterly. "A very fine example of what they call love! Where is all this beautiful love now? I thought that it was the only certain guide to a happy marriage."

Wai Hing was silent, ready to weep with the profoundest chagrin she had ever experienced.

"I wish he is killed in Singapore," said Mrs. Chu Weng, unable to control her vexation.

Wai Hing trembled in every limb and grew cold all of a sudden; she turned pale and felt like fainting. On perceiving this, Mr. and Mrs. Chu Weng gulped down their ire and spoke more calmly.

"Now, what exactly has occurred between you two?" questioned Mr. Chu Weng.

"I would rather not talk about it," said Wai Hing in the most grief-stricken tone imaginable.

Mr. Chu Weng shrugged his shoulders. "I was surprised when you left his parents' home. As you were always trying to go in for what you termed 'modern ways,' my surprise was soon quenched when I thought that it was another of your whims. I suppose you could not agree with his parents."

Wai Hing reluctantly nodded her head.

"That's to be expected," said Mrs. Chu Weng. "I am not astonished. It would have been a perfect wonder if you had gotten on well with them."

"What was exactly the matter with them?" asked Mr. Chu Weng.

"They were very old-fashioned and very strict," answered Wai Hing with a flush on her cheeks.

Mr. and Mrs. Chu Weng looked at each other in consternation.

"That seems a very good reason for hating them," remarked Mr. Chu Weng ironically. "They must have been under the impression that we were exactly like our daughter, and hence their coldness toward us."

Mr. and Mrs. Chu Weng had come into very little contact with Mr. and Mrs. Yuen Ko, though they would have liked to be on intimate terms with them. They paid them two or three visits after the families were united by marriage but were invariably received with such a marked lack of cordiality that their enthusiasm was dampened; coming to the conclusion that they were rather haughty people who liked to keep to themselves, they dropped all further intercourse. As for the marriage itself they had hardly anything to do with it; it was an affair of their daughter's, whom they had allowed to have her own way from the moment she could talk. They were not exactly modernized in their beliefs and tastes; they did love the old customs, but being extremely easygoing, they acquiesced readily enough in whatever came to pass. As for Siu Kam, they had no objection of any sort against him; on the contrary, they considered him a very suitable match for their daughter. However, their approval was of little significance; they would have consented to any choice of Wai Hing's. And now here was a fine scandal.

"Ours is a first-class family!" exclaimed Mr. Chu Weng lugubriously. Turning to his wife he continued, "We are the luckiest couple the world ever produced. We are blessed with the most disgraceful son imaginable and a daughter whose man has run away."

Wai Hing flushed and bit her lip. Just then the servant entered to announce the arrival of a guest. Tak Cheong made his entry solemnly, as befitted one of such great importance; after the customary salutations, he sat erect in an armchair and with great dignity slowly drank the cup of tea ceremoniously handed him by Mr. Chu Wang. A sudden thought simultaneously flashed like lightning through the minds of Wai Hing and her parents, and that was that the lawyer was the person who originally introduced the wretched Siu Kam into their family. They immediately looked constrained and displeased, especially the young lady, who began to cherish a hearty dislike of the unfortunate, indirect cause of her catastrophe. Tak Cheong instinctively sensed that there was something wrong, though happily he hadn't the remotest idea that, through no deliberate fault of his, he had in the space of a few seconds become persona non grata with the family. Alas! On such a frail foundation rests reputation, even the reputation of great men like lawyers!

"I hope everything is all right," said Tak Cheong.

"Oh yes," murmured Mr. Chu Weng, red in the ears.

"Nothing can ever be wrong," added Wai Hing.

"I haven't seen Siu Kam for weeks," said the lawyer. "I suppose he is well."

"He is in the best of health and spirits, so far as I know," announced Wai Hing in the same enigmatical tone.

The lawyer looked puzzled. "Where is he now?" he asked.

"In a place where none can reach him," replied Wai Hing with singular unpleasantness.

"I don't understand." For the first time in his life, the lawyer was positively flabbergasted.

"There are some things that it is best to avoid knowing," said Wai Hing exasperatingly.

"He isn't ...," Tak Cheong blurted out these words and stopped as abruptly as though a bullet had just smashed his jaw. He was going to add the horrid word "dead", but realizing that this tragedy couldn't be the cause of her queer behavior, he didn't finish the sentence.

"He has absconded!" exclaimed Mrs. Chu Weng, unable to contain herself any further.

"Who?" asked the lawyer, startled, "Siu Kam? What for? Where?"

"No other. In order to abandon his legal wife in Singapore," replied Mrs. Chu Weng in the same spasmodic manner.

"This is ridiculous," said the lawyer helplessly. "I can't believe it! Why did he want to do such an atrocious thing?"

"That is exactly what we would like to know," put in Mr. Chu Weng, puffing at his pipe vigorously.

Wai Hing did not care to give an explanation.

"I must write him and ask him to come back. He had no right to go away like this." The lawyer spoke as though he were invested with authority to control Siu Kam's movements. "What could he be doing in Singapore?"

"He might have wanted to expand his business." A bright idea suddenly struck the mind of Mr. Chu Weng hopefully. He looked round for a confirmation of his guess.

"It's unlikely that he would have run away for such a purpose without telling his relatives and friends," said Tak Cheong, his logical intellect reasserting its ascendancy. He was too astute not to be able to divine the real cause of his friend's precipitate action, though he had never received any intimation from him about his matrimonial troubles. There are some people who possess a great fondness for discussing their domestic affairs, usually the unpleasant ones, with their acquaintances; there are others, endowed with greater dignity and reserve, who absolutely refuse to divulge such secrets even to their most intimate cronies. Siu Kam belonged to the latter category; on such a subject he could find no consolation in sympathy.

Silence fell on the company. It was abruptly broken by Tak Cheong as he asked, "Did he leave any address behind him?"

"Apparently not," said Mrs. Chu Weng with a frown on her normally pleasant face. "It looks as though he didn't want anybody to know his whereabouts."

"It's doubtful even whether he has gone to Singapore," intervened Wai Hing. "He might have taken a trip to Honolulu, for all we know."

"That would be just as likely," commented Mrs. Chu Weng acidly.

Tak Cheong wasn't a detective; he had no ambition to be a keen sleuth, able to track down the steps of any person with certainty by putting two and two together. Hence he did not feel ashamed to admit that he was helpless in the present case.

"We must patiently wait for Siu Kam to come back," he said as he rose to go. "After all, he is neither a fool nor a villain. Some sudden whim must have prompted him to go to Singapore. All of us have some unaccountable impulses sometimes. He'll return sooner or later."

In the entrance hall he met Yin Pat. He lifted his brows slightly, did not exchange any greetings with him, and stalked away with erect dignity.

"What a pompous ass!" commented Yin Pat, gazing after his retreating figure with apparent distaste.

Yin Pat had arrived a few moments before to call on his very good friend, Ko San, and had chanced to hear the parting remarks of the lawyer. He sat down and began to think over this revelation. He had been paying attention to Wai Hing ever since he became acquainted with her, but as she seemed totally unaware of his advances he felt himself repulsed. Then Siu Kam had come along and married her. He felt chagrined but wasn't much concerned over it, for at that time he was more interested in getting what he could from Ko San. As time went on, however, he came to the conclusion that it was well-nigh impossible to receive anything from his friend, for Mr. Chu Weng had become so strict that he gave his son hardly a bare pittance. He began to study Wai Hing earnestly. From his observations and deductions, he arrived at the belief that her marriage was not as satisfactory as it might be, and this gave him great delight. He paid her still greater attention. From the lawyer's words he knew that the final rupture of the lute had occurred. He looked at the ceiling blissfully.

While in this attitude, he saw Wai Hing walk into the room. He jumped up and greeted her with an extraordinary show of respect, very gratifying to the unfortunate lady. They sat down and he started to exercise his utmost powers of delightful converse, frequently punctuated with soothing flattery.

"The weather today is extremely fine," he said with an ingratiating smile. "Are you going out?"

"I don't think so," replied Wai Hing, thinking how miserable even the weather had become as a result of her affliction.

"That's too bad," he remarked. "Have you anything special to do at home?"

"Not exactly," responded the lady. "I have a headache."

"Oh!" exclaimed the gentleman sympathetically as he subtly hid a smile. "That's too bad. And today is racing day."

"Is it? I forgot."

"I think the races are going to be very exciting."

"I may go," said the damsel with the headache.

"The open air will do you good."

"I hope so."

"I can never resist the excitement of betting," said Yin Pat in a tone of joyous anticipation.

"Let us go," said the damsel with the headache much abated.

They went to Happy Valley where the racecourse was located. The races had already started, and the concourse was immense. Everybody seemed to be there, and everybody seemed to be shouting deliriously.

Wai Hing made a few bets and won a little. She greeted some friends and to all outward appearance was just an eager punter like them. She did not show the slightest trace of anxiety or sadness that could cause people to divine that everything was not going smoothly in her life. She did not feel disposed to share her troubles with her acquaintances, who would probably laugh at her secretly in malicious pleasure.

Yin Pat enjoyed the races immensely and shouted himself hoarse. He managed to win a tidy sum, and his satisfaction with life was vastly augmented thereby. He paid assiduous attention to Wai Hung, who, however, appeared distrait to him. He was disappointed when she did not accept his invitation to have dinner together but hid his chagrin. He took her home and left her at the door as she did not invite him in.

Her parents were at dinner and asked her to hurry up as the food was getting cold. At the table the conversation was desultory as Wai Hing was in no mood to talk. She ate abstractedly and seemed not to care for nourishment. Mr. and Mrs. Chu Weng were profoundly disturbed and now glanced at each other and now at their wayward daughter. Finally the meal came to an end, and they adjourned to the living room where a similar silence reigned. Wai Hing perfunctorily turned over a couple of magazines but did not really read them. Her eyes filled with tears. Mr. and Mrs. Chu Weng sighed softly. Pleading a headache—the same headache again—Wai Hing retired early to her room.

She could not sleep but lay on her bed reflecting on her life and the future. She thought of the past and wondered how she came to marry Siu Kam, who turned out to be totally different from her. She did not like his serious ways; she did not like his vacillating, indecisive habits of mind. She was antipathetic to his mother, who had no love for her. His family was hopelessly old-fashioned, while she had no use for tradition. She should have known better than to marry into such a family. She felt angry with him that he did not see fit to change his ways for the better and cast off his prejudices. She wished she had never come across him, and now she hoped he was dead.

She tossed her head about on the pillow. As she became calmer, she thought that to do him justice he had not been exactly a very bad husband. He had not, so far as she knew, gone after other women. He had money and had been fairly generous to her. He didn't have a bad temper and had never spoken ugly words to her. He had not even endeavored to restrain her from pursuing her way of life.

What had gone wrong? Incompatibility of temper—that was what was the matter. It was her misfortune to have fallen in love with such a man and a greater misfortune not to have realized in time that marriage to him would eventually terminate in disaster. She was unlucky, most unlucky! Now that she came to think of it, one of her friends who had come to know that she was going about with Siu Kam in the days before their marriage had hinted to her that he was not her type, but she had brushed aside the suggestion disdainfully. And now this was the outcome!

She thought of divorce, but this was a drastic step not to be lightly undertaken. It would be scandalous, and it just did not fit in with the moral code of her family and her social circle. It would be a nine-day wonder, and it would ruin her life and make of her an embittered divorcee. Would Siu Kam agree to a divorce? She was not sure. At any rate, did he deserve to be divorced? She scrutinized this problem, viewing it from one angle and then another, and arrived at no satisfactory conclusion.

When she thought of the laughter of her friends over her unseemly situation, she writhed. They would not be sympathetic to her in any way. They would only say that she deserved what she got and that her behavior must have been outrageous to make her husband desert her. They would mock her slyly or even openly. Now, for the first time in her life, she began to realize that friendship was untrustworthy and society a sham. It was necessary to have friends, for she could not live in solitude and all sorts of pastimes needed company for their fulfillment; but basically friendship was a tenuous affair.

What was she to do? There were three courses open to her: to get a divorce, to go to Singapore, or to stay put. After lengthy reflection, she decided that divorce was undesirable, at any rate for the present. As regards going to Singapore, she had no intention of doing such a thing, for in the first place, it was not certain that she could find him; in the second place, it was undignified for her to go running after him, especially when he was the culprit; and in the third and last place, their estrangement could not be healed by such a move. As for staying put and letting things drift along, the outcome depended on whether Siu Kam returned home or remained away for good. She did not deem it likely that he would stay in a foreign land forever as, even if he cared nothing for her, he would have to consider his business and his parents. She bit her lip in chagrin when the thought struck her that he had completely ceased to care for her; her pride was hurt. When he returned, and he could not be away too long, she could have it out with him. What would happen then was left to fate to determine.

She thought and thought, and she had never thought so much in all her life on any serious problem; her head ached—she now really had a headache! She got up to smear Tiger Balm on her forehead. What a night she had; never such a one had she experienced! If Sun Hou-tzu, the monkey pilgrim of the Journey to the West, had transformed himself into a fly and watched her in her sorrow, even his mischievous heart would have been sorely tried. Dawn was approaching before she sobbed herself to sleep.

Chapter 19

The Stall-Holder

In a street of stalls that were brightly lit at night, life pulsed at its merriest. Here were sold all varieties of edibles from noodles to cuttlefish and from pork congee to a full meal of rice accompanied by a selection of diverse preparations of meats and vegetables. So much bustling activity there was, and one wondered at the concourse of customers. To the uninitiated, eating at a roadside stall might not seem high class or hygienic, but in this part of the world it was completely the fashion. Poor and rich rubbed shoulders at these eating places; the workman, the clerk, the professional man, and the tycoon alike thought nothing of wending their way to them. Men and women, adults and children came along by car, by bicycle, or on foot, singly or in groups. It would seem that eating was the great business of life and that there could be but one answer to the time-honored question of eating to live or living to eat!

Plain wooden chairs and tables were laid out in the vicinity of the stalls on the pavement as well as the carriageway. The stall proprietors were themselves the cooks and the cashiers; as waiters, they were assisted usually by members of their families. As the food was served piping hot, they were in continual enjoyment of the heat of the wood fires over which were placed the frying pans. They put the raw ingredients into the pans, stirred them as they sizzled, and ladled them out onto the plates and dishes. They did this standing hour after hour and did not seem tired or irritated.

One evening Siu Kam and Yao Wan went to this popular gourmet rendezvous and sat down at a table on the pavement adjacent to a stall kept by a middle-aged man called Ah Hing. This stall was Yao Wan's favorite and served complete rice meals. He had become thoroughly familiar with Ah Hing, who now greeted him with a big grin and came over to his table to take his order. After consulting Siu Kam for his tastes, Yao Wan ordered white steamed chicken, roast pork, and salted vegetable soup; these three dishes would go with plain white rice. Prior to the arrival of the meal, chopsticks and small plates of condiments were placed on the table. Siu Kam looked round with interest. In Hong Kong he never went out eating at roadside stalls, but one should do in Rome as the Romans do. He wondered why the well-to-do people should love to sit in the open air in this fashion instead of inside plush restaurants. His curiosity finally impelled him to seek information from his friend.

"Well," said the knowledgeable Tao Wan, clearing his throat and meditating over the problem, "I have never thought of this before. I suppose we are so used to it that we regard it as quite the proper thing to do. There is, however, always a reason for the rise of a fashion if we could only discover it. In this case, I would hazard the guess that traditionally the restaurants don't supply the kinds of victuals cooked by hawkers, victuals regarded as tidbits. Each hawker specializes in one type of preparation and is therefore more likely to produce a tastier dish than a cook in a restaurant with a lengthy menu. Then there is the convenience provided by the itinerant hawker who brings his wares right up to one's door; and then, of course, there is the question of economy. And as for the objection to stalls that the food may be insanitary, well, when you come to think of it, do we ever really fall sick on its account?"

Siu Kam nodded his acquiescence at Yao Wan's explanation. Just then, the dishes were brought to the table and the two friends commenced wielding the chopsticks with an ardor betokening that the food was appetizing. However, this did not prevent them from pursuing their conversation.

"This hawker, Ah Hing," said Yao Wan, "is noted for his food. People come from far and near to patronize his stall."

As though he was aware that they were talking of him, Ah Hing at that moment, during a lull in the cooking when his wife took over, walked to their table.

"Do you want anything else?" he addressed Yao Wan.

"No," replied Yao Wan, and he introduced Siu Kam as a man from Hong Kong.

"Oh," ejaculated Ah Hing. "And how do you like Singapore, teacher?"

"Very well," said Siu Kam.

"I haven't returned to China for a great many years," said Ah Hing. "As my native village is near Canton, I would pass through Hong Kong if I did. How I long to see Hong Kong again!"

"You should be quite rich by this time, at least to be able to go to Hong Kong at any time you like, what with your business being so prosperous," said Yao Wan.

"Rich!" exclaimed Ah Hing. "You are joking. I can hardly make both ends meet. I have to work from day to night to support my large family. I can't afford even to take a day's holiday. We hawkers are really sorry persons."

"Well, I don't know," said Yao Wan with a wink to Siu Kam. "Don't be shy to acknowledge your earnings. I am not going to borrow money from you."

Ah Hing laughed. "That's a good one. Fancy anybody borrowing money from a poor man like me."

"Do you lead a happy life?" asked Siu Kam wistfully.

"I am quite contented" was the reply. "It's no use grumbling at one's fate. Formerly, when I was much younger, I was given to complaining. I never found anything satisfactory. I was so sick of my home that I ran away when I was still a boy. After experiencing all manner of vicissitudes, I did not end as anything to be proud of but as a hawker. Such is my destined lot. I have learned to get rid of discontent and self-pity and irritability. I am happier than I ever was when I was full of youthful dreams."

"I envy you," remarked Siu Kam with evident sincerity. "I must learn from you the secret of happiness."

Ah Hing looked pleased. Just then there came a good batch of customers, and he hurried off to take over the cooking from his wife.

"He is a remarkable chap," said Yao Wan. "He works so hard—I should think fifteen hours a day—that he puts us all to shame. As he said just now he is quite contented with his lot. He is a cheerful soul. I have never heard him lamenting about anything. I suppose he is a fatalist."

"Why has he to work so many hours?" asked Siu Kam. "Is his stall open in daytime too?"

"No," replied Yao Wan. "But in the morning he has to go to the market and the shops to purchase the foodstuff and materials he needs, and then in his home he is busy cutting them up and otherwise preparing them ready for cooking. Moreover, some of the things have to be boiled beforehand."

Just at that moment there arose a clamor at a neighboring stall devoted to the sale of wafer cakes. The hawker, a slight, small man, would dexterously spread a thin circular sheet of cooked dough on a board, deposit on it diverse edibles like crabmeat, egg shreds, bean sprouts, and pork cooked with vegetables in gravy after smearing it with various condiments and then fold the sheet to form a roll. His cakes were quite popular, and customers had to wait for their turn to be served. Alas, one person's prosperity often spells adversity to another.

Further down the street there was a hawker likewise selling wafer cakes, but his were not at all popular. He therefore looked with the green eye of jealousy at this man, the more so as he had been trading in that street a good deal earlier and his business had gradually been adversely affected by the newcomer. His sense of grievance grew in proportion to the decline in his income. Thinking of a means of how to take revenge on his rival, he hit upon the idea of engaging a man to disturb him and his business. This person, short and rotund, had presented himself as a customer at the thin, small man's stall and ordered a couple of wafer cakes. Two or three times while sitting at a table waiting for them to arrive he had shouted to the hawker to serve him speedily. Eventually they arrived. He started off by looking at the cakes with an expression of great distaste and then transferred his glance to the hawker with the same toothache look on his face. The hawker, who had been vexed by his shouts previously, was now really nettled but walked away, saying nothing.

Suddenly there was a thundering exclamation from the rotund man, and the eyes of all other customers in the vicinity turned toward him.

"Hey, you!" he shouted to the hawker. "What do you call this?"

The hawker rushed forward. In the middle of a wafer cake at a broken-off end lay a cockroach that had been cooked to death. He stared at it incredulously. Some of the other customers had come forward and were now looking with horror at the insect.

"I am sure it was not in my stuff," said the hawker firmly but with a red face.

"How did it get there then?" asked the rotund man in not the pleasantest of tones.

"I don't know," stammered the hawker, casting round a helpless look.

"I suppose you don't think that I put it there myself," said the rotund man sarcastically. "Maybe I like eating cockroaches."

The hawker was silent.

"This cockroach is so big," said a gentleman with a moustache. "How is it possible that you didn't see it when you were rolling up the wafer cake?"

"I wonder how many cockroaches there are in his pots!" remarked the rotund man with a sneer. "Perhaps there are other insects too."

The hawker looked daggers at him, but the crowd had begun to look hostile and uneasy. Some of the customers went back to examine their half-eaten wafer cakes; at any rate, they did not resume eating, having completely lost their taste for them.

"Don't tell me," observed the rotund man, "that your house is full of cockroaches and to save on meat you catch them and serve them instead."

A bald man laughed and said, "His wafer cakes should be called cockroach wafer cakes."

The poor hawker in desperate straits said heavily, "I have never had a cockroach or any other insect in my wares. I believe you put it there yourself."

This accusation made the rotund man jump up, and he caught hold of the hawker by his singlet. They were both of the same height but differed in their girth.

"How dare you make such an absurd accusation?" shouted the rotund man in the angriest of angry tones. "Isn't it enough that I nearly swallowed your wretched stuff? You are now suggesting that I am mad. What do I want to put an insect for in the food for which I have to pay good money? You must be out of your wits. If you are blind others are not necessarily so. I am not going to pay you for your inedible rubbish, and I'll be hanged if I ever come to your poisonous stall again."

The rotund man then shook the thin hawker, who thereupon lifted his hands to push his assailant away. But before he could do this, the rotund man let go of his clutch and gave him a tremendous shove so that he reeled backward and fell down. He got up and rushed forward to attack the rotund man, but someone caught hold of him and frustrated his attempted onslaught. He cooled down as he realized that the crowd was by no means favorable to him.

The rotund man then stalked away muttering to himself. When he was clear of the street he suddenly grinned, apparently very pleased with himself. Late that night he went to the home of the hawker who had engaged him to expatiate on the success of what, if he had been a military man, he might have termed Operation Cockroach and to claim payment for his services. He had captured a stout member of that species of insects repellent to most people, had boiled it in a tin, concealed it in a match box, and deftly inserted it into a wafer cake when no one was looking. The two miscreants laughed heartily as at a great joke.

Coming back to the street of the fracas, on the departure of the rotund man the other customers of the thin wafer cake maker also all left the stall. Those who had not yet been served cancelled their orders; those who had partially finished their cakes disappeared without making any payments; those who had wholly eaten theirs reluctantly outlaid the money, grumbling as they did so. The poor hawker was left alone sitting disconsolately on a stool.

The excitement did not, however, die down completely. All the people throughout the entire length of the street had become aware of the incident, which now served as a topic of conversation. Siu Kam and Yao Wan had been near enough to observe the event, and they likewise were discussing it.

"Imagine such a thing happening," remarked Yao Wan. "That hawker will have no business for a long time to come if he stays in this street. I suppose he'll pack up and go elsewhere."

"What a pity!" Siu Kam commented. "To have one's livelihood destroyed is not pleasant. I wonder how the insect got there. If it were an ant or a fly he might not have noticed it—but a cockroach?"

"It is certainly curious," said Yao Wan. "But strange things happen sometimes."

Their meal came to an end, and Yao Wan called Ah Hing to pay him.

"We have had a fine meal," said Siu Kam.

"Thank you," said Ah Hing, hugely delighted with the compliment.

"I suppose you don't have insects in your food," said Yao Wan facetiously, winking to Siu Kam.

"Of course not," quickly exclaimed Ah Hing, looking pained. "I am scrupulously clean."

"Naturally," interposed Siu Kam soothingly.

"How did that cockroach—ugh! What a disgusting insect!—get into your neighbor's food?" asked Yao Wan. "Is he a dirty chap or is he half blind?"

"Neither," responded Ah Hing. "I can't understand it. Poor fellow! He is a good chap too. He'll be ruined. We hawkers must please our customers and must be alert not to give offense."

"True, true!" murmured Siu Kam politely. "I understand you have to work very hard."

"Yes, but I like it," beamed Ah Hing. "What finer way is there to spend the time than in working?"

"Goodness," laughed Siu Kam. "It must be quite wonderful when a person finds work and joy synonymous. Don't you ever take a holiday?"

"Very seldom" was the reply. "And when I do take one I find it boring. Last year I was persuaded by my family to spend three days at the seaside. I shall never forget the experience. I was perfectly miserable."

"Ha, ha!" laughed Yao Wan. "This is really a good joke. I must write an article about you in the newspapers."

"An article about me!" exclaimed Ah Hing. "There is nothing interesting about my life."

"On the contrary," said Yao Wan, "you are quite a character. I might even entitle the article 'Holidays Are a Misery.' How's that?"

"Very good," laughed Siu Kam.

"Let us go for a stroll," said Yao Wan to Siu Kam.

They took their leave of Ah Hing and went to other streets. The shops were still full of activity, and people bustled in and out of them. Siu Kam gazed curiously at the goods on display. They were truly international in character and came from all the continents of the world in a wide range of prices. He was more interested in local products like pewter and rattan ware.

Every now and then they walked past a restaurant.

"There seems to be a great many restaurants," remarked Siu Kam casually.

"Yes," said Yao Wan. "Singapore is a truly cosmopolitan city, and when it comes to food, the variety of cuisines proves its character.

For Chinese food you can have the Cantonese, Fukien, Peking, and Hainanese varieties; you can have Malay food and Indian food with their spicy curries; you can have Western food of various countries."

"It is good, I suppose," said Siu Kam, "to be able to eat an occasional meal of another race and like it, but one always prefers what one is accustomed to from childhood. Habit does not impose its tyranny more than in the realm of food. Liking for a specific dish is a cultivated taste," he added with the air of a philosopher enunciating a dictum.

"True, true," agreed Yao Wan. "It is amazing to find another person enjoying what one detests."

They were walking along North Bridge Road, which was full of traffic. They came to a cinema and moved about, scanning the posters.

"There seems to be an interesting show here this evening," remarked Yao Wan, pointing to some pictures in a frame. "Would you like to see it?"

"I have nothing in particular to do," said Siu Kam.

After booking the tickets, they entered the cinema when the screening was just about to commence.

Chapter 20

Return

Siu Kam had spent some six months in Singapore, and though life in a strange place had tended to make him forget his troubles, they were by no means completely eradicated from his mind. He was just as indecisive as ever, and no perfectly proper course seemed open to him to take. At times he thought of Hong Kong, his home, his parents, and Wai Hing and then of his business and his friends. He had scrupulously refrained from writing to any of them, except occasionally to the manager of his firm to find out what was going on with his business and once to his sister, Silver Moon, telling her he was having a holiday.

Most days he would go out and wander around, usually without any specific object in view but just to while away the time. Sometimes he would stay in his lodgings reading or daydreaming, especially on rainy days or when he felt unwell. Occasionally he took trips to the neighboring peninsula of Malaya, visiting the towns and passing through the villages and enjoying the scenery and the sights. The queer thing was that on his return to Singapore from his trips, he felt as if he was going home. He became more and more attached to the island and was quite content to let the days slip by unnoticeably.

When the fit seized him, he would ponder the difficulties and perplexities of life. At times he could not sit quietly but would pace up and down his room like a caged tiger. To be sure this simile is rather inapposite, for he was far from bearing any resemblance to a tiger. However, it may still stand just to indicate that his mind was confined in a prison of trouble from which it sought in vain to escape. He reveled in the happiness of misery.

One day he went to Raffles Place, the business hub of Singapore, just to wander about and pass the time. There was no particular reason why he wanted to go there. He had been to it on many occasions before, usually to do some shopping; he could just as well have proceeded elsewhere. He ambled round the square gazing at the shops and looking at the people. He entered a department store, not with the intention of making any specific purchases, big or small, but simply as part of his ritual of strolling around. He scanned everything and peered into every showcase. He gazed at a collection of jewels for so long that the shopman began to wonder whether he was a potential thief and stared fixedly at him. He felt uncomfortable and sidled off. He was one of those persons who could not enter a shop without experiencing an acute sense of discomfort if he did not buy something. The result was that he emerged with an article that he did not really need but that caught his fancy, the purchase being clinched by the eloquence of the salesman; to wit, a crocodile-skin wallet.

As he stepped onto the pavement, he saw with surprise Mak Gaw Lok walking in his direction. The man stopped short on recognizing him.

"Siu Kam," exclaimed Gaw Lok, "what are you doing here?"

"Gaw Lok," said Siu Kam simultaneously, "what brings you here?"

They both laughed. Gaw Lok looked as stout and prosperous as ever.

"I arrived a week ago for a short holiday," explained that gentleman. "I was told that you left Hong Kong quite some months back. Fine way to treat a friend—coming here for such a long time without wishing him farewell or giving him your address." He looked reproachful in a bantering way.

Siu Kam was nonplussed. On looking around he saw a café nearby.

"Let us go into the café and sit down," invited Siu Kam.

When they were comfortably installed, they called for drinks.

"Tell me all about you," said Gaw Lok. "What made you come here for so long?"

"Well, I felt restless," replied Siu Kam with an uneasy air. "I wanted to have a good long holiday."

"Some holiday," remarked Gaw Lok smilingly. "How is it you came here alone? I met your wife on the street the other day."

"She didn't care to leave Hong Kong for a long time," responded Siu Kam glibly, staring at his cold drink as though it contained something that fascinated him.

"She is wise then," commented Gaw Lok. "How have you been spending the time?"

"Just wandering about here and sometimes making trips to Malaya."

"I wonder whether I could find so much of interest in a foreign land to make me stay so long. I seldom travel, as you know; I am not fond of it. But if I do, I prefer to move from place to place. The strangeness of a country soon passes away."

"I am not here purely for sightseeing," said Siu Kam in an embarrassed manner.

"Indeed!" exclaimed Gaw Lok. "You are here on business? But that shouldn't take such a length of time."

"Not business," said Siu Kam. "The fact is I was feeling miserable, and I thought a change of residence would do me good. I wanted to get away from the familiar things."

"What are you unhappy about?" asked Gaw Lok wonderingly.

Siu Kam did not care to reveal his inmost soul.

"Nothing in particular," he replied evasively. "Don't you ever feel a general restlessness, a vague dissatisfaction with life?"

"Not me," averred Gaw Lok. "I find life pleasurable. I do not mean I do not have an occasional misery, but it is always produced by some tangible cause and soon passes away. I see no point in being sad about anything for long. I always look on the bright side of things."

"I wish I could do the same," said Siu Kam.

"The trouble with you is that you think too much," said Gaw Lok. "If you accept things as they are, you will have no problems to bother you."

"That's just my trouble," remarked Siu Kam with a sigh. "I can't accept things as they are, I can't be sure of the truth, and I can't decide on the right course to pursue. We live in an age when our Eastern values are shaken by the impact of Western civilization. I do not think that our traditional ways should remain unchanged, but I do not consider either that the Western ideas are right. I see only conflict between various notions of the truth and the right."

Gaw Lok reflected for a while over Siu Kam's words. To stimulate his thinking powers he ordered a beer.

"I should think," he said with the air of one pronouncing an oracle, "that as Chinese we should stick to our inherited ways. But things do not remain stationary, and I follow current innovations that are already accepted by most of the people in our community. This course of action saves me a lot of headache."

"You mean that the beliefs and practices of the majority are true and right?" asked Siu Kam.

"I suppose so," responded Gaw Lok. "They are more likely to be correct than you or I."

"That the test of an idea is its popularity is a doubtful proposition," asserted Siu Kam stoutly. "People's beliefs change from age to age and from country to country. What was popular at one time is not popular now, and what is the rage in one country is not so in another. If general currency spelt truth, then all sorts of contradictory ideas would be true, for there is no idea that has not at some time in some place been accepted as the norm. And I see no reason," he added hurriedly to forestall objection, "why the beliefs of only our particular society in our particular age should be taken into consideration."

"The way you put it," said Gaw Lok reluctantly, "it would seem that there is no infallible standard of truth and right. However, for my ease of mind and enjoyment of life, I still think it is best to do what the people around me do."

"Maybe that is the correct course to take," mused Siu Kam. "But people are born with different temperaments, and I just can't help being what I am. About this problem of modes of behavior, it seems to me necessary to determine accurately what we should follow, the Eastern or the Western. Merely doing as our neighbors do is not a justification."

"You are just climbing a tree to catch fish," said Gaw Lok in a condescending manner. "You are wasting your time. Worse still, you are making yourself unhappy for nothing. Life is short; why bother about right behavior and true belief? If I think the earth is flat, it does me no harm. I don't eat any the more heartily for knowing that the earth rotates on its axis from west to east."

"But," said the egregiously persistent Siu Kam, "to know that one's beliefs are true makes their quality different from what it would be if one recognizes that they are false or adopted merely out of expediency. Of course, the mere fact that one passionately holds that one's ideas are true does not mean that they are therefore so; they could be erroneous. It is just the certainty of the belief that is in question."

"Why then do you not make yourself accept the beliefs of society as true and have done with it?" asked Gaw Lok.

"Unfortunately, I doubt that they are, and I cannot force myself to acquiesce to them," replied Siu Kam lugubriously.

Gaw Lok changed the subject. "When are you returning to Hong Kong? I'll be going home day after tomorrow."

"I don't know," murmured Siu Kam half to himself.

"Don't tell me you are going to stay here forever!" exclaimed Gaw Lok. "The proverb says well, 'Though a tree attained a height of ten thousand feet, its leaves would still drop down on to its roots!' You don't consider this idea wrong?" he added uneasily.

"I suppose I'll return home eventually," said Siu Kam. "But I can't say when. Life is so complicated, and my thoughts are muddled. For the present I just drift along."

"What does your wife think about your staying away like this?"

Siu Kam looked uncomfortable and kept silent.

Gaw Lok gazed at him curiously.

"You haven't quarreled with her, have you? You are not separated?"

Siu Kam looked still more uncomfortable and maintained the same unaccountable silence.

Gaw Lok said slowly, "It's no business of mine, but I think you should return to Hong Kong as soon as possible." He abruptly changed the subject. "Shall we go for a walk?"

They rose and went out. Nearby was Change Alley, and Gaw Lok stared with evident interest into the narrow lane.

"Let us walk through it," said Siu Kam.

The place was crowded with stalls selling all sorts of merchandise. Bargaining was the order of the day, and unsuspecting strangers could be badly fleeced. Gaw Lok closely scanned a number of stalls and made several purchases of curios and souvenirs. The crowd made traversing the alley a jostling, hot affair. They emerged at the other end and walked along until they came to the General Post Office, where Gaw Lok stopped to send some picture postcards to his relatives and friends in Hong Kong.

Thence they proceeded to the Singapore River and stood on a bridge spanning it. Westward the river wound its way through the city, while eastward they viewed the harbor, one of the busiest and most magnificent in the world, well able to afford accommodation to the largest vessels and always thronged with a variegated assemblage of ocean liners, coastal steamers, motorboats, and sampans. Overhead, the strong light shimmered in a blue sky bare of clouds for its greater expanse.

"One of the pleasantest sights in the world is a harbor," observed Siu Kam as he gazed rapturously out to sea, for the moment forgetting his misery.

"Certainly," agreed Gaw Lok. "This reminds me of Hong Kong. I often have stood on Blake Pier enjoying the scene."

After some time Gaw Lok said, "I think I'll return to my hotel. I shall see you this evening."

"I'll go and pick you up, say, at seven o'clock," said Siu Kam.

Siu Kam walked alone in the direction of the Victoria Memorial Hall, but after wandering for a short time more, he felt tired and hailed a taxi and returned to his lodgings.

That evening and for the next two days he went about with Gaw Lok until the latter took his departure for Hong Kong. Their converse revolved round Singapore, Hong Kong, mutual friends, and the diverse problems of life. Before he left, Gaw Lok urged Siu Kam to return to Hong Kong as early as possible instead of leaving his business to take care of itself and his family to worry about him.

After seeing his friend off, Siu Kam felt more depressed than ever. In the days that followed, he would sit for long hours brooding over his home, and at night he would lie awake, his mind cogitating a multitude of problems. He felt that life had not treated him well, and sometimes the illusion crept into his brain that he was a martyr. Martyr to what? As he could not answer this intriguing question, he concluded that he was a victim of life in general. He wished that he had never been born; in such a happy eventuality he would not now be suffering from an aching head. Did not Buddha preach that all life is sorrow from birth through childhood, adulthood, and old age to death? The Enlightened One was right; it would be better to attain nirvana. But this, he ruminated, is not too easy; the life of a monk is tiresome. He groaned, and a fly that had been irritating him, repeatedly returning against his efforts to drive it off, now flew back as if in answer to his agony and alighted on his nose.

Should he return to Hong Kong? He had sometimes considered this problem before and had lightly shelved it on the grounds that there was plenty of time to deliberate over it later. But the meeting with Gaw Lok and his exhortations made him think of it constantly; he could not brush it aside. He, of course, had never intended to live in a foreign land forever and die there, however pleasant the place might be. Such a course of action was not feasible, as he was too attached to his birthplace for which he had a sentimental affection. But it was not necessary that he should return in the near future. He could very well defer consideration of the problem a good while longer; nevertheless, it still gnawed at him.

Why do most people stay in one place and never leave it? Presumably, just as a material body persists in its state of rest or of motion in a straight line unless acted on by an external force (Siu Kam recollected Newton's First Law of Motion), so a person resides in his native land pursuing the way of life and the vocation decreed for him by circumstances. It is much easier to do thus. It is only when driven by the need to escape from some misery or by the prospect of bettering one's lot that one goes and settles in another country. It is always difficult to begin life anew amid strange surroundings, and one misses the old, familiar things.

Now, in his case, so ran Siu Kam's reflections—what was there to impel him to abandon his land forever? Nothing was specific. He had a good business, and it was doubtful whether he could achieve similar success elsewhere; anyway, he was in no mood to make the attempt. A career takes years to build up; when a person emigrates, it is usually because he has no satisfactory career at home in that he has either failed to achieve it or has lost it. He had no objection to the work he had been engaged in hitherto; in fact, he had found it congenial and had never thought of pursuing a different vocation. That was not quite correct; he had thought of doing something else, but that was just a boyish fancy. When he was still in school, he read a book about famous revolutionaries and he thought it would be wonderful to live an adventurous life and achieve fame to boot. The idea did not persist long, and he never resurrected it thereafter.

He loved Hong Kong, which to him was the pleasantest of all lands. In the past, whenever he left it for a journey to another country, he would find on his return the island more enchanting than ever. The place was lovely. He was thoroughly familiar with it, and contrary to the popular saying, familiarity breeds affection. The climate was delightful, not too cold in winter nor too hot in summer. How refreshing to swim in the beautiful bays! His favorite had always been Repulse Bay. He loved even its ladder streets and its bustling, crowded lanes. There was no sight to him more captivating than the tiers on tiers of lights as he viewed them from the launch while crossing the ferry from Kowloon in the evening. He was ruminating over these nostalgic memories in a daydream when a great sadness came over him.

He had good friends back home, some of them known from childhood. Whatever acquaintances he may have cultivated in a foreign land, they could never have been the same as those. For one thing, people's behavior is conditioned and modified by their environment. He found that the beliefs, habits, customs, food, and a thousand other things were not exactly identical with what he had been used to, and however interesting they may have been, they could not be assimilated by him and he did not feel at home with them. For another, it takes time to make really good friends who, like wine, grow better with the passage of time.

Coming to his parents, he had loved and respected them but not to an excessive degree. His father was of rather a neutral character and had not exercised any particular influence over him. His mother was of a domineering type and he had always been afraid of her. Her ideas were completely of the past, and she was not to be shaken out of them. He could not blame either of them for whatever they might have done as regards him, for they had acted in accordance with their lights for his own good. It was unreasonable and unfair to expect one's elders trained in a different tradition to alter their settled traits and views. Of late he had become somewhat estranged from them, but he would not have liked to be on other than affectionate terms with them.

Siu Kam often thought of his marriage. Why did he leave Hong Kong? Principally because he was disenchanted with his married life. He had married, he reflected, just like any other man expecting to find happiness. But he had found that Wai Hing's temperament and his were poles apart, and the incompatibility had only become more evident with the passage of time. Of course, he fell in love with her or he would not have married her. But love, in his case at any rate, was blind. It was a marvel that he did not see anything in her not to his taste in the early days of their acquaintanceship. He was as though under a spell. Was it his fault or hers that they had gradually become estranged? Maybe it was the fault of neither, but it was the natural result of the march of time. He thought of the days of his courtship and the happy hours they had spent together, and a pang shot through his heart. What was he to do? Should he return home and behave as if nothing had happened? That was not so easy.

Sitting on a bench in the botanic gardens one day, he reflected on the problem of civilization. This was the age of the clash of cultures. Eastern civilization had received a tremendous shock from the impact of the West, and many of its characteristics had disappeared or were in the process of vanishing. In the material realm, all the latest Western inventions were accepted and used. Purely as conveniences, few people would object to them. Even in regard to weapons of destruction, they were willingly utilized, for any nation that disdained doing so invited destruction. However, people were more reluctant to discard cultural values and moral ideas in favor of those imported from abroad. The resulting conflict of cultures had disruptive and tragic consequences on the lives of families and individuals.

As far as he himself was concerned, he had accepted both the Chinese and the Western cultures. And why not? It seemed reasonable to do this, and it was easier to avoid extremes. It is always best to effect a compromise instead of fanatically sticking to one side or the other. But is the mixture harmonious and does it produce happiness? He had not found life happy, and he was torn by conflict between opposing values.

What was he to do? The East had its good points, and so had the West. Especially at this melting-pot stage when the individual had a choice, it was plain that it should be possible to select and adopt the best elements of each culture. But then such elements may be in conflict with one another. After further cogitation, Siu Kam finally envisaged a solution to the problem of life and civilization. Let reason decide belief. Its deliverances may turn out to be wholly Eastern, wholly Western, or a mixture; they may turn out to be new.

In any case, the resultant creed will be a homogeneous whole. Avoid a fanatic adherence to Eastern or Western civilization in toto; likewise, avoid a deliberate and conscious compromise resulting in an imperfect blend of contradictory elements. To use a scientific illustration: make a compound, not a mixture. This solution seemed to him perfectly satisfactory.

The problem of his return to Hong Kong assailed him again and again. He just couldn't make up his mind. After disposing of the problem of civilization, which in the ultimate analysis was accountable for his mental conflict and his departure from his home, he felt happier and began to review again all the pros and cons of the return. Finally, as he lay in bed one night, he came to a definite conclusion. All the factors previously considered by him—his attachment to his birthplace, his business interests, his circle of friends, his family—indicated a return. The only stumbling block was the one who in the normal course of things should be the greatest inducement—his wife.

If only his marriage had turned out right, life would have been much less complicated. However, what was done could not be undone. At this distance of time and place, Wai Hing's unsuitable characteristics did not appear so grating on his nerves, so repugnant to his sense of what was right. His conception of her in the days when he first knew her overshadowed his later self, and however it came about, it would be disgraceful to both of them.

He must return to Hong Kong and to his home within the next few days. There was no point in delaying it. He must resume his old life. He must try to live again with Wai Hing; and with his clearer understanding, he hoped they would get along well. If not, if their relationship should continue on unsatisfactory terms, should maybe deteriorate further, then there would be no help for it. Events would have to take their course. The solution was not to run away. He must wrestle with life's problems strenuously. Possibly Wai Hing had changed and would understand him better.

As slumber began to steal over his senses, he indulged in a blissful reverie of what was to come. He would soon be back in his home. Wai Hing would greet him with smiles; they would patch up their differences and there would be no discord between them. He would spend his time usefully in his office. He would be with his friends, visiting them at their residences or sitting in teahouses; their affable converse would be so interesting. He would be in the midst of his relatives, and he would be on pleasant terms with them. Familiar as he was with Hong Kong, he would make himself more familiar still and know its every nook and corner. He fell asleep with its lights glittering before him.

About the Author

Born around the time of the foundation of the Republic of China in the former English colony of British Malaya, Tan Kheng Yeang was educated in an English school. His father was from China but had emigrated to Malaya and had become a successful businessman, involved in various activities, including as a rubber merchant. From his early days he was interested in literature and philosophy, and as his interest evolved to science, he decided to study civil engineering at the University of Hong Kong, as he felt he needed a practical career.

After the Japanese occupied Hong Kong, he went into free China, where he found work in an office constructing roads and later an airfield in Guangxi Province. After the war ended in 1945, he returned to Malaya and became an engineer in the City Council of Georgetown, Penang. After his retirement, he worked as an engineering consultant and has written twelve books.